## IF YOU LIKE CHRISTINA, WAIT TILL YOU MEET HER FRIENDS!

### HELEN WILLIS
—Beautiful but a little uptight, she learns the art of abandon . . . and then can't get enough.

### JOYCE DELL
—The saucy teenager who lives her fantasy with an unlikely couple of English aristocrats.

### DIANA COLTRANE
—The glamorous Black superstar of Broadway finds a spot away from the spotlight—in Christina's arms.

### STEPHANIE McCALL
—She never suspected that the act of violation could turn so gentle, and so satisfying.

### MELINDA HOLLOWAY
—She liked company, so she loved the lavish Middle Eastern orgy—especially since she was the center of it!

# CHRISTINA'S FANTASY
## BLAKELY ST. JAMES

BERKLEY BOOKS, NEW YORK

CHRISTINA'S FANTASY

A Berkley Book / published by arrangement with
the author

PRINTING HISTORY
Berkley edition / March 1983

ISBN: 0-425-06131-0

# CHAPTER ONE

Curiosity may have killed the cat, but it only seems to give men erections. Such was the case with Malcolm Gold, at any rate, as he tried his journalistic best to infiltrate the privacy of the women's consciousness-raising group to which I belonged. Although I had done nothing to encourage it, his libidinous questions had rendered his long, slender, naked penis outrageously tumescent. Nor did my denials that the group had an erotic focus lessen the rigidity of his organ. Malcolm's fantasies were far more powerful than my reality.

"A bunch of young women meet to discuss their most intimate problems as women," he observed, his fingertips dancing idly over the scimitar of his phallus, "and you'd have me believe that they don't get into their sex lives! Really, Christina!"

"The subject is touched upon," I admitted. "It's just not primary. We basically try to understand ourselves as women in a man's world, our relationships with our parents, our siblings, with other women; we also look at our exploitation by the business world and the institutions of marriage and family. Our sex lives just aren't in the forefront of our concerns, and neither are men. At least not yet."

"When I get together with other fellows, you can bet sex is one of our favorite topics," he said proudly as his hand fell away from his stiffened member. Malcolm, poor dear, has never quite gotten past his need to boast of his masculinity.

"I'm sure it is, darling. Perhaps women are just different." I stretched my naked body, arching it toward the caressing sun.

It was one of those perfect spring days, warm and balmy, comforting to the flesh but without the fever heat of summer. The color wheel of sun rays, spreading from a cobalt blue sky frosted with whipped-cream clouds, gently caressed our naked bodies. The light breeze tickled our pubic hair, reminding us of the many passionate moments we had shared, Malcolm and I.

We were stretched out side by side in the shell of a small sailboat we had borrowed to celebrate the end of April's rainy season. The boat lay at anchor in a small deserted cove off Long Island Sound, and while the Sunfish itself was easily visible from the sailboats spread over the Sound like a swarm of multicolored butterflies, we were effectively hidden from view by the sloping sides.

After lying in the sun awhile longer, I began to think that it wasn't just Malcolm's imaginings about what went on at my women's consciousness-raising group that had raised his penis. Perhaps it was the sun's heat that had drawn it erect like a sprouting plant shoot. Surely that was the effect of Old Sol's touch upon the nipples of my breasts. Right now they were swelling and hardening in the intense heat.

Malcolm noticed. He didn't miss much. Not Malcolm. Not when it came to anything having to do with sex. It was flattering, of course, to have him looking at me in that hot-eyed, hungry way of his, even after all the times we had made love, but my satisfaction was tempered by the knowledge that Malcolm was unusually sensual. He was a connoisseur of the libido—that, darlings, was what Malcolm was. Or, rather, what he had become over the five or six years that we had known and loved each other.

His sexuality showed, most of all, in his mouth. It was sensual to an extreme, telegraphing its cunnilingual ability, framing a tongue calculated to lick the clothes from one's body, twisting into smiles to make the vagina shiver, jeweled by dimples one ached to fill with one's sharp-tipped, tingling nipples. Ahh, Malcolm's mouth! If the rest of him had been totally unlibidinous, his mouth alone would have made him a seducer par excellence.

But of course there was more to Malcolm than his mouth. There was also his long, curved, sharply pointed dagger of a penis—the Toledo blade of an expert Hidalgo swordsman. And most of all there was technique—the subtlety of lovemaking which makes perception and sensitivity better than brute force. There was nothing clumsy or brutal about Malcolm's coupling. His touch was gentle and the pleasures he provided were prolonged. He rarely overwhelmed me, but he always gave satisfaction. And he was always in demand for return engagements.

His background was not, perhaps, congruent with this role. Malcolm Gold grew up in the Pelham Bay Park section of the north Bronx, the son of immigrant parents. He worked his way through the Columbia School of Journalism. His IQ was high enough for him to spurn membership in MENSA—the organization composed of people who test out at the genius level. Indeed, Malcolm had been quite the grind before he met me but eventually he was released from all his inhibitions to become the masterfully erotic being he is today.

Nor, as far as outward appearances are concerned, does

Malcolm look the part of the consummate lover. He is rather gangly and not overly muscular. The hair on his chest is sparse and the hair on top of his head is sandy and receding. His manner is easygoing and affable and not very macho. Yet over the long haul I would have to say that Malcolm is perhaps the most satisfying lover I have ever known.

If I seem obsessed with Malcolm as a sex object, it is probably because I, like him, have a constant and abiding interest in the pleasures of the flesh. More than ten years ago, when I was a Vermont schoolgirl in my early teens, I discovered the delights of my erogenous zones. If a boy kissed my neck, my nipples grew hard. If he touched my nipples, the lips of my vagina bit at my panties. And if he touched me between my legs, I would disgrace myself by drenching his fingers with honey.

On the heels of my discovery of my sexuality came the realization of my desirability. Boys' eyes confirmed what my mirror told me: I was developing into a voluptuous young woman. My legs were long, gracefully curved, silky; my breasts were large, creamy, and wondrously firm, tipped with bright red, half-dollar-sized aureoles and pointed maroon nipples. My hips were round and inviting, my waist narrow, and my bottom—seemingly always in sensual motion no matter how I tried to control the sway of my gait—was plump and high and made to bear the weight of a man between my legs.

I was fair of face, with high cheekbones and a delicate peaches-and-cream complexion that deepened into golden tan in the summertime. My eyes were jade green with yellow flecks and they were set wide apart in a way which seemed to accentuate their depths. My mouth was round, the lips set in a sort of permanent pout as suggestive of fellatio as Malcolm's mouth was of cunnilingus. (In truth, the hard flesh of an erect penis in my craw is one of my greatest pleasures.) And my jaw, while round and feminine, could set quite stubbornly when I set my mind on the fulfillment of some specific desire.

Life had been good to me. I had just passed my twenty-fifth birthday that day with Malcolm in the sailboat. Since my teens my body had filled out ideally. I had inherited a secret fortune and owned and ran *World Magazine,* a successful monthly of which Malcolm was the editorial director. My life was very pleasant indeed. And yet I had my secret dissatisfactions, many of them common to all women, which was why I had joined the consciousness-raising group in the first place.

"Are you awake?" Malcolm inquired.

"Yes." I had closed my eyes against the sun and, truthfully, I had been half dozing, but now his voice brought me fully awake. "What is it?"

"I can't get that women's group of yours out of my mind."

I turned on my side to look at him. The bottom of the boat was rough against my bare skin. I reached for my shorts and put them under my hip. I stretched out my halter-top under the weight of my thigh. "I can see that," I told Malcolm pointedly, eyeing the erection protruding from his fist.

"Why don't you tell me what you *really* talk about," he insisted.

"I told you already that there's nothing to tell. We don't actually get into sex very much."

"Oh come on, Christina. After all we've been through together, why hold out on me, of all people?"

I considered it. His erection looked raw and pink in the sunlight. The swell of his balls was not concealed by his sparse, sandy pubic hair. And his mouth—ahh! darlings! Malcolm's mouth—was positively Rabelaisian in its silent curlings.

My naked breasts were caressed by the gentle sea breeze. The nipples quivered. They ached. My thigh muscles clenched, the inner flesh grinding together. I tried to hold back the warm wetness trickling over my clitoris.

Malcolm! Under the proper circumstances he really turned me on. These, it was becoming obvious, were the proper circumstances.

"All right, darling," I told him. "I won't hold out on you. I'll tell you whatever you want to know."

"Then you do talk about sex in your women's group!" He tugged at his hard prick triumphantly.

"But of course, angel," I lied.

"You tell each other about your experiences?" he panted.

"Naturally."

"If we make out today, will you tell them about it?"

"In minuscule detail, my sweet."

"Then they'll all know just how I fuck you?" The idea was getting Malcolm hot. His flat, thin chest was working like a bellows.

"If I let you fuck me," I teased, "then my description will be a testimonial to your talents. If all goes well, that is," I added as an afterthought.

"Come on now, Christina. Have I ever forced myself on you?"

"Never, darling—perhaps you ought to try it." I squeezed my breast casually, stroking the nipple with a fingertip, inflaming Malcolm with the caress as well as myself.

"It's not my style," he said as he leaned over and licked my other nipple with his wondrous tongue. "Tell me the horniest experience you've heard since you joined the group."

It was a challenge to my creativity. Clutching Malcolm's mouth to my burning breast, I thought for a moment. "It's hard to choose," I said carefully. "Maybe it was Helen being ravished in the grease pit of the garage."

"Grease pit! Garage!" Malcolm came up for air. "Helen? Who's Helen? What does she look like?"

"She's a young housewife in our group. Maybe a year older than me and much thinner, but with very big breasts. She has brown hair and eyes and is sort of timid, which makes what happened all the more curious."

"Does she swing?" Malcolm's long hard-on was flat against my belly now, his balls tangling hotly in the golden fleece of my pubic triangle.

"Oh, no! Not Helen! She's absolutely faithful to her husband—except for this one time." I stroked Malcolm's rather bony bottom and was rewarded by the thrust of his cock as he writhed under my caress.

"What happened?" He licked the little pulse at the base of my neck.

"She'd gone out to this vegetable farm on the tip of Long Island," I improvised, "and on the way back she got a flat tire. It turned out the spare was flat too, and so she walked down this deserted road until she came to a gas station in the middle of nowhere." My voice was purposely husky as I launched into the make-believe story; my hands were impudent and busy on Malcolm's ass.

"Helen," I continued, "told the man she had a flat and asked him to come and fix it. He said it would cost her eight dollars and she'd have to pay in advance. Helen opened her purse and that's when she realized she'd spent all her money on produce. So she told the man she'd have to pay him with her VISA card. But he just laughed and said he didn't take credit cards. She said she didn't have cash, and what was she supposed to do? She offered to mail him a check, but he just laughed at her again. Then, finally, he sort of looked her up and down and told her that there might be a way. It was obvious what he meant."

"What was she wearing?" Malcolm is a stickler for details.

"A sundress," I decided. "With nothing underneath but cotton bikini panties." I slid my mouth over Malcolm's chest until his flat nipples started to stand up. "Aren't you tired of holding your prick?" I inquired. "Why don't you let me do it for you, darling?" I sat up to shift position and noticed out in the Sound a pair of binoculars zeroing in on my swaying naked breasts and stiff, elongated nipples.

"Sure!" Malcolm eagerly offered his long pecker to my hand. "But don't jerk it too hard, Christina. I have other plans."

"I'm not an amateur, darling. Certainly not with you." And on impulse I bent so that my long golden hair cascaded over his thighs and bestowed a quick, sucking kiss on the ruby crest of the cock in my fist.

"Ahhh!" Malcolm reached between my legs and stroked from my anus to the lips of my vagina. "Go on with the story of Helen, Christina. What did she do when the garage mechanic propositioned her?"

"She became indignant. She voiced her outrage. But she's basically a shy person, as I said, and she was ineffectual. Her voice was very shaky and she couldn't seem to get enough breath into her lungs, which made her too-large breasts heave and strain against the thin material of the sundress. And in the end she realized that her anger was only making the garage mechanic hornier. She couldn't help seeing that he'd developed a large, arrogant hard-on in the crotch of his grease-stained overalls." Malcolm's prick was throbbing in my hand, a compliment to my Scheherazade-like abilities.

"Was he a handsome young stud, this garage mechanic?" he asked, perspiration beading his brow. Perhaps the springtime sun was warmer than it seemed, or the reflecting green water was magnifying its heat. More likely it was my tickling fingers under his balls that were raising his temperature.

"No," I answered. "He was the furthest thing from young and handsome. The way Helen told it he was short and very muscular, but with a beer belly. He had a three-day stubble of beard and a bald spot. There was grease on his hands and grease on his face. From the first he struck her as an animal." My thighs were quivering with the investigations of Malcolm's hand between my legs. My panting breasts were becoming shiny with perspiration. My nipples burned.

"Why didn't she just walk away from him?" Malcolm asked. "I mean, a flat tire hardly seems reason enough to—"

"That's what we asked her." I stopped talking long enough to receive Malcolm's kiss. It was a long kiss, hot and cloaked in silence save for the rhythmic sound of the water lapping at our small sailboat. Our bodies entwined while we kissed and it felt as if the sun were smiling down even more strongly at this spectacle. Malcolm's hard cock was like a long branding iron sizzling against my squirming belly. I dug my nails into his shoulder blades as his talented tongue thrust and twirled deep inside my mouth. The sensations it provided sent thrills all up and down my naked body and made me slightly faint.

I was a moment recovering my voice after the kiss, and then I continued. "We asked her why she didn't just walk away, and Helen couldn't really answer us. She was repelled by the mechanic, by his slovenly appearance and his garage odor, by his very persona. She was appalled at his having propositioned her so baldly. And yet her legs in the sundress—her slim shapely legs in the mini-sundress," I elaborated, "—did not seem able to carry her away from him. Instead she embarked on the one course sure to seal her fate. She tried to bargain with him."

"Bargain? Bargain how?" Malcolm had straddled one of my legs and as I held it bent at the knee he moved up and down it, his burning balls riding the length of my smooth thigh.

"She said she might be willing to give him a kiss if he would change the tire," I said, then cupped one of my breasts in my hand and drew designs on Malcolm's chest with the nipple.

"That's absurd. It's childish."

What did he expect? After all, I'm not a professional writer. I hadn't had time to polish the plot, to revise and refine it. "Life is often absurd and childish, darling," I told him. "In any case, Helen offered him a kiss and he said he was willing to try it, to see if it was worth the trouble of changing the tire."

"And she went for that?" Malcolm jeered, stroking the squirming cheeks of my ass.

"She was very upset about being stranded, so she kissed him." I rubbed one of my nipples up and down the length of Malcolm's cock.

"Jesus!" He took both my breasts, pressed them tightly around his prick, and slid back and forth in the perspiration-slicked cleavage. His long, thin, hard prick was throbbing with jism. "Go on. Tell me about the kiss."

"As soon as her lips touched his, he bit her lip so she had to open her mouth wide and he stuck his thick tongue all the way down her throat. He grabbed her ass with both hands through the sundress and began rubbing up and down against her. His cock felt thick and hard and brutal through his overalls. He was right on target with it and it pushed her pussy lips wide apart and rode the cleft right through her sundress and cotton panties. It was the kiss of a beast in rut and it filled Helen with disgust. But at the same time she couldn't help being excited by it."

"Why not?" Malcolm panted. "*I'm* excited by it. By just hearing about it!" He pushed higher so that the tip of his prick was at my lips. "Lick it a little, Christina," he suggested.

"I saw someone watching us through binoculars before," I told him. "He looked as if he could focus right in on my nipples."

"He can't see us as long as we're lying on the bottom of the boat."

"He can if I raise my head to lick your prick."

"Does it really bother you?" Malcolm asked as his fingers moved expertly in the honey of my cunt. He knew me all too well!

"No," I admitted. "It excites me even more being watched." I licked my way up his cock, from his balls to the tip and then back down again. My suspended breasts panting, I repeated this three or four times. Then I raised my head toward the binoculars and stuck out my tongue impudently. "Don't you want to hear what happened to Helen then?" I asked Malcolm.

"Sure." He pushed his head between my legs, his hot, clever mouth against my cunt. "You talk. I'll just amuse myself while you go on with the story." His tongue snaked out and traced the outline of my sensitive, swollen, pulsing pussy lips.

"Lick me!" I moaned, raising my bottom so that the pussy lips parted to present the raw pink inner flesh to his tongue. "Lick me, angel, and I'll tell you about what happened to poor, dear Helen."

His tongue made wordless answer . . .

"The beast did not release Helen when the kiss was over," I gasped. "Instead he held her by the ass with one hand and pulled down the top of her flimsy sundress with the other. Her large, panting breasts came tumbling out—a naked surprise package contrasting with the rest of her slender, nymphet body. Immediately the animal grabbed for them with hands black with grease. His uncut fingernails raked the wide copper breast-tips. He squeezed the long, cinnamon nipples, then grunted and pumped with his hard-on against her pussy through their clothing. "Don't do that!" I squirmed to eject Malcolm's tormenting tongue from my smarting quim but then changed my mind and closed the lips of my pussy around it. Better to be tortured than empty, desolate.

"Sit on my face and play with my cock and balls," Malcolm ordered.

Not caring that the upper half of my naked body—my erect nipples and perspiring breasts—could be seen by the man with the binoculars, I did as Malcolm said. Before my staring, frenzied, green-liqueur eyes, a kaleidoscope of sails glided over the green-blue surface of the Sound. The passion of my sex-contorted face and heaving bosom was there to see for any who cared to look. I didn't care. Malcolm's lips were inside my cunt now and his tongue was on my erect clitty. I was grinding over him, clutching at his long, hard cock, and forcing myself to continue my improvisation about Helen and the auto mechanic:

" 'What are you doing?' Helen had demanded when he pulled down her dress. She meant to be indignant, to stop him, but her voice was weak and the pressure of his cock rubbing against her made her resolve even weaker. 'Aren't you going to fix my flat?' she asked him. 'These don't need fixing, lady!' He laughed and squeezed her big breasts. 'Any more air and they'll bust!' Helen was frightened now by his aggressiveness. 'Then what are you going to do to me?' she asked him. He laughed again and pulled up her skirt in back and began rubbing her ass through her cotton panties. 'Play with you,' he told her. 'I'm gonna play with you and you play with me.' And he licked her big breasts and then unzipped his fly. His cock was very hairy and black with car grease. There was a lot of sweat visible on his balls. And the aroma was really zoolike."

Malcolm sucked at my clitty as I squeezed his cock. A second pair of binoculars focused on my now hard-bouncing breasts from across the Sound. The blue of the sky was sheer Van Gogh, and the sun toasted my nipples. Once again I forced myself to go on with the story:

" 'Look,' Helen said, cornered now, desperate, 'if we're going to play with each other the way you say, then maybe you should wash up first. You know, get the grease off your hands and out from under your nails. Clean up your genitals a little.' But the grease monkey was merely insulted by the suggestion. 'Don't get high-and-mighty on me, lady,' he told her. 'You're as horny as I am! You think I can't tell? You think I can't see it in the way your nips are standing up? You think I can't feel how damp your crotch is getting? Now quit playing games!' And he grabbed her quim through her sundress and panties and began squeezing it. 'You're getting grease all over my clothes!' Helen protested. 'Jeez! I don't wanna do that!' he answered and reached under the dress and put his hand between her legs. She was embarrassed because, just like he'd said, her panties were sopping. 'Squeeze my cock!' he told her. 'It's all sweaty and greasy!' Helen exclaimed, protesting. 'Squeeze it!' He raised a hand like he was going to hit her. She squeezed it, and revolting as it was, when it began getting hard and jerking in her hand, Helen could no longer hold back the horniness she felt!''

"Listen, Christina!" Malcolm said, easing me off his face and coming up for air. "What were all you girls doing while Helen was telling you this?"

"*Women,*" I corrected him automatically. "Not girls. *Women.*" I had been on the brink of coming in his mouth. Now it subsided.

"Women. Sorry. Women. What were you doing while she was describing the incident? Were you playing with each other? With yourselves?"

"Of course not!" I was indignant. "We don't come together for sex! I told you that!"

"Sure, but this was pretty erotic stuff. Exciting. Hell, it's got me excited!" He stroked his long, thin hard-on. "Why wouldn't it have excited you?"

I stared at Malcolm, appalled at where my imagination had led us. It was obvious that the idea of a bunch of young women sitting around fondling themselves and each other while one of them related a bizarre sex experience was a major turn-on for him. I think his vision of what we were doing was even more exciting to him than the raunchy tale of Helen and the grease monkey.

It crossed my mind to cater to his fantasy. The hotter Malcolm became, the more my own ultimate erotic satisfaction increased. "We licked each other's breasts and sucked each other's pussies and writhed together in one mass of flesh while Helen told us how the beast entrapped her." That's what I thought of saying, that's how I thought of luring his tongue back to the nest of my quim. But I stopped myself. Quite simply, there are lines which must not be crossed—not if one is going to live with oneself. I had already compromised my feminist commitment by inventing a sex story which had never actually been related at our consciousness-raising sessions. I would not betray that commitment completely by drawing a false picture of the group's concentration on and participation in erotic experiences.

"No," I told Malcolm. "Nothing like that happened. Helen told her story and we listened. That was all."

"Oh," he pouted, disappointed, his mouth a sensual magnet. "Well, go on with the story, then."

"And you go on with what you were doing." I raised up and offered the steaming cup of my *yoni* to his lips, a demand for a quid pro quo.

"All right," Malcolm said, his head sliding under my

bottom. A moment later there was the delicious thrill of his tongue licking long and deep between the pinkened cheeks of my derriere.

I resumed speaking. "They were in the garage now, Helen and the chunky, balding grease monkey. His cock was sticking out of his overalls and his balls were hanging out too. The top of her sundress was down and her over-sized breasts with their wide tips and long nipples were bouncing up and down to the rhythm of his unclean hand squeezing her cunt through her cotton panties. She began jerking him off, not caring how filthy his cock was. Then she remembered that she'd have to be going home to her husband and kids. 'Listen,' she panted. 'Be careful! Don't come all over my dress!' She looked down at his trun-cheon of a cock and she couldn't stop the honey from her cunt spurting out over his fingers. It went right through the cotton of her panties. 'You've already got grease on my dress,' she said. 'I can explain that away. I'll say it happened when I was changing the tire. But I won't be able to explain away your cum all over my dress.' And all the time she was talking she was pressing her big hot bare breasts against him and pulling on his thick cock with both hands and squatting so his fingers could push the panties higher up her snatch."

"Snatch?" Malcolm asked, pulling his head out from under me just enough to speak. "I never heard you use that word before, Christina. It isn't like you. Your euphe-misms are usually so much more elegant." He then slid back under me and sucked at my anus and vagina indis-criminately with his marvelous mouth.

"I got carried away by the imagery," I confessed. "It's the sort of word the Beast—that's what Helen called him—brings to mind. Anyway, he pulled away from her long enough so she could take off the sundress. Then he backed her up against a car that had just been simonized and lifted her breasts so he could suck them. The wax was getting all over Helen's back and the seat of her panties, but the way his mouth was going at her nipples she was beyond caring about it. She didn't even protest when he pushed her down on her knees on the hard, dirty cement floor and made her suck his cock. It was enormously thick and hairy and it was all she could do to stretch her mouth open wide enough to get it in. The odor of grease and grime almost suffocated her. His balls were bouncing against her chin, large as eggs, and the hair over them was so wiry that it scratched her. But his hands were tight over her ears and she had no choice but to keep on sucking."

Malcolm, too, kept on sucking. My cunt was wide now, enveloping, greedy to spread over his entire face, to swallow it, to drench it with honey, to explode over it with the glory of orgasm. I stopped talking for a moment and moved over him, grinding into his mouth, throwing back my head, my golden hair streaming in the breeze, my breasts thrusting toward the hot-licking sun. Hazily I noticed that there were now three sets of binoculars focused on my lipstick-long nipples. I wondered if the watchers were masturbating. Well, why not, darlings? It was a beautiful day for it! Sunny. Warm. Blue skies and frothy clouds hanging over the tranquil waters of Long Island Sound. Yes, a beautiful day for sucking pussy, making up ribald stories, playing with Malcolm's cock, putting on a show for sea-going voyeurs, thinking about them pulling on their peckers because my hot nipples and bouncing breasts turned them on, thinking about the streams of white jism spurting from their cocks when they could no longer contain themselves. Yes! A beautiful, beautiful day for it!

"I think I want to fuck, Malcolm," I decided. "I think I want to finish telling you Helen's story while you fuck me."

"Great!" His face appeared, glistening with my honey. "How—?"

"Just lie there the way you are." I moved over him. I knelt with one knee on either side of his flat hips and lowered myself. With the tip of his cock just barely wedged in the gateway to my pussy, I resumed talking, swaying from side to side, teasing him, titillating him, my breasts grazing his face, but my position prevented him from penetrating my hungry cunt any deeper.

"Helen was kneeling in that drafty garage wearing nothing but her cotton panties now," I resumed. "Her mouth was stuffed with that thick truncheon cock and her nostrils were stopped up with its strong aroma. She thought he'd come in her mouth for sure and she was torn between her desire to get it over with and her fear of choking on it—he wasn't the kind of animal who would come considerately; he was the kind to let it pour down a woman's throat without caring if he killed her. Yet, even with these two heinous choices facing her, her cunt was burning with desire. She couldn't keep her hands away from his tool while she sucked him. She had slim hips and thighs and so, not being too fleshy, her brown-haired little cunt was the sort which exposes itself easily and completely. Looking down between her legs as she sucked, Helen could see her clitty sticking out and her finger strumming it. Everything down there was red and swollen, raw and wet. She shoved two fingers all the way up her quim and got ready to come."

"Damn it, Christina! Let me in!" Malcolm was tugging at my hips, trying to force my cunt to lower itself further on his long, slender, stiff cock.

"Don't be impatient, darling," I said, settling myself so that my tight quim sucked in another inch of his prick. His lips nipped at the tip of my breast, a titillating reward. I rocked back and forth without allowing him to penetrate me any further. The heart-shaped tip of his prick swelled against the inner walls of my pussy. I gasped, and then I tickled the underside of his balls.

"Christina! Christina!" Malcolm laughed. Despite his demand of a moment before, I knew that he loved to be teased. "Go on telling me about your fallen housewife and her repulsive seducer."

"Well, darling, as I was saying, Helen was sucking that huge cock and frigging herself and on the verge of coming. But the Beast, it seems, had other plans. All of a sudden he pulled his brutal cock out of her mouth and grabbed Helen's big breasts and pulled at them until she got to her feet. 'I'm gonna fuck you now, lady,' he told her. And he grabbed her cotton panties and ripped them right off her body. 'In the grease pit,' he added, guffawing like a rhinoceros in heat. Well, as you might imagine, Helen protested. But to no avail. He was quite simply too strong for her. He twisted her arm behind her back with one hand and he managed with the other hand to unbutton his sweaty, grease-stained overalls and shuck them off. He wasn't even wearing any underwear. And his body, which was heavy with muscles, but big bellied too, was covered with gorillalike hair, and parts of him were caked with grease. Nudity, according to Helen, didn't improve his aroma any either. And so he forced her down into the grease pit."

Meanwhile, Malcolm's long, slender middle finger slid between my buttocks and invaded my anus. I fell forward at the same time that my pussy slid down the length of his cock to settle over his balls. He moved his finger, tickling me. It drove me wild. I began to move in small, hard, grinding circles. The motion made his thin prick spin inside me. The sensation was like a shower of sparks over my clitoris. I pressed one of my breasts to his lips, forcing it into his mouth. I began moving up and down, his finger deep in my anus, guiding me. "Fuck me, darling," I moaned. "Fuck me deep!"

"Like this?" His groin rose and his hips rotated. "Do you like being fucked like this, Christina?" His cock moved in and out of my cunt, his tormenting finger in and out of my bunghole.

"Yes! Yes!" My pussy clenched at his long, slender, pumping rod; my honey drenched his balls.

"What happened in the grease pit?" Malcolm panted.

"The Beast made Helen get on her hands and knees," I told Malcolm, exciting myself even more by closing my eyes to envision the scene as I spoke. "He made her do this with her knees wide apart so that her raw cunt was completely open and exposed. It put a strain on the muscles of her arms and legs and made them stand out in a way that accentuated Helen's slenderness. This in turn made her oversized breasts seem even heavier as they hung down all wet with perspiration. The Beast mounted her from behind, palming her breasts in his huge, hairy hands, clawing the bronze aureoles, pulling at the long cinnamon nipples. At the same time his filthy prick—thick and hard as a billy club—was stretching poor Helen's narrow quim to its utmost limits. His greasy, hairy belly was spread out over her small, smooth ass, and his large hot balls were bouncing against her. Grunting like a pig, pulling on her perspiring breasts, he started to fuck her."

"Like I'm fucking you?" Malcolm asked, then pulled my face down to his and kissed me. His tongue slashed in and out of my mouth in cadence with his long finger in my ass and his hard prick in my cunt.

The triple sensation was delicious to the point of delirium. "No!" I gasped when the kiss was over. "Not at all like you're fucking me, angel. Your movements are subtle and slowly—albeit excruciatingly—provocative. The Beast had none of your finesse, as Helen described the experience. His was pure, hard-driving animal lust. His huge cock tore at the flesh of her pussy. His screwing of Helen was most painful to her. And yet pain and pleasure can be so close in the act of making love . . ."

"Can they, now?" Malcolm asked, deliberately pushing his finger all the way up my anus so that it hurt. Then, with perfect timing, he slid the entire length of his stiff cock over the swollen tip of my clitoris.

"Bastard!" I raked his chest with my fingernails and kissed him and bit him at the same time. "Fuck me!" There were tears in my eyes, but I didn't care. "Fuck me hard!"

"Like this?" He shoved his cock all the way up and twisted it so that the head caressed the mouth of my womb.

"Yes!" I panted. "Harder! Faster!"

"Very well!" Malcolm pushed back on my shoulders, forcing me backwards. He moved with me and when the maneuver was complete, I was on my back on the bottom of the sailboat, the rough planking bruising my skin, his long, rigid cock still buried inside me. Now he put my legs up on his shoulders and pushed in even deeper. "You want it harder? You want it faster?" he panted. He began pumping with long, brutal strokes. "Then you shall have it, Christina!" Doubling my legs back so that my toes touched my shoulders and my cunt was strained open as wide as possible, Malcolm fucked me as only Malcolm can fuck. "Go on with your story," he demanded. "Tell me how the Beast raped your friend."

"It wasn't really rape," I panted. "Pain and all, Helen wanted it just as much as I want you right now." I rocked to his pumping. I was on fire now, beyond worrying about the binoculars focused on us from the sailboats which had been moving in closer to achieve a clearer view. His weight was on my naked, burning ass and his thrustings— as hard and fast as I had pleaded for them to be—were like the lash of a whip goading me to expend more energy, urging my flesh to fiery orgasm. "It wasn't rape," I repeated. "Helen didn't care anymore that he had a big belly, that he was hairy, that he was balding, that he was filthy and greasy, that his body odor was unpleasant. She didn't care that she, a respectable housewife and mother, was at the bottom of an automobile grease pit, was actually wallowing in the black gook, that her thin, naked, big-breasted body was splattered with the slippery, scummy oil and slime and carbon of cars. She didn't care that she was on her hands and knees like some cow rutting in the fields, her nose pressed to the filth, her ass high in the air, her cunt spread to the Beast like a bitch in heat. No, Helen didn't care. She just wanted that thick donkey-cock to never stop pumping inside her burning cunt. During those moments she never wanted to go home to her nice clean house, her nice clean husband. All she wanted was to stay in that filthy garage grease pit forever, panting and snorting like an animal, snorting and growling like the Beast, shaking her heavy breasts and pushing back with her skinny ass and fucking and being fucked until she came and then came again, and again . . ."

"Only once for us, Christina," Malcolm teased me. "It gets too cold out here after the sun goes down." He pumped into my exposed cunt, his shoulders holding my body doubled in half, his pink balls slapping against my ass.

"Once is all I ask," I told him fervently. "I'm so hot! I want to feel you coming inside me, darling. I want that spurt of cream to scald my womb. I want to feel it and then I want to wrench your cock from its roots with the violence of my coming!''

"Easy, Christina," he laughed breathlessly. "I may want to use it again."

"Come inside me!" I begged. "Do it!"

"The way the Beast came inside your friend Helen?"

"Yes!" I screamed, clawing at his ass, drawing blood. "Oh God, yes!"

"Tell me about it."

" 'I'm gonna come, lady!' That's what he told Helen. And he pulled down on her heavy breasts until she fell forward. Then he came down full force on her ass with his cock up her cunt and started shooting his load inside her. Flattened, pinned, Helen couldn't hold back. She started to come with him, all of her climaxing movements inside her painful, but not to be denied. She came with him while he kept on pumping, his jism filling her quim, and then running out and down the insides of her legs. She was completely debased and she hated it, but she couldn't stop coming. She was shrieking with it. Coming and shrieking, coming and shrieking . . . Now, Malcolm! Please!'' My imagination and verbalizing had pushed me to the brink of orgasm. "Give it to me now, darling!"

"Yes!" His thin frame bore down on my doubled-up body. His balls forced their way between the lips of my quim, the tip of his slender cock brushing the entrance to my womb. And then he began to come—long, hot, creamy spurts that pushed me over the edge.

I screamed wordlessly. The blazing sun spun in the blue sky overhead, and the gentle lapping of the water at the sailboat was suddenly like a roar in my ears. My clutching cunt twisted and wrenched at the spurting cock inside it. I came. Malcolm came. It lasted a long, long time. It lasted for what seemed an eternity . . .

When I opened my eyes, the sun was back in its usual place in the blue sky. The sailboat lay at rest, no longer rocking frantically with our lovemaking. The soft breeze of Long Island Sound was like a rebuke to the perspiration drying on my smooth skin. I was stretched out full-length, the energy drained from me, a sort of smug contentment filling me like balm. Malcolm was beside me, his slender body also at rest, his marvelously sensual mouth uncharacteristically slack, his long penis curled over his flat belly like a napping eel.

Finally I sat up and reached for my bag. The gesture was automatic. I wanted a comb for my hair.

At the same moment Malcolm also sat up. He desired his usual after-sex cigarette. He reached for his jeans to retrieve the pack from his pocket.

Both our gestures were aborted by a sudden burst of applause. Mouths agape, we saw that half a dozen assorted sailboats, mostly brightly colored Sunfish, had circled us at the mouth of the cove where our own craft had lain at anchor. I recognized the binoculars worn by some of the occupants of the sailboats. But they hadn't really been needed. While Malcolm and I had been occupied making love, they had moved into easy eyeshot of the exhibition we were providing. They were a young crowd, both male and female, and now they were showing their appreciation of our performance. Their laughter was good-natured as they clapped their approval.

Embarrassed, Malcolm and I looked at each other. "What should we do?" I wondered.

"There's only one thing to do," he pointed out.

He was right, of course. And so, when he bowed, deeply, his penis flapping in the wind, I curtsied. The gesture made my naked pussy pucker under the setting sun, but I didn't care. I owed it to my public.

Then I put on my shorts and halter. Malcolm pulled on his jeans and T-shirt. We hoisted anchor. We raised our sail. And, trailed by our fans, we headed back to port.

"Tell me something," Malcolm said as we docked. "That story about your friend Helen—is that really a true story?"

"Of course, darling," I assured him. "Why would I lie?"

Why indeed? I didn't know the answer myself.

# CHAPTER TWO

One reason that I lied—and it is so often the case, is it not?—was that when I told the truth, I had not been believed. Malcolm had rejected the very idea that six young women might meet to discuss the problems of being women in a man's world and not zero in on sexuality. It had seemed inconceivable to him. And yet our meetings so far had barely touched upon the topic of our erotic lives. So many other things had seemed so much more pressing.

But Malcolm was incapable of understanding this. After all, he and his obsessively bonding male friends enjoyed nothing so much as standing around the bar bragging to each other about their sexual conquests. Why would not women do the same?

Men!

Such was my attitude that evening when, after showering away the residue of my interlude with Malcolm and changing into slacks and a blouse, I hired a limousine to take me from my Park Avenue apartment to Forest Hills where our consciousness-raising meeting was being held at the apartment of Helen Willis. (Although I can easily afford to keep my own car and chauffeur, it seems an unnecessary nuisance in Manhattan.) Traffic was light and so I arrived early. Helen greeted me at the door and offered me a glass of wine. We sat down to chat while we waited for the others to arrive.

Helen Willis—the Helen of the invented story I had told Malcolm—was pretty much as I had described her to him: a slender and shy young woman with brown hair, her sweater bulging remarkably with the impressive package of her oversized breasts. Her face was attractive but nervous, and she was constantly ducking her head as if to apologize for whatever she was saying. At the moment she was discussing her husband. It seemed he had objected to going out that evening so that Helen might play hostess to our meeting. His obstreperousness had interfered with her getting her two toddlers to bed, and so this was her first chance to draw a deep breath all evening.

Listening, I realized that this was the first time Helen had really talked about her husband and children except in the most superficial manner. She had never mentioned his name before. As it turned out now, it was Bruno.

"What sort of work does Bruno do?" I asked casually.

"He's an automobile mechanic—a grease monkey in a garage . . . Christina? . . . Christina, why are you laughing?"

"I'm sorry," I gasped. "I'm sorry." But I couldn't seem to make myself stop.

"It's not funny," Helen told me. "It's not so great being married to a grease monkey, believe me! He's always got the stuff under his nails. He's always sort of grimy. And sometimes he gets it on me."

I was seized with another convulsion of laughter.

"You think it's so funny being married to a man who falls into bed without remembering to wash off the damned garage?" Helen was indignant.

"I'm not laughing at you." Somehow I managed to get the words out. "Really I'm not."

"Not that it happens so very often." Helen was pitying herself now, whining a little. "Sometimes I think he'd rather drink beer than—you know."

"He drinks beer?" I asked, trying to maintain control.

"Oh, sure. Bruno's got a real beer belly."

"A beer belly!" I lost the battle. I burst out laughing again.

The doorbell saved me momentarily from Helen's indignation. Melinda Holloway followed her back into the room. She cocked her head at the spectacle of me snickering while trying to stop by sipping wine. "What's with Christina?" she inquired.

"She thinks my lousy marriage is hilarious." Hostess or not, Helen was bitter.

"Listen," I said, chagrined at my effect on her. "It's not that. It's the irony of the situation."

"What irony? What situation?" Melinda asked. She was a tall, voluptuous, statuesque redhead. She was in her late thirties, recently divorced, and was always the member of our group who insisted on clarification.

"It's really not important," I told her. "It's just something that happened with my lover today." I took Helen's hands in mine. "I apologize. Really I do. I wasn't laughing at you and your husband. I was laughing at myself."

"Well, all right," Helen said, mollified. She went into the kitchen to fetch some potato chips to go with the wine. She would probably have made canapés except that we had decided at our very first meeting that we weren't going to let ourselves be trapped into that traditional role of providing nourishment for one another and competing to see who could make the fanciest hors d'oeuvres.

"Lover?" Melinda asked. "You never mentioned a lover before, Christina. I didn't even know you had one."

"Had one what?" The speaker was Joyce Dell, the baby of our group. When Helen had admitted Melinda, she had left the door ajar and Joyce had let herself in. Now the eighteen-year-old Joyce, leggy in jeans and pert-nippled against the tank top she was wearing, flung herself into a chair and pouted. The pout was meant to insist on an answer to her question.

"A lover," Melinda explained. "Christina has a lover."

"Oh?" Joyce yawned. "Is that all?" She yawned again. (Is there anything so sophisticated, so hip, so blasé as an adolescent girl?) "Only one?" she added as an afterthought.

"As a matter of fact, no," I replied. "I've had many, many lovers if the truth must be known."

"And it certainly must!" Stephanie McCall announced as she sailed into the room, a striking brunette in a flowing scarlet gown by Pierre Cardin. A successful advertising copywriter about my age, Stephanie might have stepped out of the pages of *Vogue*. Such was her poise, and her uniquely personal style as well. She was an original, this Stephanie, and her forceful personality was rarely to be denied. "Tell all, Christina," she insisted now. "Start with your first lover and don't leave anything out."

"That's not what we're here for!" Helen complained. "Leave that sort of thing to the men. We're here to try to understand our female nature, to probe ourselves as women. We're not here to look at ourselves as the sex objects men would have us be."

With the exception of Stephanie, there was general agreement with this. She was silent, obviously formulating some counterargument. But she was saved from having to voice it by the arrival of Amanda Briggs, the sixth and final member of our consciousness-raising group.

"Nonsense!" Amanda proclaimed from the doorway. She was a blonde like me, only heavier, perhaps five or six pounds overweight, all of it in her hips and bottom.

We had teasingly nicknamed Amanda "Earth Mother" because of her sweet and supportive nature and because, of all of us, she was the most womanly. Hers was the sort of glowing fleshiness Rubens loved to paint. "We can talk about sex from a woman's point of view without falling into the trap of looking at ourselves the way men do," Amanda said. "I mean, we probably all have problems in that area, hang-ups—"

"Not me!" Joyce Dell tossed her head, her ponytail swishing arrogantly. "I don't have any hang-ups."

"Ah, youth!" Melinda interjected, regarding Joyce with blue-eyed envy. "Wait until your first divorce, my dear."

"I'm never going to get divorced because I'm never going to get married. Who needs it? I'd rather play the field."

"You'll grow out of that," Helen told her.

"Why should she?" I wondered. "I never have. And I'm pretty satisfied with my life."

I should have known better than to draw attention to myself. Melinda was nothing if not persistent. "Tell us what happened with your lover today, Christina." It was said as a demand.

Keeping a nervous eye on Helen, our hostess, I made full confession of my activities with Malcolm Gold that afternoon. Sipping at her wine, Helen's delicate face became flushed when I got into the more graphic parts of the story I had made up for Malcolm. However, she wasn't at all offended at having been used in such a manner. On the contrary, she was obviously flattered to have been the subject of my fantasy.

She giggled at my descriptions of the grease pit. In a voice that was soft, but nevertheless ironic, she made the mock accusation that I must have been peeping through the keyhole of her bedroom to have described Bruno's technique so accurately. And when I had concluded my account, Helen sighed and said how odd it was that *my* fantasy was *her* reality, while her own fantasy was not really so very far from *my* reality.

Melinda's reaction was quite different. The flame-haired amazon was quite indignant at my having "distorted" our group experience to titillate Malcolm. When Joyce countered none too tactfully that Melinda was overreacting, probably because of her age, it sparked a free-for-all discussion regarding the ethics of my misrepresenting the group's focus on sexuality.

This went on for a while, and finally Stephanie said something that got to the heart of the matter and gave us all pause. "Methinks the ladies doth protest too much," she pointed out with that Bryn Mawr inflection of hers. "It seems that we are more comfortable with debating the relatively minor matter of Christina's misrepresentation of our meetings than we are dealing with our sexuality. I would submit that it doesn't matter one damn whether or not we fulfill her lover's image of how libidinous our proceedings are. What is important is that we should stop evading the subject. I think the time has come when we must discuss the eroticism of our lives." She strode back and forth across the room nervously as she spoke, and yet her poise was never for a moment in doubt. Her shoulders were back, her bosom thrust upward, her derriere tucked in, her long, perfectly manicured hands molding her hips as she moved in a swirl of scarlet Cardin.

"You mean like fucking and sucking and like that?" young Joyce said, and yawned.

"I'm glad Bruno isn't home to hear that language in his living room." Helen's wifeliness asserted itself.

"You can't be serious!" I reacted. "Bruno works in a garage. He must hear that language all the time."

"Sure. But not in his house. And not from women!"

"Where have we failed?" I moaned, disappointed in Helen.

"I think Stephanie is right." Amanda said, smoothing over our little flare-up. "And Joyce has a point, too. We probably shouldn't be shy about using those words. They keep us from being vague; they keep us honest. And since we've been honest with each other where everything else is concerned, why not about our sex lives?" Her roundish face dimpled as she turned to Helen. "If Bruno comes in," she assured her, "we'll cut off the discussion. You don't have to worry." She took Helen's hand in hers and squeezed it reassuringly.

"Sisterhood!" When it comes to gestures, Stephanie's timing is perfect. She picked up the carafe and poured wine into each of our glasses. "Sisterhood!" Proposing toasts, I'm sure, is a knack perfected in the better finishing schools. "Sisterhood!" She raised her glass with an aristocratic flourish and drank.

The rest of us followed her example.

"And now let's talk about balling and blow-jobs," Joyce said. There were definitely moments when her outrageous frankness was most refreshing.

"Since it's her house, why don't we start with Helen?" Amanda said, still holding her hand. "What did you mean before when you said that your fantasy wasn't so very far from Christina's reality?"

"I guess I was envious," Helen sighed. "You see, I spent the afternoon with two whiny children, cooking spaghetti for my husband who's already too fat and who 'banged' me last night—his word—just to get his rocks off and without giving a damn that I didn't even come close to an orgasm. Christina spent her afternoon with a suave, sophisticated lover who was sensitive to her mood, her desires, her reactions. While I was in the kitchen, she was out in a sailboat with a soft breeze and the warm sun and an accomplished and considerate lover. My life is such a drag and hers seems so damned romantic that I can't help being jealous.''

There was no reason, I suppose, that I should have felt guilty, but I did. I didn't know what to say. Still, it was obvious from the silence that everybody was waiting for me to say *something*. ''Nobody's reality lives up to their fantasy.'' It was the best I could come up with. ''Not mine any more than yours, Helen. Not really.''

''My reality is being skewered in bed like I was a chunk of liver,'' Helen said bitterly.

''But you have the power to change your reality,'' Melinda told her. ''Have an affair.''

''I don't know any men I'd want to have an affair with. All the men I know are like Bruno. I don't move in Christina's circles.''

''Wait a minute!'' Stephanie interjected. ''Is that the best you can do by way of a fantasy? To be Christina? What about before you knew her? What was your fantasy then?''

Helen thought a moment. Then, unexpectedly, she giggled. ''Jeremy Irons,'' she said. ''Someone very suave and debonair.''

''Your fantasy lover is British?'' Melinda was, as always, a stickler for nailing down the details.

''No. Not necessarily. Jeremy Irons was just an example. I could have said Robert Redford. It's a certain kind of person I'm talking about.''

''Like Mick Jagger.'' Joyce sighed.

''No. Not macho. Not youth culture either. My dream lover . . . Well, I guess the best definition would be that he has to be as different from my husband Bruno as possible. He has to be the kind of man who might cover my naked body with flowers before he possessed me.'' Helen closed her eyes and an almost voluptuous smile played over her lips. "Yes, he would be all golden tan, with piercing blue eyes and curly hair. Not much body hair though, and what there was would be soft and light and sensual. His belly would be flat. So flat! And his flanks would be smooth. Most important of all, he'd be clean. His hands would be clean, and his fingernails. There would be no pouches in his flesh where dirt might collect. He wouldn't have to be too muscular, just as long as he wasn't paunchy. And—oh, yes!—as long as his penis and balls weren't too hairy and were clean." Helen's hands clenched and unclenched around the apron in her lap.

"What would you do with him?" Amanda asked softly.

"You mean what would he do to me!" Helen's eyes were still closed and her slight, top-heavy figure rocked back and forth as she continued. "Maybe we'd meet in the woods," she said. "Perhaps a picnic lunch. Wine." She finished the glass in her hand and although she was the hostess, held it out to be refilled. Stephanie, ever gracious, poured from the carafe. "Yes, definitely wine." Helen's eyes opened to reveal an uncustomary sparkle. She closed them again and resumed speaking. "It would make us sleepy and we would curl up on the picnic blanket in the shade of a large oak tree. The sun would speckle us hotly through the leaves and after a while he would murmur how lovely I was. I would demur, of course, but he would insist. I would blush a little and without my willing it, my tongue would lick my lips. He would bend toward me tentatively and then, reading the willingness in my eyes, he would kiss me."

"About time!" Young Joyce was impatient. "I thought the two of you might perish of old age before he got around to that!"

"He would definitely not be the kind of man to rush things," Joyce told her. "The success of our liaison would depend on that. After the kiss," she mused, "we would resume our walk in the woods."

"Jesus!" Joyce's ponytail wagged in disgust.

"We would walk with our arms around each other's waists." Helen ignored her. "We would come to a river-bank and being very warm from our stroll, we would decide to go skinny-dipping."

"How daring!" Joyce said sarcastically.

"Still a bit shy of each other, we would go behind separate bushes to take off our clothes."

"Why not wear blindfolds?"

"Be quiet, Joyce! We're here to be supportive of one another. Have you forgotten?" Amanda said, coming to Helen's rescue.

"When we stepped out from behind the bushes," Helen went on, her voice quite husky now, "he would look at my breasts and his eyes would light up. I have very heavy breasts for such a thin person, you know, and he would be surprised to see how firmly they stand out and how excit-ingly they're shaped—like melons with bright berry tips. Anyway, he would stare and this would embarrass me, and so I would run to the bank of the river with my breasts bobbling and I would dive in. From there I would watch him as he approached. I would see his long, thin, rapierlike penis."

"Cock, dammit! Can't you say cock?" Joyce was perspir-ing. Impatient as she was, in some strange way Helen's imagery was turning her on.

"Cock," Helen said, licking her lips. "Pecker. Shlong. Prick. Dick. Wang." She smiled. "But I prefer to think of it as a sword. Anyway, as he stands there on the riverbank before diving in, his you-know-what is sort of halfway to an erection from his having seen my big naked breasts. His pink balls are swollen and bouncing against his tanned thighs. When he dives, his bottom in the sunlight is like a Greek sculpture.''

"Isn't he ever going to fuck you?'' Joyce wriggled.

"Shh!'' Amanda silenced her. But her usual farmgirl composure had also been ruffled and she was shifting from one substantial buttock to the other and back again as she hung on Helen's words.

"We would frolic in the water,'' Helen decided. "My naked breasts would float on the surface with their big, hard berry nipples inviting him. When they grazed his chest, his penis would uncoil beneath the surface and stretch against my thigh like a water snake seeking warmth. Perhaps he would kiss me again then. Our tongues would clash. His hand would cup my breast, toying with the nipple, arousing me. Our flat bellies would press wetly and hotly against one another. I would hold onto his slim hips, and then perhaps his smooth, sleek bottom. Slowly we would make our way to shore.''

"About time!'' Joyce panted. "You've got me coming in my jeans and he hasn't even stuck it in yet.''

"Shut up, Joyce!'' The three of us admonished her with one voice.

"We would lie on the grass, our bodies wet and glistening and hot. We would kiss and our drenched limbs would lock together. His chest would be hard against the softness of my panting breasts. His hands would run over my slender body—my hips, my buttocks—as if it were made of glass. Then, slowly, he would push me back on the grass and stroke my slim thighs until they parted. His erection would be full-blown now, and he would rub it between the lips of my vagina. He would not put it in, not at first.''

"Of course not,'' Joyce hooted. "Why would he want to do a dirty thing like that?''

"I would cup his balls and play with them. He would

kiss my breasts, my straining nipples. He would lick and suck them. I would take his erection in my hands and stroke it. We would talk about what we were doing. He would ask me if I liked this or that and if I said yes, why, then he would do it—but delicately, sensitively. He might kiss the lips of my vagina, for instance. Or he might nibble my buttocks.'' Helen giggled. ''I've always wanted a man to nibble my buttocks—right at the cleft, you know; but nibble, not bite. I'd never even dare suggest that to Bruno,'' she added bitterly. ''I'd be too afraid he'd sink his ugly teeth into my bottom-flesh.''

''Why did you marry him if you feel that way about him?'' Melinda blurted out.

''Why does anybody get married? I was young. I didn't know any better. It was the thing to do. He asked me.''

''Why do you stay married?'' Melinda demanded. ''Why don't you get divorced like I did?''

''The kids . . .'' Once again Helen sighed.

''That's no reason!'' Melinda was firm. ''Believe me, it's better to cut loose at your age than at mine.'' Her red hair shimmered like a flame of conviction as she nodded her head.

''That's for another time,'' Amanda chided her mildly. ''Go on, Helen.''

''Finally he would spread my legs more widely. He would open the lips of my vagina as if they were flower petals. He would take his stiff penis and he would insert it in the entrance.''

''Hooray!''

''Be quiet, Joyce!''

''He would just barely insert it. I would look down the length of my slim body and I would see it embedded there. It would excite me and I would pant. He would lick my heaving breasts and push his saber in a little more. The head would press against my clitoris and I would start to writhe and my honey would pour over it. He would ask me if that felt good and I would say it did. He would kiss me and his tongue would slide in and out of my mouth as his organ stabbed deeper into my tight, twisting tunnel of love. I would be moaning by then and my legs would be stretched as wide as I could stretch them. I would dig my nails into his sweet behind and my reward would be the full penetration of his long erection. His balls would bounce hotly against my bottom and the lips of my vagina and he would move in and out of me with long, deep, hard strokes. I would move with him, moaning, pleading with him to hurry, to make it last, to hurry, to make it last. Then, and only then, we would in our frenzy talk dirty to each other. 'Do you like the way I fuck you, Helen?' he would ask. 'Yes,' I would say. 'Your cock feels wonderful in my cunt. Stroke my clitty with it.' And he would do that. He would do anything I asked. His main pleasure would come from satisfying my carnal desires. 'Take it out for a minute and lick my pussy,' I might tell him. 'Of course, my dear.' And he would suck up my juices with gusto. 'Would you like to taste them on my cock?' he might ask. And I might deign to do that, licking my own honey from his wonderful prick. Of course he would know just when to put it back in. And he would tickle my asshole as he fucked me again. This would drive me wild and I would begin laughing as if hysterical. But I wouldn't be hysterical. I would be happy! So happy! My cunt would be filled with his prick and there would be rainbow colors in my brain and then I would dig my nails into him and perhaps scream, and I would start to come. As soon as he felt that, he would stop holding back, and he would come with me, his cream—his clean white cream—gushing into my cunt, burning it, cleansing it, while his erupting prick jerked one orgasm after another from me.''

Helen opened her eyes then. She smiled. She didn't say

anything else. She was obviously waiting for some response from the group. When she didn't get it (we were too affected by the picture she had drawn to find words so quickly), she decided to say one other thing. "The best thing about that daydream," she told us, "is his coming as I start to come instead of before. Bruno always comes fast and just as I start to react, he pulls out. I'm always left all sticky and hung up. I usually have to go in the bathroom and finish myself off."

"Why don't you get him to use his hand or his mouth to finish you off?" Stephanie wondered.

"He'd never do that. He doesn't think women are supposed to be horny. Not even when they've just been laid. Not if they're wives, anyway."

"Goddamn men!" Amanda was uncharacteristically bitter.

"Tomorrow, Christina, you can tell your lover that fantasy." Helen grinned at me.

"It's too idyllic," Melinda said, then strode across the room on her long legs and poured herself another glass of wine. "Even fantasy should be grounded in the realities of the flesh. For me, at least, they have to be if they're going to work." She ran her fingers through her long red hair. "Helen's fantasy may be fine for her, but for me it's too much like a fairy tale. I want something very different from that. I'm thirty-eight years old and my husband was a pussycat in bed with me before the divorce. Now, from what I hear, he's a tiger with his new lady. But of course she's got all that youth to turn him on with."

"Don't low-rate yourself, Melinda," Amanda said. "You're gorgeous and you know it. You look like a young Rockette—tall and bosomy and with those gorgeous legs. I'm ten years younger than you are and I don't have half the things going for me that you do." Amanda hugged her briefly and returned to her chair.

"Thanks." A surge of emotion caught Melinda off

balance and she took a moment to wipe a few tears from her eyes. "You're beautiful and I don't believe a word of it, but thanks, darling. Anyway, I was digressing. What I wanted to say was that what I want out of sex isn't all sugar-coated and shimmery like Helen's vision. My dream has sharp edges. It has the smells of rutting and the feel of sweating flesh. I don't want men to call the shots for their own pleasure any more than Helen does. On the other hand, I don't want all that polite conversation, all that consideration and consultation, either. I want hard, raw fucking and sucking and what-have-you. I want it all, unvarnished, unadorned, before I'm too old to enjoy it, before my energy starts to decline and undermine my performance. Just once I want it down and dirty the way I never had it with Herbert."

"You were faithful to him?" Joyce asked Melinda, wide eyed.

"Oh yes, baby. I was a creature of the fifties, albeit the late fifties. I cut recipes out of *Good Housekeeping* and planted rosebushes and read everything I could on how my marriage could be saved and never, never uncrossed my legs in the name of adultery. It's the way it was, sweet. Herbert didn't beat me, and I didn't cheat on him. That was the deal."

"The past is past," Amanda told her gently. "And the future is now."

"Down and dirty," Stephanie reminded Melinda. "What exactly do you mean by that?"

"Four young studs." Melinda's breasts swelled, parting the strands of her long red hair. "All four taking me on at the same time. Shifting patterns." She licked her lips. "Athletic types with the bodies of young men. Shiny bodies, bulging with muscles. All with thick, juicy cocks and heavy balls. I would spread myself over a bed and take them to me. I would hold a stiff pecker in each hand." She was panting now. "I would take one in my mouth and lick it, glorying in the feel of the hot, hard flesh choking me. The fourth stud would climb over me. He would part my red gash with both hands. He would shove his cock all the way up it and he would fuck me hard. And fast. Hard and fast . . . I would come, but that would only be the beginning. I would turn on my side and a cock would slide up my ass like a hot poker. I would force myself to relax so that my anus would stretch wide to allow him to pump in and out of me there. His balls would bounce like burning ingots against the cheeks of my ass. Another cock would be between my breasts, ass cheeks riding up and down on my nipples, shaft dragging balls and pumping in my perspiration-slicked cleavage. The third stud would be standing off a little and jerking off. He'd be really turned on because I'd have the fourth prick, the one that had just fucked me and come in my cunt, in my mouth now, and I'd be licking and sucking it back to hardness. The balls would be dripping with his cum and my honey from before, but I wouldn't care. I'd be lapping it all up and squealing and slapping my ass back against the stomach of the stud with his prick up it and squeezing the cock between my breasts and watching the cock that was jerking off as it started to come and shoot its stream of jism all over the rest of us . . . We would have to rest, I suppose, but then we would begin again. I would take two of the cocks in my mouth at the same time and suck them. I would be on my hands and knees. A stud would slide under me and pull me down by my hips until my cunt slid over his cock. Then the last stud would mount me from behind and stick his cock up my ass. I would feel the two cocks fucking inside me as I sucked the other two cocks. The two in my mouth would be rubbing against each other as I licked them with my tongue. Four balls would bounce and roll over my chin. Perhaps I would stick a finger up each of their assholes. And down below, through the little partition of flesh separating my ass from my pussy, I would feel the two cocks rubbing against each other. I would be crammed with cock—my mouth, my cunt, my ass. I would go berserk and I would start to come and when I did, the two cocks in my mouth would begin shooting at the same time and the cock in my ass would erupt and by so doing would bring off the cock in my cunt. Jism would be dripping from my mouth and my cunt and my ass. I would be having it all, down and dirty, for the first time in my life, letting go at the age of thirty-eight, and I would love it!''

"Holy shit!" Joyce shouted, the first to find her voice. "Holy shit!"

"Please," Helen protested. "I don't like bathroom language."

"But we've all been using dirty words."

"There's a difference."

"That's true," I agreed with Helen. "Sex words turn most of us on. Words related to elimination turn many of us off."

"But not all," Joyce told me flatly. "When you're young, you don't have hang-ups like you do when you get older."

Twenty-five years of age, and already I was being consigned to the older generation. Ah, the cruelty of youth! The unthinking cruelty of youth!

"Let that be a lesson to you, Christina," Stephanie said, amused. "Never rule out anything where the Young Turks of the sexual revolution are concerned."

"Are you really into bathroom games?" I asked Joyce.

"Why not? It's natural, isn't it? Whatever's natural doesn't turn me off."

"And that's your fantasy?" I asked, repelled but interested. "Urination? Defecation? Enemas? Water sports?"

"There's nothing natural about an enema, or water

sports,'' Joyce informed me with the snotty expertise of youth. ''But as for the rest—''

''Defecation?'' Melinda couldn't hide her shock.

''Well, no,'' Joyce relented. ''Too messy. But peeing could be fun.''

''Have you ever—?'' Amanda left the question hanging.

''No,'' Joyce admitted. ''But I sure have thought about it. I mean, we're supposed to be talking about fantasies, aren't we? Well, I have a lot of fantasies about that.''

''Such as?'' Stephanie wouldn't let Joyce off the hook.

''Oh, taking a shower with a guy and peeing on each other. I mean, the water would wash it right off, so it wouldn't be yicky or anything. Or holding his thing while he pissed. The idea of doing that really turns me on. I mean holding it all hot with water and watching the stream of yellow gold piss spurting out! Wow! Also, I like the idea of his watching me pee. I mean getting right down there where he can see it coming out of me and wetting my bush when it comes.''

''Have you ever suggested doing any of those things to your boyfriend?'' Helen wondered.

''I don't have any one boyfriend. I play the field. I like variety.''

''Well, then have you ever thought about it with one of the field?''

''No. You see, my fantasy isn't another kid. It's some mature guy, a guy who's been around, a guy who would know what he's doing. That's the kind that turns me on. I've never made it with anyone over twenty-two. But what I want is to have a really wild scene like that with an older man.''

''But young men have all the energy,'' Melinda protested.

''Maybe so. But I'm not looking to run a marathon with the guy. All the energy in the world doesn't mean much if he doesn't know how to use it.''

"From the mouths of babes," Stephanie murmured.

"I've had too many young guys jump my bones like they were going out for the team. I want somebody who'll go a little slower and who has imagination and know-how and is willing to experiment. And if he's a little short on wind, why I don't mind slowing down."

"It sounds to me like a father fixation," Helen remarked.

"Oh, come on!" The comment irritated Stephanie. "Labels are too easy. You can attach one to anybody's fantasy if you want to. They don't really mean anything, or explain anything. Joyce's fantasy may be different, but it's as legitimate as anybody else's."

"You don't see infantilism in her obsession with urination?" Helen asked.

"Maybe. So what? I see a hell of a lot of frustration in your fantasy, too. But that doesn't make it any less valid."

"We're not here to psychoanalyze each other," I reminded Helen. "We're here to try to understand and be supportive."

"Besides," Joyce added in her own defense, "I don't see what's so hard to understand in my wanting to make it with an older man. The young guys I've made it with always seem to be in a hurry to catch a train to the ball game. And believe me, they've got hang-ups, too. But an older man . . ." She sighed contemplatively.

"It might not be all you expect," Amanda told her gently.

"And the fantasies the rest of you have?" Joyce was sharp. "What guarantee do you have that they'll be up to snuff?"

"I'm not sure I quite get the picture you fantasize," Stephanie said.

"I'll flesh it out for you," Joyce said, thinking for a moment. "An older man, but slim and tall and well built. Gray at the temples perhaps, and with a closely trimmed mustache. Maybe a salt-and-pepper Vandyke beard—very neat and classy, you know. Probably he should be rich because that sort of goes along with being urbane. He should have a swanky beach house like the rich people do in the Hamptons. Or maybe it should be on the French Riviera.''

"You want to make love on the beach?" Amanda inquired.

"Yes," Joyce giggled. "The other night I saw this old Hollywood movie on TV—*From Here to Eternity*. It was so old it was in black and white. Anyway, Burt Lancaster and Deborah Kerr make love on the beach in it. Well, they don't actually fuck or anything like that. I mean, those old movies are pretty prissy. But with the waves crashing and everything, it's pretty damn sexy. As long as I'm dreaming up this fantasy, it might as well have a background like that. I mean, I'd sort of like a long, hard, slow fuck with the surf pounding in the background."

"Wouldn't the pee you're so hooked on get lost in all that water, dear?" Melinda inquired.

"We wouldn't pee on each other in the water. That would come later. Although—" Joyce had a sudden inspiration "—maybe that's how we meet. Maybe I'm behind a sand dune taking a pee and he stumbles on me and it turns him on. If he's urbane enough, maybe he could even carry off sticking his hands under me and washing them in the golden shower. And then I'd tell him to pee over my pussy and—"

"Just like that?" Helen was dubious. "I mean, you've just met—"

"You mean it's okay to screw when you just met, but not to pee on each other? Listen, this is my fantasy!"

"Quite right! Go on with it, baby," Stephanie told her.

"Okay." Joyce crossed her arms and hugged her pert

young breasts. Her smile was strictly cat-devouring-canary.
"He'd sort of gently ease me over on my back and he'd
lick the last few drops from my pussy. Then he'd lick my
pussy lips. He'd ease into eating my pussy in earnest. I've
always wanted a really experienced older man to eat me
properly. Most young guys just want to get blown without
returning the favor. He'd be wearing yachting clothes—a
navy blazer with gold buttons and white ducks and one of
those white captain caps with gold braid. Of course he'd
take off the cap to lick my pussy. And he'd open his pants,
too. His prick would hang out big and hard and I'd fondle
it while he went down on me. My youth would really turn
him on. I'd be wearing this bikini, but I'd have taken off
the pants to pee, and now he'd remove the top. He'd go
ape over my breasts. He'd play with them and stroke the
nipples until they were very hard and then he'd kiss them
and suck on them. His mustache would tickle and so
would his little Vandyke beard. Then he'd go back to my
pussy. He'd suck at it hard and his mustache would tickle
me more down there and I'd feel like I was going mad.
He'd squeeze my ass and play with it while he sucked me.
His hard cock would be sort of waving over my face and
every so often I'd stick out my tongue and lick his balls.
His tongue would stab my clitty and then it would go all
the way up inside me. He'd be sort of licking and sucking
me at the same time and that would make me start to
come. He'd know just how to use his mouth to make it last
a long time. My thighs would lock around his cheeks and
I'd grind back and forth, coming . . . coming . . . coming . . . At some point I'd pull his cock into my mouth
and he'd come, too. Then maybe he'd piss on my pussy
again, or I'd piss over him. Or maybe we'd take a shower
in the beach house and do it there. Maybe we'd go to bed
and fuck and then get up and do it again—piss, I mean.

And all the time the surf would be pounding . . . pounding . . .''

"I would say that our Joycie is a young woman who knows just what she wants!" Stephanie McCall licked at her blood-red lipstick.

"And you, Stephanie?" Amanda asked, tuned in to her aroused reaction. "What is it that you want? What's your fantasy?"

"I'm afraid of what you'll all think of me if I tell you."

"Oh come on, Stephanie. We're being honest with each other. Nobody's going to judge you."

"I know, but I still can't help thinking you'll disapprove."

"Does it involve another woman?" Amanda inquired. There was the oddest note—almost of hopefulness—in her voice.

"No. It's not that." Stephanie hesitated.

"Well, what is it, then?" Melinda asked impatiently.

"My fantasy is of being raped."

There was an awkward silence.

"I know what you're all thinking," Stephanie said. "Stephanie the feminist. Stephanie the decrier of woman's traditional role. Stephanie who's always quoting Susan Brownmiller. Stephanie who refuses to cast herself as any man's sex object, let alone his victim. Yes, that's how I've presented myself. Well, moment of truth, sisters. Both ears and the tail. I have this goddamn sick fantasy of being raped and I can't shake it. I'm ashamed of it. I feel like a hypocrite, but there it is. In the privacy of my bed in the darkness of the night, what little old liberated Stephanie is lusting after is good old-fashioned macho rape!"

Agitated, Stephanie raked her blue-black hair with the nervous comb of her fingers. It was the first time any of us had ever seen her drop her customary Bryn Mawr composure. "How's that for selling out the women's movement, sisters?"

"Easy, darling," Amanda said, putting a comforting arm around her shoulders. "Sit down." She led Stephanie to the couch. "Now listen. If we have sick sex fantasies involving men and women in traditional roles, we have to look at them for what they are. They are symptoms of our persecution as women. They are evidence of it. We fantasize in keeping with how we have been taught to fantasize. Your fantasy is imposed on you by all of your experience in a male-dominated world. All the books you've read, all the movies you've seen, all the TV shows you've watched have conspired to teach your subconscious that the most heinous and forbidden act of rape is somehow the most delicious. To have sex without responsibility because you are forced—what could be more of a relief for women who are brought up to believe that having sex voluntarily is somehow evil? As much as you consciously may have overcome that notion years ago, at some subliminal level, you have never gotten over it. None of us do. So why not rape? If it's inevitable, as the old saw would have it, then indeed why not lie back and enjoy it? Especially in fantasy."

"That's all very well," Stephanie replied. "Except that the only real way to banish a fantasy is to actualize it."

"What do you mean?"

"I take chances."

Amanda stared at her, dismayed.

"I deliberately put myself in the sort of situation where my fantasy might come true. I do exactly what the god-damn men always say women who get raped do. I dress provocatively and ride the subways late at night. I walk down dark streets with my hips swaying. I strike up conversations with men in bars and lean against them when I talk so they can feel I'm not wearing a bra. I never leave with them. I'm always playing the Russian roulette of walking out alone and wondering if they'll follow me; I'll be scared stiff but wondering if they'll rape me."

"But you could get hurt!" Joyce said, upset. "Do you want to get hurt?"

"You could get killed!" Helen chimed in.

"I don't want to get killed. I don't want to get hurt. Well, maybe I do in a way. I'm not really sure. I want to be forced, and there's certainly pain mixed in with the pleasure I anticipate, but even in my fantasy there's a limit as to how much of that I want. Oh, I don't know! It's so sick!"

"The only way to exorcise it is to talk about it," Amanda told her. "Just what is your fantasy? How do you see it happening?"

"I'm all alone on a deserted subway platform," Stephanie began . . .

(But I immediately had a problem. I could not visualize Stephanie McCall with her *Vogue* magazine poise, her wardrobe by Cardin and Dior and de la Renta, her Bryn Mawr accent, riding the subways. Not even in a late-night effort to get herself raped!)

". . . all alone at the end of the platform furthest from the change booth," Stephanie continued. "Then this man appears on the platform. He's youngish. He needs a shave. His hands are very dirty. He's wearing one of those cheap sailor's pea coats—the kind you see in the window of those Army and Navy stores—and a work shirt and corduroy pants. As soon as he sees me, he starts ambling toward me. It's summer, very hot, and I'm wearing a loose linen beanbag mini—midthigh and nothing but gauzy bikini panties underneath. When I see him I get frightened and I start to pant and that makes my nipples get hard and they stand out against the linen so he can see them. When he sees this, he sort of grins a cruel grin like he's decided I'm asking for it. He comes closer, maybe ten feet away from me, and he just stands there grinning. Then he reaches down with his hand and he grabs his joint through his pants and he shakes it so I can see it's hard. I want to look away from him, but I'm too scared to turn my back on him. He laughs out loud because I'm staring at the erection in his pants. He moves in on me then. I want to back away from him, but I'm at the end of the platform and there's no place to go. 'No!' I plead with him. 'Please! No!' But he just laughs again and grabs me with his dirty hands.

"You're gonna love this, baby!' he says. He grabs me and he kisses me. He forces his tongue into my mouth. He bites my lip so it bleeds. He keeps on kissing me, sucking the blood. Meanwhile his filthy hands are all over me. He squeezes my breasts through the linen and it hurts. He claws at my ass. He forces his knee between my leg. He raises it up under the minidress and rubs it against my pussy through my panties. Then he reaches down with his hand and feels there. When he finds it's wet, he really gets excited. He unzips his pants and pulls out his prick. It's big and brutal and hard. 'Suck this for me, baby!' he says. 'No!' I protest. I pull away from him. He doesn't try to grab me. Instead he reaches in his pocket. He comes out with one of those switchblade knives. He presses the button. The blade snaps out long and sharp. 'I said suck it!' he tells me. Sobbing, I fall to my knees. My skirt rides up over my crotch and he can see my sopping gauzy panties. He pricks my neck with the tip of the knife. His other hand tangles in my hair. He pulls my head to him and shoves his big cock in my mouth. I choke on it, but I've got no choice. I suck as hard as I can. Now he reaches down and starts playing with my breasts through the dress while I'm sucking him. My hot, hard nipples really seem to turn him on. I think he's going to come in my mouth and then my nightmare will be over, but he fools me.

" 'That's enough!' he says abruptly. 'Stand up!' I do what he says. 'Take off your dress,' he says. 'I want to see your jugs.' He stands there holding his bare cock in his hand while I do what he wants. It's all glistening with my saliva and it's cleaner than his hands are from my having sucked it. When the dress is off, he makes me kneel again and then he kneels in front of me and rubs his cock and balls over my breasts and nipples. He's really turned on because I have these sort of sharp oblong breasts that curve like bananas and my nipples are very pointy and sensitive. He grabs one of them and tries to force it under his balls and into his asshole, but it won't reach. 'I'm gonna fuck you now!' he says finally, breathing hard. 'Don't!' I try to scramble away from him again. 'I'll scream!'

"He grabs me by the shoulders and flings me down on the subway platform. 'Scream? Go ahead and scream, bitch! Scream your head off, cunt! Who's gonna hear you?' And he smacks me hard across the face. Then he reaches down and rips my panties off. I cross my legs but he opens my thighs brutally with his hands. He takes almost all of my breast into his mouth and bites it, drawing blood. He reaches under me and shoves a finger all the way up my asshole so that my cunt rises up in an effort to get away from the pain. 'Don't hurt me,' I sob. He ignores me. He shoves his prick in my cunt and brings his full weight down on my pelvis as he starts to fuck me. I scream and that seems to excite him even more. He slaps me. He twists my breasts. He pinches the nipples. And all the time his finger is up my ass and his huge cock is in my poor tight pussy and he's fucking me as painfully and brutally as he can. I fight him. I scratch and I bite. His cock is tearing at my cunt. The pain is excruciating. And yet when I feel him starting to come, all of my agony can't stop me from coming with him. In the end we come together, two animals locked in mortal combat.

"Finally he pulls out. He looks at me. I am covered with jism and blood. My cunt is bruised and battered, but still gaping. My banana-curved breasts are black and blue. There are welts all over my face and naked body. A subway train whistles in the distance. I see his hand draw back and turn into a fist. I see it barreling toward me. That's all I see. Everything goes black. When I wake up, the train is gone and so is he. I am lying naked and bruised on the cinder-covered platform. My beanbag mini, all crumpled up, is lying nearby. I get to my feet and put it on. It hurts me to move. Waves of pain spread out over my body from my pussy when I do. I've been raped. And—" Abruptly Stephanie stopped talking.

"Yes?" Amanda prodded. "And?"

"And it's the best fuck I've ever had!"

"She was right before," Helen said. "That is one hell of a thing for a feminist to say. That being raped is her most satisfying experience!"

"We're not here to judge!" Amanda was firm. "What is . . . is! We can't argue with Stephanie's feelings. Not any more than you can argue with mine!"

"Yours?" Melinda asked, looking at the sweet, round blonde curiously.

"Yes, mine. I'd never intended to reveal them to our group. I didn't think you'd all be able to handle it. Or maybe I was afraid I wouldn't. But now with the example of Stephanie's courage in confessing feelings so unpopular with the rest of us, I've had a change of heart."

"Whatever are you talking about, Amanda?" I asked her.

"I'm a lesbian," she announced. "That's what."

"Oh, my goodness!" Helen looked nervously toward the front hallway as if she expected Bruno to appear at any moment.

"Now, Helen, don't look so stunned." Amanda showed her dimples. "A lot more people are homosexual than you'd dream."

"But you don't look mannish!" Helen blurted out.

"Are you bi?" Joyce was curious.

"Not any more."

"Is one of us your fantasy?" Stephanie wondered.

"Is that a firm offer?" Amanda wondered impishly. "No, my dears," she added. "You can all relax. You're all safe. The object of my fantasy is Diana Coltrane."

"Diana Coltrane!" I exclaimed. That did surprise me.

"Why not? Lots of people fantasize about people in public life. Particularly performers."

"Is it because she's black?" I wondered.

"That's not unrelated. I find that dark mahogany skin color of hers very exciting. The contrast! I think about that a lot."

"I know you're going to make fun of me for being so naive," Helen said, "but I've never understood exactly what it is that lesbians do. I mean, your fantasy. What is it that you see yourself doing to Diana Coltrane?"

"It's more what I see her doing to me." Amanda sighed. "She's slender as a willow, you know. She has these long, narrow hands. I see us naked together in a bed. There's a mirror overhead. My body is all soft and pink and white. Hers is black and sleek. I see her Afro cradled on my breasts. Her breath is hot on my nipples. My nipples are very wide and pink. They don't stand out much. They sort of spread when I get excited. They're spread now from her breathing on them. Diana's nipples are like bright red lipsticks against the midnight of her breasts. If she has aureoles, they're lost to the blackness."

"You seem to know an awful lot about how she looks naked," I observed. Once again I was surprised.

"I saw pictures of her in one of the men's magazines. They were stills from this movie she made."

"I see."

"Anyway, to satisfy Helen's curiosity: I see Diana as the aggressor. I see her kissing my breasts and licking them. I see her sharp nipples stabbing into my wide pink ones. I see her kissing me, her tongue warm and insistent in my mouth. I see her hands kneading my buttocks. I'm too heavy down there, I know, but that would turn Diana on. She would turn me over and hold onto my too-heavy hips and sit on the pillow of my buttocks and rub up and down the cleft with the curly black hair of her pussy. Then she would reach between my legs and make a fist and it would be small enough for her to force my pussy open with it. I would turn over and I would play with her gushing clitoris while she fist-fucked me. Then—"

"Listen," Helen interrupted. "I don't want to be a wet blanket, but Bruno's due to come through that door any minute now. If he walks in on you talking about two women doing things like that to each other, it's going to confirm all his worst suspicions about this group. I'll never hear the end of it. He'll make my life miserable. So if you don't mind—"

"Oh sure, honey." Amanda patted her hand and smiled to herself a little when Helen snatched it away. "It is getting late. It's time to break up. This has been one mile-stone meeting, all right! And I guess we can cover any unfinished business next time."

We all got up and started milling around preparatory to leaving. As we straggled toward the door, Joyce suddenly turned. "But we've heard everybody's fantasy except Christina's," she exclaimed.

"That's right," Melinda agreed. "Come on, Christina, before we go, tell us what your fantasy is."

"There isn't time," I replied.

"You don't have to get into it. I didn't. Not really," Amanda told me. "Just give us a hint of what it is."

"It's a mystery." I laughed.

"That's not fair, Christina!"

"Maybe not. But it's true. That's what my fantasy is. A mystery!"

Of course they wouldn't believe me. Just like Malcolm that afternoon, they thought I was being evasive. Well, perhaps I was. But I was also being truthful. I had described my fantasy accurately. That's just what it was:

A mystery!

# CHAPTER THREE

Diana Coltrane! Chance often moves in ways more mysterious than any deity. What I'm trying to say, darlings, is that I had not set out to play the role of deus ex machina in the fantasy of one of my five sisters (let alone in the fantasies of all five of them!). There is, however, no way to stop a coincidence whose time has come.

The first step in the coincidence was, of course, Amanda Briggs's choice of Diana Coltrane as the object of her lesbian fantasy. I knew Diana, you see, knew her intimately, even if the intimacy had been (for me at least) casual. The second step occurred a few days later when Malcolm Gold came into my office at *World Magazine*.

"Diana Coltrane," he said by way of greeting. And he tossed a half-dozen eight-by-ten glossies onto my desk.

I looked at them. They were publicity photos of the singer-dancer-actress. Like most such shots they were glittery with highlights and bland with retouching. They caught the sparkle in Diana's jet black eyes without the impudence. They made a coiffed helmet of an Afro which was vibrant and untamed in real life. The high cheekbones were perfect and symmetrical, but the tilt of angular sensuality was completely lost. The chin was subtly rounded, its stubbornness concealed. The mouth was libidinous enough, but its humor was missing, and its compassion as well. The face was Diana Coltrane, but the spirit behind the photos was strictly Madison Avenue packaging.

Two of the shots were what in a bygone era used to be called "cheesecake." They froze Diana in moments of conscious provocativeness. In scanty dance costumes they caught the gloss of Diana's blackness without its richness. The dampness of perspiration which comes with strenuous exercise had been blotted up, and with it had gone the carnal aliveness of Diana in motion. The long, sleek, lightly muscled dancer's legs were on display, but there was no hint of the hot rippling of inner thighs attesting to Diana's passionate nature. Pains had been taken to angle the shots to catch the ebony swelling of Diana's breasts and the deep, exciting cleavage between them. And yet with the long red nipples concealed by the retoucher, the aroused and therefore arousing Diana had been lost to the camera.

Most of all, it was her blackness which had been sacrificed. Standard glamour photography had turned the rich skin tones into a black as flat as the white of the segregated flesh in old Ziegfeld chorus line stills. "Dey done make me look lak a honky chick dipped in melted chawklit!" I could just hear Diana with her exaggerated cottonfield put-on jeering at what the photos had done to her.

"Lousy art, angel," I told Malcolm succinctly.

"Publicity handouts." He shrugged.

"Have one of our staff photogs get better," I told him.

"Problem. All our shutterbugs are tied up. I could hire a free-lancer, maybe . . ."

I thought a moment. "That won't be necessary," I decided. "I'll shoot her myself."

"That's right." Malcolm grinned his cunnilingual grin.

"I keep forgetting you were a *World* photographer before Dame Fortune dumped that inheritance in your lap and made you publisher."

"And a damned good one, too," I reminded him.

"Not bad." The grin again. "Not half bad."

"Better than this garbage," I said, pushing the glossies aside contemptuously.

Malcolm hadn't bothered to spell out for me the reason *World* needed photo art on Diana Coltrane. Although I hadn't given it any thought until he threw the photos on my desk, and although it had never occurred to me when Amanda Briggs had identified Diana as the focus of her fantasy, the reason was nevertheless self-evident. Diana had just opened to rave reviews as the star of a Broadway musical which had brought her more personal acclaim than any female performer had received since Mary Martin lit up the sky washing her hair in *South Pacific*. Naturally *World* would be featuring her in its Entertainment Section.

"Do you want me to set up your session with her?" Malcolm inquired.

"No thanks, darling. It will be better if I call her myself. We're old—ahh!—acquaintances, you see."

"I see." One of Malcolm's eyebrows described an impertinent arc. He knew me too well. My nuances were never lost on him.

Even so, my attitude may have been misleading. In truth, I didn't know how to define my relationship (if such it could be called) with Diana Coltrane, not even to myself. After Malcolm had left my office, I leaned back in my executive swivel chair and thought about it.

We had run into each other—met? encountered?—many times over the last two or three years. At certain social levels and certain heights of celebrity, such contacts are inevitable. Elaine's, Regine's, Studio 54, et cetera—the haunts of New York's haut monde may be constantly changing, but they are also tiresomely infinite. This is also true when one goes abroad. Diana and I had seen each other in Cannes at the film festival, at Ascot during Derby Week, in Nassau and Bermuda at regattas and dinner parties. The tenth time we were introduced, we both laughed. The eleventh time was during Hunt Week at the Scottish estate of Lord and Lady Smythe-Turnbull. That had been in autumn of the previous year. It was also the last time I'd seen Diana Coltrane.

Yes, the last time I'd seen her—perfumed and naked and black and beautiful—Diana had been quite out of breath from our exertions. She and I had just finished making love to each other for the first (and as it turned out, the only) time. Her eyes had the heavy-lidded look of the sexually sated. We had smiled lazy smiles at each other and dozed off in each other's arms. When I awakened, Diana Coltrane was gone.

Not just from my bed, but from Castle Turnbull as well. She had left a note of explanation and apology for Lord Alfred and Lady Violet, but none for me. I had felt terribly rejected, but as time passed the feeling receded and I had rationalized that whatever had provoked her to bolt had been her problem, not mine. Probably she could not handle a lesbian interlude. Possibly the cold dawn and sobriety had been traumatic for her. Whatever the truth, time would either sort it out for Diana and me, or it would not. *Que será será.*

It had not been my first lesbian experience by a long shot. I have long been bisexual and while I definitely tilt in favor of men, I am attracted to certain women as well. Given our proximity during Hunt Week at Castle Turnbull, Diana Coltrane was definitely one of those women. Her sultriness was palpable, her black dignity a challenge. Our sharing a room and a bath and the same dressing and undressing times was bound to turn the challenge into a fait accompli.

The reason we had to share a room and bath despite Castle Turnbull's thirty-six-guest chambers was that like most of these drafty old Scottish mansions this one had an extremely iffy heating ventilation system. Shortly before our arrival, a pipe buried somewhere in the six-foot-thick concrete walls had rotted away and the east wing had been rendered suitable for refrigeration rather than habitation. Since the hospitable Smythe-Turnbulls had invited a full house for the hunt, some of us had to double up. Diana and I drew each other as roommates.

Well, to be more precise, we drew each other as bedmates. Each boudoir in Castle Turnbull was outfitted with a large, canopied double bed. Short of one of us sleeping in the oversized bathtub, or an armchair, we had no choice but to share it.

It was large enough so that we slept, for the most part, without touching, until the last night of Diana's stay there. That was the night when, following the excitement of the hunt, I suppose the stimulants got somewhat out of hand. Starting with martinis before dinner, we proceeded through several bottles of Piper-Heidsieck '59 to marijuana scones (ah, Scotland!) and finally to a hashish water pipe. Diana and I looked at each other and nodded our mutual agreement to leave when the cocaine-sniffing began. I never use snow; runny noses are a turn-off for me, and as for Diana, she told me on the way up to our room that she had seen too many lives broken by it during her youth in Harlem to ever be able to regard it lightly as the champagne of drugs.

As I recall, that was about as serious as our conversation got. We were both quite high, and neither of us was averse to remaining so. With this in mind, I had scooped up half-a-dozen joints and brought them upstairs with us while Diana had brought a bottle of champagne and two goblets.

Lying side by side on the bed, we smoked and drank and talked.

I have no memory of what we discussed. Whatever it was, it created an empathy between us. This closeness continued as we finished the last of the champagne and decided to undress and get under the covers. Even in the west wing the heating alternated with bone-chilling Scottish drafts.

The wine and the grass had dispelled our reluctance to allow our bodies to touch. Indeed, our inhibitions had quite vanished. We clung together against the cold like schoolgirls, giggling and bundling.

"These nightgowns are absurd," I remember observing. "We should have brought flannel."

"I don't own a flannel nightgown," Diana had replied.

"Neither do I. That's why we're freezing our derrieres off in gossamer and silk."

"Poor Christina."

"Poor Diana." I put my arms around her and rubbed my hands up and down her back to warm her.

We had turned out the light, but we had neglected to draw the heavy draperies. The autumn moon was streaming through the arched window like a beacon. Its rays turned Diana's face into a delicately carved ebony sculpture.

"That feels good," she cooed, wriggling against me. Her breasts were very firm, the nipples like dagger points.

I let my hands wander down and stroked her bottom. Like her breasts the cheeks were firm and resilient. They were also fleshy and quite feverish to the touch.

"I think I'm warming up." Diana sounded breathless.

"You *feel* warmer."

"I'll bet I do." Diana giggled.

We were both really quite high . . . quite high! As I have said, I had been with women before. I was not inexperienced. And yet, I can also say quite honestly that there had been no premeditation on my part of what followed.

Diana put her arms around me just as mine were around her. Her long, slender, deft fingers played over my bottom. I could feel the sharpness of her nails through the flimsy silk of my nightgown. I moved in closer to her. Our breasts flattened against each other and bulged up over the bodices of our nighties. Our stomachs rubbed together.

Looking down at the juxtaposition of our breasts, I caught my breath sharply. Four mounds were visible—two chocolate, two vanilla, both cherry-tipped and shimmering in the Scottish moonlight. I raised my eyes and found Diana's deep, dark eyes looking into them.

"Christina—" she started to say.

"Hush!" I kissed her on the lips.

It was a gentle kiss at the start, a gentle women's kiss, tentative and sweet. Then, suddenly, as if overwhelmed, Diana's tongue was in my mouth, fierce and stabbing. I groped and found her breast and squeezed it and played with the hard, blood-filled nipple. Panting, it inflated and strained under my hand. And then both of Diana's slender hands were on my larger, fuller breasts, trembling, caressing. Thus we prolonged the kiss, our first.

"Christina—" Finally the kiss was over.

"I know. I know." I soothed her, hugging her tall, slender body close to mine.

"The pot—the bubbly—"

"Shh. It's all right." I took her firm black breast from the bodice of her nightgown and cupped it to my lips. My tongue fluttered over the nipple, which strained to become even harder and longer, even more erect. "It's all right." I put my lips around the tip of Diana's breast. The long nipple shivered there. I pulled the covers over our shoulders against the fickle cold. I tongued and sucked and nibbled at her panting black breast.

"Jesus!" Her head was thrown back, her eyes closed. Her nostrils flared in the moonlight. Her tongue, licking her lips, was pink against the midnight of her flesh. "Lord Jesus!"

Under the blanket I caught one of her hands with both of mine. I pressed it between my legs and held it there with the muscles of my thighs. Again I felt her long nails through my silken nightie.

I stroked her thighs through the gossamer garment she was wearing. Her eyes came open, slowly, sultry and heavy with desire. She pressed her belly against my hand and then guided it lower. I felt her velvety black pubic curls through the flimsy material. Stroking between each other's legs, we kissed again.

"I'm cold," Diana said, shivering. "Now I'm burning up."

"It's the interaction between the wine and the grass, angel." I tugged at her nightgown and then my own. When they were pulled high enough, I covered the shivering flesh of her naked thighs with my own. "Relax," I told her. "You're tense. That's why you're getting these flushes."

"Well." Suddenly she giggled again. "I knew it wasn't just the booze and the Mary Jane." And then, unexpectedly, she inserted her long, slender fingers in my pussy. "I thought so!" she exclaimed. "You're all wet just like I am."

I writhed under her ministrations. Using both my hands, I parted the lips of her quim and dipped into it. Yes, she was warm there, and sopping with honey. I moved two fingers up her narrow cunt and then she was riding up and down on them.

"Good Jesus!" she started to say. "I never—"

But I silenced her with another kiss. When it was over, I removed her nightgown entirely and then my own. Despite the cold, I drew back the blanket. I wanted to look at her nude body in the moonlight.

It was beautiful. Her pointy breasts were thrusting upward, the red tips glowing. Her hips, flaring from her long, narrow waist, were writhing, a blur of ebony motion against the white sheet. Her delicious derriere was bouncing up and down impatiently. Her cunt was parted and glistened wetly. The purple lips were folded back from the pink, meaty interior. Her bright red clitty stuck out with all the arrogance of a man's erection.

I could not resist it. I bent to her, holding my own breast in my hand. I guided it to her pulsing pussy. I stroked the hard stub of her clitty with my straining, rigid nipple. My white breast fluttered like a dove between the shapely black pillars of her open thighs.

Diana's hand moved inside me, frigging deeply. I pushed my nipple as deeply inside her cunt as I could get, trying to emulate the motion. It wasn't too successful, but even the failure was titillating. When I sat up, she tugged me to her and sucked at my honey-coated nipple. It was her syrup, to be sure, but Diana—and I, too—had passed far beyond considering such niceties.

Indeed, her mouth at my sticky breast made me aware of my own mouth, my own hunger. I bent my head to her slavering quim. My blond hair spread out over her flat raven belly. In the moonlight it gleamed like gold on sable. Her gleaming thatch tickled my nostrils. I inhaled deeply, aroused by the perfumed female aroma. I licked the excess juices from her thighs with my tongue. Somewhere above me she moaned. The soft night sky of her thighs caressed my cheek. I kissed the deep purple lips. Both her hands tangled in my blond hair. The tip of my tongue found her clitty. I deliberately tantalized it. Her hands twisted in my hair. Her pelvis rose to claim the contact. Her open pussy kissed my lips and claimed my mouth, drawing it inside her. I sucked her clitty. I probed the long, tight, wet glovefinger of her pussy with my tongue, holding it stiff, trying to use it the way a man uses his prick when he's fucking. I did it rhythmically, knowing that was what I myself enjoyed most. I brought her just to the brink of quivering orgasm, and then I pulled out my tongue and broke off contact between my mouth and Diana's pussy.

"What—?" The word torn from her lips was both a sob and a pleading.

"Shh," I said, putting my hands under her and raising her squirming bottom. Now the moonlight illuminated the sweet curve of her firm young ass. I kissed the quivering flesh and found it hot and firm and tender. I ran my pink tongue lightly up and down the cleft separating the pert half-moons.

"Sweet Jesus!" Diana exclaimed again, shaking all over as if possessed by some uncontrollable ague, some all-encompassing fever. "Oh, my sweet Jesus!"

I probed more deeply with my tongue, and felt the tight coil of her anus. I stabbed at it gently, and then more insistently. Slowly, it relaxed. I thrust my tongue up as deeply as I could. At the same time I pushed two fingers up Diana's cunt and frigged her.

She screamed and started to come. She came for a long, long time. Her sphincter locked my tongue in place. Her climaxing quim wrenched at my fingers. And she kept on coming for a long . . . very long time.

When it was over, Diana fell back on the bed exhausted. I released her and went into the bathroom to wash my hands and face and rinse my mouth. But I had not yet come myself and so I hurried to return to her.

She was waiting for me, panting, tired, but not *too* tired. She looked up at me questioningly, as if asking what I had in mind to do next. I guided her with a kiss.

I threw back the covers, unmindful of the cold, too aroused to even note its contrast to my burning body. Diana's chocolate figure looked delicious. I raised one of her lithe dancer's legs and slid one of mine under her. We merged, scissor fashion, the syrup of her orgasm still on the lips of her pussy as they pressed against mine. I took her by the shoulders and raised her to a sitting position. We rocked back and forth gently, our bobbling breasts grazing, the nipples sending thrills through us as they touched. Our quims smacked wetly against one another, kissing, grinding. We rocked, panting, kissing, licking at each other's tongues, belly to belly, open devouring cunt against open devouring cunt.

"Jesus!" Diana squealed. "Again!"

I clutched at her, my red nails raking the sides of her tensed ebony thighs and the soft, writhing swell of her hips. My breasts swung violently as the fire in my pussy erupted. We froze to stillness against each other, both our pussies suspended in midair, the double fulcrum of our bodies held in the ecstatic madness of mutual orgasm. Hot and splashing, we came and came . . . and came . . .

When it was over we had regarded each other with indolent, still half-drugged eyes. We had pulled up the blankets and put our arms around each other. Snuggling closely, we had drifted off to sleep. And when I woke up, Diana Coltrane was no longer there.


It seemed long ago, although in reality it had only been six or seven months. We had not run into one another in the intervening period. Other erotic experiences had turned the images of our erotic combat into barely seen pentimento. In truth, she had almost faded from my mind.

Still, the vision of her rushed back sharp and clear when I heard her voice on the other end of the telephone. I had gotten the number from Celebrity Service. A secretary had answered and I was on hold a long time after I gave her my name. Finally Diana came on the line.

"Christina"—her voice was carefully neutral—"what a surprise to hear from you."

I explained that it was a business call. I told her *World* was doing a piece on her. I explained that I wanted to take some fresh pictures rather than use the publicity shots we had on hand.

"You intend to take them yourself?"

"Yes. If that's all right with you."

Again there was a long pause. "Why wouldn't it be?" she said finally in that same flat tone. "Come by tomorrow at noon if that's convenient."

"That will be fine." I said goodbye and hung up the phone.

The next day I arrived at her Sutton Place penthouse on the dot. A maid let me in. She told me that Miss Coltrane was on the roof patio sunning herself. She led me there and then went back to her duties.

There was a high wall with fieldstone set into it around the sundeck. Obviously it had been designed to block prying eyes. (Later I would see that it was only partially successful.) Diana was stretched out on a chaise lounge in the center of this closed-in area. She was nude. The deep blackness of her flesh gleamed voluptuously with coconut oil. Her breasts stood straight up, the nipples erect. A gentle breeze rippled the sablelike fur fringing her pussy. A bright pink slash separated the purple lips.

Seeing my eyes on her, Diana reached languorously for a white terrycloth robe on the patio floor and put it on. "Hello, Christina," she greeted me. She picked up a sponge from a basin of ice water and wrung it out. She reached inside the terrycloth robe with it and began wiping the coconut oil from her body. "Sticky." She made a face.

"Why bother with it, then?"

"Because I sunburn easily. Painfully, too. White folks think blacks are impervious to the sun because the results don't show up on our skins. But it's not true. You can get just as badly sunburned if you're black as if you're white."

"I know that," I told her.

"Do you?" There was a hint of her sarcastic down home drawl in the way she said it. "Lawsy, Miz Christina, Ah 'pologize for doubtin' y'all."

"Hostile, darling," I said, refusing to be provoked. "You're angry with me. Why?"

"Angry?" She cocked her head and thought about it. "No," she decided, serious now. "I have no reason to be angry with you."

"I didn't think you did."

"The truth is I suppose I'm angry with myself." Diana sighed. "Although I really thought I was over that."

"Why should you be angry with yourself?"

"Because of what happened between us in Scotland," she told me frankly.

"It upset you."

"Yes."

"That's why you left so abruptly? Without even saying goodbye?" I asked her.

"Yes."

"And you hold me responsible?"

"No. I'm a big girl. I'm responsible for my own actions," Diana told me in a grave voice.

"But you think I took advantage of the situation. Of the dope and the wine. Of you."

"No. Logically I don't think any such thing. We both did what we did."

" 'Logically.' " I repeated the word thoughtfully. "But

emotionally," I guessed, "emotionally is a different story. Isn't that so, angel?"

"Shucks, Ma'am! Seems y'all jes' too smart for this pore little black girl. Ah declare, white folks has theyselves such insight!"

"Knock it off, Butterfly."

She looked at me, startled. Then a slow, sweet, uncomplicated grin spread over her face. "You're right, Christina." She nodded. "I'm being bitchy. And it really wasn't your fault. You didn't seduce me. I was as horny as you were."

"It was your first time with another woman." I was sure of it.

"That's right."

"Then you shouldn't be upset with yourself for being upset. Lots of people can't handle homosexuality. Lots of them go to pieces when they wake up to realize they've actually indulged themselves in the experience for the first time."

"Really?" Diana's laugh was charitable. "Is that the cotton-pickin' truth now? Oh, Christina," she patted my cheek, "do you really think I can have spent the last five years scrambling to Broadway stardom, clawing my way through the sex jungle of show biz, and still be as naive as that last statement of yours would make me?"

"I don't understand." I was truly puzzled. "You said you were upset because of what happened between us. I was just trying to put it in some kind of perspective. Why are you putting me down?"

"Because it wasn't the sex that bothered me—at least not per se. It's a lot more complicated than that."

"Then explain it." I was suddenly feeling quite frustrated.

"No. I don't think so." She stood up. "You came to take pictures." She nodded at the camera and other equipment slung over my shoulder, "let's get with it. What would you like me to wear?'' The terrycloth robe fell open. Her supple body emerged naked in the sunlight.

"I like that." My eyes affirmed her nude appeal.

"I hardly think so. *World* is your magazine, isn't it? Not *Playboy*?''

"Not *Playboy*," I confirmed. "Still, a little sex appeal never hurts.''

"I'm not selling sex appeal. Not any more. I'm not selling my body, not even in pictures. All I'm selling is talent. And so far that's been quite enough. The public seems quite willing to buy it.''

"Okay." She certainly was touchy. "Why don't we do the star-relaxing-at-home bit, then. In the kitchen. Doing the bills. Painting. Sculpting. Whatever it is you do for recreation.''

"I make quilts." Diana laughed. "Now, that shook you up, didn't it, Christina?''

"Yes." But she would never suspect how much. Talk about coincidence! Amanda Briggs's hobby was quilt-making, too. It was the third link in the evolving chain.

I followed Diana inside. Together we chose a simple house dress for her to wear. For the next two hours I photographed her doing a variety of household tasks including quilt-making. The quilts—Navaho patterns—lent wondrous splashes of bright color to the shots.

Finally I was done. From crawling and climbing to get the proper angles for the effects I was after, I was quite disheveled. My blouse and slacks were rumpled, my underarms clammy with perspiration, my hands and even my face streaked with the dust and grime kicked up by my efforts. "I must look like a coal miner after a hard day," I remarked to Diana.

"Well, Christina, I have seen you looking somewhat less soiled." She cocked her head and reflected a moment.

"Why don't you have a shower," she offered. "You'll feel a lot less grungy for the trip home."

"Thanks. I do believe I'll take you up on that."

"Give your clothes to Bridget. Maybe she'll be able to shake some of the dirt loose from them. You'll find a robe hanging in the bathroom. You can put it on when you're through showering. I'll be out on the sundeck evening out my tan." She laughed ironically.

I did as she suggested. Under the shower I wondered at her hospitality. Was there more to it than that? Despite her having run away, did Diana secretly want to pick up where we had left off at Castle Turnbull?

After toweling myself dry and putting on the robe I found in the bathroom, I went back out to the terrace. Diana was stretched out on her back, naked, soaking up the sunshine. Seeing me, she motioned to the second chaise lounge beside her. "Lie down and relax," she said. "Bridget will be at least another twenty minutes with your things. Soak up some sunshine. You look anemic, Christina."

"I am not!" I said indignantly. "I'm already getting a tan. I was out sailing just the other day. Look, see how dark I am."

"It all depends where you're coming from," Diana laughed. "From where I'm sitting, you're Rinso white, Christina."

"That is a racist remark!" I told her haughtily as I removed the robe and stretched out naked under the blue sky.

"All my life I've wanted some honky to say that to me." Diana laughed again. "Now don't get offended. Racism is when you hurt someone. Us black folks, why, chile, we ain't got the muscle to swat a fly iffen she be a white fly."

"You've got me trapped here without my clothes," I

told her frostily, "but that's no reason to get on my case. I haven't done anything to you."

"Haven't you?"

"No." I had a sudden insight. "You're back where you were before, aren't you? It's what happened in Scotland that's making you so negative toward me again."

It brought her up short. "Yes," she sighed. "I'm sorry. I suppose you're right. I really have no other reason to put you down."

"You said before that it wasn't the sex that bothered you. Do you want to tell me what it is now?"

"I don't know. I'm not even sure that I can explain it so it would make any sense to you. Let me think about it." She fell silent.

The silence lasted a long time. I relaxed into it. Beside me Diana's full, red-tipped black breasts were rising and falling evenly. Her pussy was like a flower opening its petals to the sun. I felt a lazy sensation of desire spreading over my body. It tickled my nipples to hardness and warmed my inner thighs. The mattress of the chaise burned hotly against the fleshiness of my buttocks. A slow syrup developed in my vagina.

But I did not act on these feelings. I knew instinctively that Diana wasn't ready for a repeat of our lovemaking. She might be sorry later, but still she would reject me now. I felt it in my bones.

And so we lay side by side in the balm of the afternoon, naked, a tall, delicate, small-boned black woman with lissome legs and firm breasts and aristocratically narrow hands and feet, and a more earthy, voluptuous white woman with a semisuntan and a twin-melon bosom and flowing roundnesses defining hips and thighs and bottom. We lay stretched out in separate chairs, not touching, eyes darting against the brightness to sneak appreciative peeks at each other's bodies. Our desire was like live electricity crackling between us, but Diana blotted it out and I did my best to follow her obvious wishes and ignore it.

The sun had its effect. Our bodies began to gleam with perspiration. Diana spread coconut oil over her skin. She didn't ask me to help her and I didn't offer. When she was done, she handed me the bottle. I applied the oil to the surface of my body. My own fingers made me tingle with a sort of desire. Diana didn't offer to spread it over the places I couldn't reach. It was just as well. I doubt I could have controlled myself if she had touched me.

Suddenly there was a great noise and a large shadow blotted out the sun. "What the hell is that?" All I could make out was a metallic surface where the sky should have been.

"Network television affiliate." Diana sat up. "They check in here every afternoon around this time." She shook her fist. "I'm going to buy an antiaircraft gun and shoot you down!" she shouted.

Refocusing my eyes, I realized then that it was a helicopter. It was so close to us that I hadn't made out the details of its shape at first glance. Now, angling my head back, I could read the lettering on the side of the craft. TRAFFIC REPORT was what it said. The designation was preceded by three letters identifying the network to which the affiliate belonged.

"They must really be going ape today," Diana told me. "A naked white chick! Up to now all they've been getting is black meat."

"They must like it, or they wouldn't keep coming back."

"Oh, yes. They like it all right. Just like Mister Thomas Jefferson and all those other slave-owning types." She stood up and took her naked breasts in her hands and shook them at the copter. "Hey, honky, you like this?"

she shouted. "Or this?" She bent over and thrust her behind out and wiggled it. "Well, eat your heart out, white boys! This is one black ass you ain't never gonna have!"

"Hey, Diana, take it easy, darling."

But she was beyond hearing me. "You like them, Christina. Well now, you can have them. Hey, white boys!" she shouted. "Here's some pale skin for you—blond hair and all. No black girls for sale today, only white. Prime white meat. What am I offered?" Her upper lip was beaded with perspiration and her dark eyes were darting wildly. "One woman slave for sale! You can work her or fuck her! Do I hear an offer?"

"Diana! Stop it!" I grabbed her by the wrists and forced her to sit back down on the chaise. "Come on now, angel." I stroked her hair back from her forehead. "Calm down."

The whirlybird circled the rooftop, the occupants obviously intrigued by my hugging Diana's face against my naked breast. The rotors drowned out the sound, but when I looked up I could see that two of their faces were red from whistling at us. Suddenly I understood—at least in part and for the moment—Diana's outrage. "Get out of here, or I'll call Air Traffic Control!" I shouted at them.

Perhaps they could read lips. Or perhaps it was simply time for them to leave and go about their business. At any rate, they made a final sweep for a last, lingering ogle, and left.

I turned my attention to Diana. Her face was still buried against my naked breast. Her breath was hot on the nipple. It excited me, but this definitely wasn't the time to follow up on my desire for her. Gently, I disentangled myself from her.

"Sorry." She was more composed now. "I just get really ticked off at the gall of them."

"It's all right. I understand. I was getting pretty ticked off myself."

"It's not the same thing."

"Why not?"

"Don't you understand, Christina? White men have been insulting black women for three hundred years in this country. Of course," she added as an afterthought, "insults are really the least of it."

"I guess I just didn't think of it that way."

"There's picking cotton, ante and post bellum, right up to the present slave wages. And there's cleaning toilets. And there's cooking and cleaning. And most of all, and always, there's spreading the legs for Mister Charlie's pleasure! Sons of bitches!!" She pounded her fist against the flagstones. "No matter how far a black woman gets, no matter how successful, there's always some white bastard thinks she should be spreading her legs when he snaps his fingers!"

"Hey, slow down. They were just peeping Toms. They'd be here all the same if I was sunbathing here all by myself. And I'm white."

"Oh, sure. But it wouldn't be the same, Christina. Not really. Believe me. You wouldn't be black salvage available to be claimed by any white man who wanted you!"

I didn't argue with her. I understood her outrage, even sympathized with it. But I also thought she was greatly overreacting.

"You wanted me to tell you what it was that bothered me in Scotland," Diana said abruptly. "Well, Christina, that's what it is." Her breasts were rising and falling quickly with her anger.

"That's what is?" I was bewildered.

"A black woman being used by a white."

"But I'm not a white man! I'm a woman. Just like you."

"It doesn't matter. You're white."

"I didn't use you," I protested. "It was mutual. We used each other."

"That's not quite true, Christina. Think back. You were the aggressor."

"Well, you didn't seem to object."

"No. That's true. I didn't object. I didn't fight you off. I wanted it as much as you did. And when it was over it didn't bother me that we were both women either. But what did bother me was that I'd just laid back and enjoyed it for a white person."

"I can't help being white any more than you can help being black."

"That's not the point. I'm not blaming you. I'm not angry at you. I'm blaming myself. It's myself I'm mad at. If I'm going to make love with a white woman, then by God I want to be the one to call the shots. I want to be the aggressor! You're too damn macho a woman for me, Christina. Particularly for a white woman! What I want is a white woman who'll be subservient to me and glad of the chance!"

"Is that what you want?" I sat down slowly and stared at Diana. "Is that really what you want?"

"Sure."

"To have a lesbian experience with a white woman and be the aggressor all the way? Have I got it right?"

"Well, yes . . . Why are you looking at me like that, Christina? You look like Machiavelli about to pull off a coup. Positively diabolical! What is it, Christina?"

"Nothing really, darling. I'd just like to ask you to a small dinner party. Will you come?"

"When is it?"

"Whenever you say."

Diana stared at me, puzzled. "Sure I'll come," she said. "Why not?"

"Good. Good. There's a friend of mine I want you to meet. I think you two will really hit it off."

"Oh? What's her name?"

"Amanda Briggs." Inside my brain my grin was a mile wide. "Her name is Amanda Briggs."

*And,* I was careful not to add aloud, *her dream is about to come true!*

# CHAPTER FOUR

When I was a child reading fairy tales, most girls my age
identified with Cinderella. A few, more liberated, identified with the stepsisters. (Why not? Going to the ball sure
beats cleaning the ashes out of the fireplace.) One or two,
the most perceptive, identified with the Prince in spite of
the gender difference. (Rich is better than poor, to do the
choosing better than to be chosen.) I, however, always
identified with the Fairy Godmother. I recognized from a
very early age that it's more fun to manipulate than be
manipulated, and on the whole, I'd rather have the power
to turn a pumpkin into a coach than to be bounced around
in one pulled by six rodents turned into equines. Yes, far
better to be able to create a glass slipper than to have one's
future hinge on the correct fitting of one!

And so I waved my magic wand and threw an *intime*
dinner party to which I invited Diana Coltrane (the Prince
cast as ebony Princess for my fairy tale) and Amanda
Briggs (my blond, dimpled earth mother Cinderella). It
would be perfect. Diana wanted a physical relationship
with "a white woman who'll be subservient to me and
glad of the chance!" And Amanda desired sex with super-

star Diana Coltrane with "Diana as the aggressor." Having set up the glass slipper, all I could do once the dinner party was under way was cross my wands and hope that they might ball happily ever after—or at the very least get it on once or twice.

There were twelve people at the dinner party. Ten of them were male-female couples, including myself and Malcolm Gold. That left Diana and Amanda. Seated next to each other at dinner, it was only natural that they should pair off after coffee. Also, I confess I had confided Amanda's fantasy to Diana, swearing her to secrecy, of course. It was obvious from the gleam in Diana's eye that she found Amanda to her liking. When they departed together— ostensibly to share a taxi—I thought the prognosis for the fulfillment of Amanda's fantasy was excellent.

Naturally I was impatient to find out what happened. To be cool, however, is the modern-day essence of discretion. I restrained myself. I didn't call Diana. I didn't try to contact Amanda. I made myself wait for our next women's consciousness-raising meeting to learn the results of my Fairy Godmothering.

But I was disappointed. Amanda Briggs did not attend the meeting, which was held at Stephanie McCall's posh apartment on Seventy-third Street just off Central Park West. Nobody knew why she wasn't there. Indeed, her absence receded to the backs of our minds as we focused in on the problem Joyce Dell brought to our attention.

"It's that bastard president of ours!" Joyce complained. "For the past three years, ever since I was fifteen, I've always had a summer job in the library. I did a lot of filing, but sometimes I'd make posters for the children's library, and I was also being taught how to tell stories to the little kids. I really enjoyed the job and it gave me a chance to put a little money away toward college. Now I'll be starting college next fall and I'll be without a job this summer. That fucking president has cut out the program. I don't even know if I'll be able to make my first semester's tuition. There's talk of him slashing student aid too. I just don't know what I'm going to do!''

''Maybe you can find a different job somewhere,'' Helen Willis said, trying to comfort her.

''There are damn few jobs for young people,'' Melinda Holloway pointed out. ''Joyce has a real problem.''

Indeed she did. We spent the whole evening discussing it, not solving it, of course, but being supportive of Joyce and trying to make her feel better about her situation. That, despite Malcolm's wishful projections, is really what women's consciousness raising is all about. Even so, sex did reenter our discussion via humor just before the meeting broke up.

''Maybe you can combine your two concerns,'' Stephanie McCall suggested. ''Perhaps you can find a job somewhere urinating on an old man.''

''Not *too* old,'' Joyce laughed ruefully. ''I mean, I'd want him to be able to go on from there.''

''Put an ad in the paper,'' Stephanie persisted. ''Young woman seeks job as mutual urinator-cohabitator with responsible older man.''

Many a true word is spoken in jest! I thought. Likewise, many an idle jest has been redefined as reality. Who could have guessed that Stephanie's would turn out that way?

Not me. I wasn't even considering the idea of playing Fairy Godmother again. I was too concerned over what might have happened to my first Cinderella to think about waving my wand over a second one.

For three days after the meeting, I tried to call Amanda Briggs. There was never an answer. I tried to phone Diana Coltrane. Same result. How odd! Surely her maid should have answered even if Diana herself wasn't at home. Then I saw an item in the *New York Times* Drama Section announcing that Diana had taken a short leave of absence from her show to go abroad. I concluded that Amanda must have gone with her and stopped trying to call either one of them.

It was around this time that I myself received a call from Lady Violet Smythe-Turnbull. In addition to having played hostess to Diana and myself at her Scottish estate during Hunt Week, Lady Violet is a very old and very dear friend of mine. Some of my most memorable (and more than occasionally erotic) experiences have occurred in the company of Lady Violet and her husband Lord Alfred.

Lady Violet is a statuesque brunette who was born into a working-class family in Liverpool. She had married into English nobility straight from the topless chorus line of a London supper club noted for the permissive atmosphere afforded the gentlemen who dined there. (I had covered the wedding for *World* during my days as a photographer prior to my having inherited the fortune which enabled me to purchase the magazine.) Her husband, Lord Alfred, is some twenty years her senior, which places him now somewhere in his early fifties. He is a lanky gentleman with the ruddy face of one who traditionally rides to the hounds, and a drooping mustache which sometimes gives him the look of a sorrowful walrus. They had what has come to be known as an "open marriage," although to Lord Alfred it would always be simply a matter of noblesse oblige. Lady Violet, who has great humor, never questions his grand seigneurial insistence on erotic tradition, but she has been known to wink at his assumption that such rights—even in this day and age—are limited to the privileged classes. "Serfs do the old in-out too, ducks," she would tell him. "You nobs don't have a patent on it!"

"By Jove!" Lord Alfred would reply, blinking his rheumy eyes in astonishment. "By Jove!"

It was his way of acknowledging that Lady Violet was

still quite a handful. Her strong will had carried her from the topless chorus to the peerage, and she always made it clear that she was not about to change.

Now she was on the other end of the telephone. "Christina, my sweet!" Kissing noises crackled in my ear. "I'm so glad I could reach you."

"It's wonderful to hear your voice, angel." I meant it. "Are you calling from Scotland?"

"No, ducks. We're here in New York. At the Sherry Netherland."

"Lord Alfred, too?"

"Oh, yes. He's right here mixing some martinis. Won't trust an American bartender, you know. Says they've frozen their taste buds with too many ice cubes."

"Say hello for me."

"Alfred!" she called. "Alfie! Christina says hello."

"By Jove!" Lord Alfred's voice was faintly discernible. "Alfie says hello back."

"Will you be in town long?" I inquired.

"Afraid not. Just a couple of days. Then we're on our way to California. We've taken Buzzy Armbruster's place for a month."

"Lucky you!" I said enviously. Buzzy Armbruster, the millionaire playboy, had built a mansion on the California shore a little north of Santa Barbara which has been compared to San Simeon. The locale was spectacular, with mountain foothills running to the edge of a wide, sandy beach delineated by sea-smoothed rock jetties. It was a place of blue skies, bright sun and high, crashing surf. And the mansion itself was filled with the gadgets and gimmicks of a millionaire who both believed in convenience and enjoyed elaborate practical jokes. "Beware the hangover room," I warned Lady Violet.

"I've seen it," she laughed. "And besides, Buzzy won't be there. Alfie and I will just close it off for our stay."

"Pity." The hangover room was where Buzzy had the servants bring guests who had overimbibed and passed out. Everything in the room was upside-down. When an unfortunate drunk came to in it, he would find himself lying on the ceiling looking up at the furniture hanging down from the floor. He wouldn't know whether to make a dive for the chandelier and cling to it until help arrived, or try to inch his way over to the wall so that he might crawl to safety. "Still, you really should make use of some of Buzzy's other thingamajigs while you're there, darling," I added.

"Oh, we will," Lady Violet assured me. "After all, that's half the fun of having taken the place. Listen, Christina," she went on, "are you free for dinner tomorrow night? It's the only time Alfie and I have available, but we'd so love to see you before we leave."

"I am. And I'd love to see you, too. Say when and where."

"The Palms at eight, then. Alfie will make the reservation."

The Palms! How like Lord Alfred. Prime beef, and sawdust on the floor to prove how proletarian the aristocracy is at heart. And a hundred dollars per dinner just to not be outdone by the bloody Yanks!

Despite the casual atmosphere of the Palms, I dressed for dinner. I was sure that Lord and Lady Smythe-Turnbull would, and I was right. Lord Alfred wore soup-and-fish dated by the lapels—a prerogative that went with his title—while Lady Violet was Aphrodite-like in a black Valentino evening gown with a sculptured bodice and a double-tiered skirt edged in lace. The provocative design was enhanced by straps which deliberately fell over the upper arm rather than the shoulder, and a deep rounded V to display her ample cleavage. The floral design of the lace was intermittently transparent, showing off Lady Violet's long, shapely show girl legs.

She and I embraced by way of greeting. Then Lord Alfred stood to kiss my hand. His beagle-pouched eyes managed a decided sparkle as they took in my gown. It was a prime example of just how lascivious haute couture can be in the hands of a master like Givenchy. A slim, ruffled dress, it started just above the nipples of my breasts and ended halfway down my thighs. It clung to the intervening curves in a deserved panic at the precariousness of its grip. Indeed, when I took off my ermine evening wrap, all sounds of steak being masticated were silenced—the women's in envy, the men's in chewless lust. Ahh, Givenchy! Such artistry—true art!—is rare, is it not?

"By Jove!" Lord Alfred's mustache felt like a raccoon's tail drawn across the back of my hand as he kissed it. "By Jove!"

We sat down and ordered aperitifs. Famished, we ordered our steaks before the second drink. It was while we were waiting for them that Lady Violet confided her problem to me.

"Servants," she began. She had long since mastered the upper class British accent and what followed came out quite as snotty as the complaint dictated. "One simply cannot find servants in the United States. You Americans do not come to grips with the problems. Either you rely on slaves, as you did before the Civil War, or on overpaid, underworked, and inevitably too familiar hired help who openly resent every moment of their employment. It is the one area, my dear, where even in its current state of decline the British Empire is far ahead of you."

"It's inevitable," I agreed. Despite the underlying snobbishness, I saw no reason to argue the point. "Upward mobility causes it. Your lower classes have a tradition of accepting their lot in good faith. A butler takes pride in being a good butler, a footman in being a qualified footman. But in the United States, a waiter is very likely studying law nights at Columbia. A cab driver may be saving to start his own business. A cleaning lady may have her eye on an executive training program. America's upward mobility may be more myth than reality—particularly under our current administration with its philosophical debt to the Bourbons—but the fact that it's widely believed has all but banished the obsequious attitude from our servants' behavior patterns. So resign yourselves to it, darlings. While you're here, there will be no faithful old family retainers to lick your Lordship's and Ladyship's boots.''

''By Jove!'' Lord Alfred shook his head, signifying his extreme disapproval of such a circumstance. *What was the world coming to?* he was probably wondering. ''By Jove!''

''Must you be so smugly American, Christina?'' Lady Violet asked, her tone humorous. ''I am in the most dire straits and you lecture to me on egalitarianism in our former colonies. How tiresome!''

''Sorry.'' I laughed with her. ''But then you haven't really explained how desperate your situation is.''

''I am without a lady's maid!'' Lady Violet answered, her expression straining for a tragic effect.

How completely the topless chorus line had been forgotten! I thought. I did not, however, think it my place to remind her. Despite the striking of such poses, I am quite fond of Lady Violet. And I knew that under the haughty veneer she was capable of laughing at herself. ''It is, I fear, a common situation in the wilderness of America,'' I told her. ''I don't think I can help you. Our universities have been quite derelict in their duty as to turning out qualified lady's maids.''

''But what shall I do? I am told that it is simply not possible to hire such a functionary on the California coast.

It is bad enough in the East, my friends tell me, but in the West they say, it is impossible.''

"Alas," I mocked her. "I fear it is true."

"I shall have no choice but to find a girl and train her myself.''

"By Jove!" Lord Alfred displayed a sudden interest at this prospect.

"But where does one find such a creature in your country, Christina?" Lady Violet wondered.

"Have you tried the alms houses?"

"Are there really such places? Oh!" Lady Violet laughed her hearty, prearistocratic laugh. "You are making a joke. But seriously, Christina, are there no young women in need of such employment?"

Before I could answer her question, our steaks arrived. It would have been sinful not to eat them immediately while they were at the sizzling height of their carefully prepared flavor. So I mulled over Lady Violet's quandary while devouring the Palms' compelling argument against vegetarianism.

"By Jove!" Lord Alfred rolled his eyes with delight at the savory meat. "By Jove!" His reaction revealed a sensuality he usually reserved for orgies of sex rather than eating. "By Jove!" he climaxed.

So pronounced was the lasciviousness of his tone that my attention was distracted from my own plate. Looking up at him, I saw a mature man in a state of epicurean delight. So lewd was his expression that it jolted my memory. "Joyce!" I exclaimed aloud. "Joyce Dell!"

"Beg pardon, Christina?" Lady Violet said, cocking her head questioningly.

"Nothing," I assured her. "I just remembered a friend of mine, that's all." But my mind, as you may imagine, darlings, was positively racing!

*Joyce Dell! Of course!* My palm tingled with the Fairy

Godmother wand once more ensconced there. *A mature man into Golden Showers! Lord Alfred, by Jove! A Lady of the British realm in need of a wench to train for service! A sweet young thing in need of employment! An open marriage, noblesse oblige, and young womanhood in search of mature guidance! Something for everyone, by Jove!* And all I had to do was once again wave my magic wand!

I waved it the very next morning. I called Joyce Dell at her home. "She's still in bed." The man who answered, doubtless her father, didn't sound happy with that. "I'll get her."

"Hullo." Joyce's yawn was sulky. "Who is it?"

I told her. Then I explained why I had called.

"Wait a minute!" She had come awake. "Let me get a handle on this, Christina. You've got a job for me as a cleaning woman in California?"

"Not a cleaning woman. A lady's maid."

"A maid, then. Same thing. Listen, I'm not trying to be snooty, but I don't think I really want to travel across the country to do some English dame's shitwork."

"It's not the same thing. You won't be doing any cleaning," I assured her. "A lady's maid helps her mistress to bathe and dress. She takes care of her clothes and jewelry. She makes her up."

"Mistress?" Joyce picked up on the word. "What am I, a goddamn cocker spaniel?"

"It's a British term. It doesn't mean the same thing there that it does here. Now, you listen to me, Joyce! Get off your high horse. This is a chance for you to spend the summer at one of the most beautiful places in the world, right on the Pacific Ocean, and get paid for it. And you really won't have to work very hard either. Lady Violet and Lord Alfred are really very decent people, even if they are aristocrats.''

"Lord Alfred?'' As if by instinct, Joyce was suddenly interested.

"Yes. He's Lady Violet's husband. You'll be her lady's maid, but I imagine you'll be seeing a lot of both of them.''

"Lord Alfred,'' Joyce repeated. "I don't suppose he has a Vandyke beard?'' she inquired.

"No. But he does have a mustache.''

"Close clipped?''

"No. Kind of droopy.''

"But is he a mature aristocrat? I mean, he's a man of the world? Experienced and—you know?''

I thought about it. Yes, it was true. Lord Alfred was all those things. He was a bumbling dear to me, but as I made the effort to look at him through Joyce's eyes, I readily acknowledged that he might fit the mold of her dreams. No Vandyke, but I was reasonably sure that he did pee.

"Lord Alfred is all those things,'' I told her.

"Golly!''

"You must not use such language,'' I told Joyce. "Lord Alfred and Lady Violet will think you provincial.''

"Gosh, Christina, I don't know. A lady's maid! Gee, I don't know the first thing about it.''

"The first thing about it is not to say 'Gee' or 'Gosh' or 'Golly.' As to the rest, I believe that Lady Violet is willing to train the young woman she hires.''

"But why the fuck would she hire me? Oops! Sorry! I'll watch my language. I promise I will.''

"Watch the gees, the goshes and the gollys. You don't have to worry about 'fuck.' That won't bother Lady Violet and Lord Alfred. And she'll hire you because I recommend you.''

It really was that easy. Having no place else to turn,

Lady Violet was quick to act on my recommendation. She interviewed Joyce Dell the very next day. Joyce must have been on her very best behavior because Lady Violet hired her on the spot. A few days later my eighteen-year-old friend followed the Smythe-Turnbulls out to the coast, her fare prepaid by Lord Alfred.

A week later I received a short letter from Lady Violet. It was to be followed by others, but I didn't know that as I read it. The first letter went as follows:

Dear Christina,

Just a line to let you know that Joyce seems to be working out quite well for an American girl. She is quick to pick up the knack of her various duties. Would that she were as adept when it comes to vocabulary. Still, that is coming along too. I feel reasonably sure that the day is not far off when she will no longer say "Holy shit!" Wherever did Americans get the idea that excrement is in any way sacred? Likewise bovines. Hallowing cattle, I'm sure, will also soon be a broken habit for our dear Joyce.

She is really a delightful young woman and you must not let my carping lead you to believe that I am less than completely satisfied with her performance. There is, however, one habit of hers which puzzles me. It concerns the rinsing of her kidneys.

Joyce has a routine during her free time of going to the beach to urinate. Is this some peculiarly American custom of which I am not aware? She seems not to care that passing men may see her. Indeed, I sometimes think that she goes out of her way to attract their attention. Doubtless I am wrong. Doubtless mine is simply the perception of a stranger in a strange land. Still, if it is otherwise and there is some kidney problem, I would like to know about it. How else can I help her?

Do write and say, Christina. I wait for your answer.

As always,
Vi
(Lady Violet Smythe-Turnbull)

I wrote back that Joyce's kidneys were as sound as a dollar. I assured Lady Violet that urinating in public was not, generally speaking, an American custom. I implied that Joyce's routine was no more than a personal peccadillo and that Lady Violet need not be overly concerned with it.

A second letter from Lady Violet arrived very soon after mine was sent. It concerned Lord Alfred rather than Joyce Dell, although Joyce was mentioned in it at some length. Lady Violet had this to say:

Dear Christina,

It is quite balmy here, which is to say slow-paced, and so I feel impelled to write more often than is my usual custom. Adding to the dreariness is the fact that dear Alfie seems to have discovered mortality. His own, that is. This has lent a decidedly *triste* intonation to his customary "By Jove!"

He is fifty-three years old, you know, and that is traditionally a time of introspection and evaluation for upper-class Englishmen. It is also the age of gout, but Alfie, thank goodness, has been spared that. Alas, he has not been spared the mandatory Church of England ticket on the Biblical route.

I don't mean to imply that Alfie has gone religious on us. No, no. Alfie could never be so hypocritical as to turn his back on a lifetime as a reprobate. What he has done, though, is turned to the Bible for guidance in dealing with the fact that fifty-three is bloody well not middle age, since very few upper-class Britishers survive to their one-hundred-sixth year. The poor dear has definitely heard Death rattling his scythe, and so he's put his nose to the Good Book to ferret out how to outwit the Grim Reaper for an extra decade or two.

He has zeroed in on King David, for whom he seems to feel some special affinity. I suppose it is because King David, like Alfie, was really an unconscionable libertine for most of his life. (Do you recall how he got rid of Bathsheba's husband, Uriah? He put him in charge of an army going into battle. Then he issued orders for Uriah to advance while at the same time issuing orders to the rest of the army to retreat. Deliciously evil, what? And yet there are still those today who say that Open Marriage is not an improvement on that old-time morality!) In any case, Alfie identifies his situation with that of King David's towards the end of his life. You will recall that David's royal physicians kept Death at bay by sandwiching him between two naked virgins in his sickbed. Now Alfie has gotten it into his head that this should be the desired route to his greater longevity. He says, and he may have a point, that the exercise afforded lungs and heart by such a prescription is more efficacious than jogging.

I cannot help thinking—and rest assured, dearest Christina, that there is not the slightest censure implied here—that our young Joyce's presence has been somewhat key to this conviction of Alfie's. In truth, I myself am sometimes carried along into libidinous fantasy by the youth and energy and eroticism of her Lolita-like persona. Ahh, to be young! But if one cannot be young, why then the next best thing is to contrive some form of co-optation of the sexuality of youth, is it not? The need for this, I suppose, becomes particularly pressing when one reaches Alfie's age.

Look at our Joycie, if you will, dear Christina, through Alfie's cynical old eyes. See her in her bikini as she sets out for her afternoons on the beach. Such a wisp of a bikini, Christina. More suggestive than nudity, but of course that's the idea. Consider her leggy, adolescent body, all firm flesh and slender thigh muscle. See how clearly that tiny silken triangle outlines the high mount of her *mons veneris,* its upward tilt, the twin ridges of its lips and the cleft between them. Observe the skyward thrust of her small, compact, round, saucy *derrière* as she departs. See how it sways as if motored by the sweet young hips flaring out from the tiny teen-age waist. (Ahh, where do the years go? Where do the inches come from?) Note the jiggle of her breasts, a bosom so firm and well-molded as to render the support of the deliciously insufficient bikini bra quite superfluous. See how the nipples jut out—so long! so hard! Are they always in such a state of excitation? Is that adolescent half-smirk which seems always on Joycie's lips an acknowledgement of the demand implicit in the bouncing of her breasts?

She is, I must admit, a comely child above the neck as well as below. The bone structure of her face is quite charming, the cheekbones high, according to the British standards of beauty, the chin rounded but firm, the nose small and straight with no hint of the Hibernian, no Irish pug. Yes, quite comely except for the constant petulance of expression so peculiar to her generation here in the Americas. It is an expres-

sion, I am sure, which has much to do with the
conflict between expectation in what is surely the
most sexually permissive society in civilised history
and the frustration of not meeting *that expectation*.
All of which leads me to the key question, my dear
Christina, the question which has more to do with
meeting Alfie's needs than Joyce's, the question which
it is my hope that you can answer, will answer, and
shall answer promptly. It is this:

Can it be that Joyce is a virgin suitable for the
warming of Lord Alfred's bed? How impatiently I
await your reply!

> As ever,
> Vi
> (Lady Violet Smythe-Turnbull)

I answered immediately. While my letter was chatty,
and somewhat nostalgic, the reply to Lady Violet's "key
question" was succinct and to the point. *No!* Joyce Dell
was not a virgin! She had passed the point of no return on
more than one occasion, if such a paradox might be permitted. She might indeed be frustrated, but it was by no
means her permanent condition. If virginity was the ad-
mission price to Lord Alfred's bed, then he had better look
elsewhere.

It was not. Lady Vi's next letter made that quite clear. It
was a most entertaining missive:

My dear Christina,

Events here have taken a most happy turn. Dear
Alfie has been most effectively distracted from his
*angst*. Our sweet young Joycie has banished the adolescent curl from her moistly pursed lips. Since, as
you know, jealousy is not in my make-up, I am truly
enjoying their mutually arrived at solution.

The ability to enjoy comes straight from dear old Buzzy Armbruster. When he furnished this place, incorrigible voyeur that he is, dear Buzzy put in every gadget imaginable to be sure he would be privy to the erotic activities of his guests. There are high-powered telescopes to provide intimately close-up views of every part of the beach. Even those which might be considered safely private are visible from the raised terraces of the beach-house. Also, there are one-way mirrors through which one may view the action in various boudoirs. There is even a video system, complete with audio of course, by which every corner of the house and grounds may be observed. That specifically includes bathrooms.

Yes, it is bizarre! Quite bizarre! But also entertaining! Very, very entertaining!

Let me start at the beginning. In truth, dear Christina, that was innocent enough on my part. Poor Alfie had been sinking deeper and deeper into his depression. Every time I looked into his eyes they were saying, "What does it all mean? What does it all matter?" Each morning when he greeted me, and each evening when he went to bed, his "By Jove!" was coming to have less and less *joie de vivre*. Hopelessness hung from his jowls as from an unowned mutt on his way to the municipal pound's gas chamber. Truly, my concern for him turned to fearfulness. I worried that he might do himself some harm. In particular, I was fearful when he went off by himself to the beach. In the mood he was in, I feared the waves might seduce him to attempt suicide. Well, probably I am exaggerating this possibility, but the important thing is that my fear of it was quite real. It led me to keep an eye on him during his beach strolls via one of Buzzy's strategically placed telescopes. Thus it came about that I saw what I saw.

Dressed in white ducks and the shirt of his polo team, Alfie was strolling on the beach when he felt the pressure to relieve his kidneys. I know this because I was keeping an eye on him through the telescope and I saw his hand clutch at his crotch. I am Alfie's wife and I have long known what the clenching of his fingers in such a manner signifies.

He unbuttoned the fly of the white ducks. (Alfie considers zippers to be vulgarly American and refuses to have them installed in his custom-made trousers.) He took out his thick, craggy old pecker. Zeroing in on it with the telescope, I saw that it was quite heavy and indeed semi-tumescent with his need. He took aim at a waist-high tangle of sedge grass and let fly. His stream was quite like liquid gold in the sunlight, arcing high and very strong for a man convinced he is on the waning curve of Life.

"By Jove!"

I could not hear him make the exclamation, of course, but I am familiar enough with the twistings of Alfie's moustache when he pronounces these two syllables to recognize what he said. I followed his sudden stare with my telescope to see what had provoked his verbal reaction. And there was our young Joycie!

How romantic! you say? Well, not quite. Traditionally speaking, the elements of romance were somewhat askew. But then for all his millennia of family background, when it comes to sexual adventures, my sweet Lord Alfred does not *always* follow in the footsteps of tradition. In this case, at any rate, circumstance did not give him any choice.

Our Joyce, you see, dear Christina, had herself removed the bottom of her bikini and was squatting behind the sedge grass to pee in the dunes. (You will recall that I wrote to you previously of her predilection for such cavalier urinary behaviour.) Her own golden stream was pouring healthily from her pussy, the droplets clinging to the sparsely adolescent hairs fringing it. Truly, the expression on her face testified to a sensual enjoyment in the performance of the act. A positively ecstatic transcendence transformed this expression when Alfie's patrician geyser arced over the sedge grass to despoil the fragile bikini top over her breasts, and then changed angle to spray her belly and the hands holding her thighs apart, and finally her own peeing cunt. Ahh, Christina, you should have seen the child's expression when Alfie's sun-heated piss mingled with her own! It was this expression which prompted Alfie to exclaim again, and to repeat it:

"By Jove! By Jove!"

He moved closer. He aimed more accurately. She removed her hands from between her legs. She placed them behind her on the sand and leaned her weight on them. She tilted her bottom. Her still pissing pussy lifted to Alfie's stream. He pee'd into it, his *angst,* I am sure, quite forgotten.

Why was I so certain of this? Because his big, crusty old broadsword, even as the stream poured from it, was becoming quite tumescent. Yes, quite, quite *rigid!* The close-up zoom lens of Buzzy Armbruster's telescope confirmed this.

As happens, they both ran out of liquid. (The penile stiffness, as it were, did not however abate.) Young Joyce came erect from her rather awkward urinary position. She made no attempt to retrieve the bikini panties lying on the sand. Instead, she reached behind her to remove the top of the bikini.

"It's all wet," she explained. (I had no difficulty reading her lips via the telescope.) She tossed the bikini top aside. Her healthy breasts, the long, hard red nipples shiny with Lord Alfred's pee, bobbled like firm, ripe melons under the California sun.

"By Jove!" Alfie was impressed. His pee'd-out pecker was full-blown now. He had to hold it down from his belly with his hand it was so hardened with jizzum, so randy and ready. "By Jove!"

My nubile lady's maid took one look at that patrician prick and I could see the greedy passion spreading over her immature face. Her breasts began to pant visibly. A reddening lust spread over her flesh, an uncontrollably randy rash. She lifted one of her breasts in both her hands and licked the remains of Alfie's hot, pungent pee from it. Then she cupped her pussy with both hands and thrust it forward, offering it to him, shaking it as if to tempt him with the remains of urinary wetness.

Alfie fell to his knees in front of her. He was obviously not about to inquire as to her virginity. He recognized the salvation he had been seeking without putting too fine a point on its details. His sandpapery old tongue rolled out and he licked the wet from her firm young thighs. He worked his way up to the sparse silk of her young bush and sucked the droplets from it. Then his clever, experienced old tongue dipped between the swollen, purple lips of Joycie's squirming pussy.

"Eek!" (Still reading her lips.) "Eek! Eek!"

She gave a sort of little jump, the result of which was that she was sitting on his shoulders, facing him. Her thighs gripped his ruddy old cheeks and her lower legs locked behind his head. Her gaping young pussy was grinding against his mouth and tickling walrus moustache. Her hands were tangled wildly in poor Alfie's greying hair and pulling most awfully at it with no regard whatsoever to its having been somewhat thinned by the years.

Poor dear Alfie! There was no way that his kneeling position could sustain such youthful exuberance. He toppled over on his back and his ruddy old face was quickly and completely obscured by the raunchy hoyden's sopping cunt. It spread over his visage like a wet sponge.

Behind Joyce, dear Alfie's cock was still standing up from his white ducks, straight and firm as a flagpole flying the Union Jack for the honor of the Empire. Indeed, my eyes misted over as I surveyed it through the telescope. There is a sort of pride in having a husband who can raise such a pecker on the declining side of his middle years. It arouses emotions not unlike those felt when our fleet set sail to reclaim the Falkland Islands. It is hard for Americans to understand I know, Christina, but these last gasps of Empire are very important to us British. Indeed, such aristocratic erections as Alfie displayed on the beach may well be the final symbol of all dying Western civilization.

Ahh, how bloody pompous I must sound. How King-and-country jingoistic! Do forgive me! We are a foolish race, we British, patsies for national pride, stiff-necked suckers for the Anglo penis. But enough of that! Meanwhile, back on the beach . . .

Joyce, hard-titted breasts bouncing, had ridden Alfie's buried face to orgasm. Now she had turned around and was crouching over him, her bum sticking impudently up at the sun, her pussy moving lightly back and forth over the tip of Alfie's nose, her breasts squinched against his still-flat belly, her mouth hover-

ing over his dancing erection. Her tongue darted out
to lick his rugged, egg-sized balls, and I clearly saw
Alfie's eyes pop. His tongue darted out again and
began moving in and out of the honeyed entrance to
Joyce's pussy. Her lips turned into an O around the
rough-sculpted crest of Alfie's cock. She began to
suck it . . .

Standing at the telescope now, my hand was between my legs. You know how it is, Christina darling. I had opened the zipper of my Gloria Vanderbilt
jeans and my hand was well inside my panties. I was
disgracefully wet and my poor little clitty was all
swollen. That, however, did not stop me from frigging myself as I focussed on young Joyce and my
husband licking and sucking at each other's genitals
on the beach.

Ahh, how avidly they went at it! It was as if the
crashing surf had fired their blood. I was reminded of
that old war movie with dear, sweet Deborah Kerr
and Burt Lancaster. The waves roaring. The surf
shifting the sands. The entwined bodies. The moonlight . . . (Well, of course this was sunlight, but then
it's the *general* ambience I have in mind.)

Anyway, Joyce seemed to be a child to me again as
she licked Alfie's randy old cock, for all the world as
if it had been a lollypop. Lord, how that sweet young
thing did enjoy it! She sucked his balls and kissed the
shaft and finally pulled it all the way down her throat
and ate it as if she was never going to give it back to
him. And all the time Alfie was going at her succu-
lent young cunt again. He was licking and sucking the
honey from it as only dear Alfie can. Watching, I
could feel his expert tongue between *my* legs, licking
the juices from deep inside *my* pussy.

Suddenly he rolled over and shoved his cock down

Joyce's throat to the hilt. His craggy old ass started to bounce and I knew he was coming. I also knew (from my own experience with him) that he had contrived to get her clitty between his lips and was sucking it as his tongue frigged deep inside her cunt and his cock shot gobs of his sweet British cream down her hard-swallowing young throat.

It was too much for me, of course, Christina. I fell away from the telescope and held tight to my writhing cunt as my own orgasm exploded. It was wonderful!

So wonderful that—re-living the episode now as I write—I am seized once again with horniness. Forgive me Christina. I find that I must end quite abruptly.

> Most *raunchily* yours,
> Vi
> (Lady Violet Smythe-Turnbull)

Naturally I was quite delighted with this communication. It certainly sounded as if Joyce Dell's fantasy had come true. Egotistically enough, I suppose, I felt confirmed in the potency of my Fairy Godmotherhood. All I had to do was wave my wand to make my sisters happy. *Poof!* And their most lascivious dreams would come true!

I became quite heady at the prospect of pursuing this course. What I had contrived for Joyce Dell and Amanda Briggs would also be possible for Helen Willis and Melinda Holloway and Stephanie McCall. (And for myself? Ah well, the time had not yet come for me to consider that.) Thus was I carried away by the idea of manipulating reality to suit fantasy. All things were possible, all situations contrivable, all desires attainable. *Poof!*

This illusion of power, alas! was to be shattered by the abrupt and unhappy return of Joyce Dell from California.

# CHAPTER FIVE

Prior to Joyce's return, however, I was still riding the crest of my role as manipulator. It was during this period, when my ego still reigned, that the weekly meeting of our consciousness-raising group took up the question of Stephanie McCall's obsession in depth. This session, combined with my genuine feelings of concern for Stephanie while under the influence of my self-proclaimed Fairy Godmotherhood, led me to seek the counsel of Pogo the Player.

"Rape?" The tone was flat. The hooded eyes betrayed nothing. It was no idle conceit that Pogo the Player was completely unflappable. "You want me to help you to arrange to have a friend of yours raped?"

"It's for her own good," I assured him.

"Of course." His head bobbed compulsively—the pogo stick–like movement which had earned him his nickname. "Why not?" He stroked his angora cat calmly and then brushed a few stray hairs from the lap of his Pierre Cardin slacks.

"She wants to be raped," I explained, babbling a little. "She puts herself in dangerous situations so that it will happen. It has become an obsession with her and she takes more and more foolish chances. I fear for her safety. Truly I do.''

"And so you wish to have her raped to keep her from being raped." The hooded eyes strayed momentarily to the original Franz Kline hanging on the wall of his Central Park South apartment. They blinked approval. "I see."

"I don't think you do. That's not quite what I mean. I want to have Stephanie raped so that she doesn't get herself killed trying to get herself raped."

"How involved your world can be," Pogo said, stifling a yawn. "But why do you come to me, Christina? I am a player, not a rapist, a procurer who deals in flesh and only peripherally in violence."

It was true. Pogo is a player—which is to say a pimp. I had first met him some years before while working as a photographer for *World*. I had been working on a photo story about the subculture of procurers and prostitutes. Pogo was one of the major players on the New York scene. In fact, with some twenty subpanderers working for him, he was a veritable Prince of Players.

Like all such sovereigns, Pogo had his court favorites. They changed with some frequency, but there were always two or three very special ladies of the night whom he handled directly. They drifted in and out now—languid, indolent, as at home as the angora, and as eager to please him. Occasionally Pogo would bestow a caress on one or the other of them—or on the cat.

Unlike the feline, these beautiful young women were quite plastic looking. There was a blankness to even the adoring glances they lavished on Pogo. Were they on drugs? This occurred to me, but I rejected the notion. Pogo regarded his $500-a-night specialty girls as thoroughbreds subject to certain strictures. The every-night whores who were the dray horses of his stable might be kept in line by maintaining them on the knife edge of a heroin habit, but not these beauties. They were forbidden drugs as well as alcohol, tobacco, and fattening foods.

They functioned for love of Pogo—nothing more, nothing less. And they were hooked on the need for his approval the way an addict is hooked on a drug habit. He might have sex with them once in three months, and it might last only twenty minutes, and yet his psychological hold on them was so strong that it was for this that they lived. It was the high-water mark of their emotion—and the measure of their shallowness.

Such Svengali-like power defined the success of Pogo the Player. It earned him his luxurious quarters, his collection of Impressionist and Abstract avant-garde originals, his designer wardrobe and his custom-crafted Mercedes limousine. It brought him in contact with Brahmins and financiers, statesmen and powerful politicians, visiting prime ministers and potentates. He catered to the wealthy, the powerful, the blue of blood. Quality was his stock-in-trade, discretion the hallmark of his reputation.

Less obviously, Pogo was also a practical man. (Always he maintained the addicted street whores as a hedge against a rainy day.) This—given the nature of his business—brought him into contact with other "practical" men. His contacts in the Organization were so highly placed as to insure only the finest vintage Chianti in Pogo's wine cellar. His standing was high—solidly high—in the world of professional crime. Knowing this, I had felt it natural to turn to Pogo for help with Stephanie McCall's problem.

I had no doubt that Pogo would help me if he could. He liked me based on my never treating him judgmentally. At the same time, I had never bothered to hide the fact that as a feminist I was appalled at the way his profession exploited women. He admired both my honesty and my ability to refrain from moralizing on an individual level. It was a fine line I had drawn for myself; Pogo was one of the few people I knew who could appreciate the subtlety of the distinctions I made. This understanding put him firmly in my corner.

I relied on that now. "I come to you," I told him, "because I thought you might put me in touch with someone suitable."

"A rapist?"

"Well, yes . . ."

"You think that among my associates I count career rapists?" Pogo asked, amused.

I shrugged, feeling a little foolish, but still sure that if anyone might help me it would be Pogo the Player.

"Rape is an impulse crime," he pointed out.

"I know that."

"The Cosa Nostra has not yet seen fit to put it on an organized basis."

"Spare me your irony."

"I'm serious. There is no profit in rape."

"Nevertheless, there are recidivist rapists."

"You don't understand. Since there is no profit, there is no professionalism involved. This makes rape strictly an amateur's crime."

I absorbed this. Pogo the Player did not have to tell me that the word "amateur" was anathema to him. His professionalism was his pride. He dealt only with other professionals. This feeling ran very deep. Like others in this field, he was convinced that amateurs were ruining the business. "Then you can't help me," I concluded.

"I didn't say that."

"Then what are you saying?"

"Fantasy is illusion, Christina. Would you agree?"

"Yes, I suppose I would."

"Then understand this, my dear. When it comes to the erotic, reality is illusion, too. Do you understand?"

I thought about it. "I think I do," I told him. "But I

don't really think the illusion of rape will satisfy my friend."

"It is not the illusion of rape I'm talking about. The rape will be real enough. Brutal, etcetera. It is the illusion of the rapist to which I refer. A genuine rapist, you see, is not a possibility. Too hard to locate. Too untrustworthy. Too schizoid. Such a one might really do your friend harm, which is what you're trying to avoid. And so we must find someone who will provide the illusion of a rapist. And this illusory rapist will then commit your rape."

"But Stephanie has to be convinced," I pointed out.

"Of course. I do not deal in shoddy illusions. You should know me better than that, Christina." Pogo sounded hurt.

"I'm sorry."

"Give me a few days," he said, standing up. Our meeting was at an end. "I'll call you."

Two nights later he did indeed call me. "I have arranged a meeting for you with two men," he told me.

"Two?"

"Yes. It seems that for all but the impulse rapist, rape is a very difficult crime to commit singlehandedly. All exceptions to the contrary, it is hard to insert one's penis in a moving vagina and hold a knife to the victim's throat at the same time. It's also difficult to tie and gag a victim with one hand. My contacts in stir assure me that the most successful rapes are committed in tandem. One man holds the struggling victim while the other ravishes her, and then they switch places."

"Then I will be meeting with both rapists?"

"Not exactly. In the case we are contemplating, only one man will rape while the other holds."

"Oh? Why is that?"

"One of the two men is gay."

"I see." Well, the truth is that I didn't see at all. But I did trust Pogo. I wrote down the time and place of the meeting. "How will I recognize them?" I asked.

"You won't have to. They'll find you. *Au revoir.*" Pogo had his conceits. Dropping a French phrase now and then was one of them.

*"Au revoir, mon cher. Merci."* I hung up the phone. Little did I know that his choice of language was meant to be prophetic.

The meeting place was a bar on St. Marks Place. It was long and narrow and quite dimly lit. There were tables at the back. As I made my way to them through the crowd at the bar I noticed that there seemed to be at least five distinct genders represented. A sixth ambled up to me in chains and codpiece, miniskirt and waitress cap and took my drink order. I stayed with the ambience and ordered a light beer.

As I was sipping it, a man strolled over to me. He had a Viking haircut, a large nose, and a gold chain. He was twisting a wedding ring off his finger as he arrived. "Lonesome?" he inquired.

"I don't think so," I told him.

"Married?"

"No."

"Well, that's okay," he decided.

"I'm relieved."

"Can I buy you a drink?"

"Thanks, no. I already have one." I held up my beer to show him.

"Mind if I sit down?"

"As a matter of fact, I do mind. I'm waiting for someone."

"Why didn't you say so in the first place?" He was indignant. "I wasted my time, and I haven't got much time to waste."

"Of course not," I sympathized. "After all, you do have to get back to your wife sometime, don't you?"

He glowered at me and moved off.

Almost instantly he was replaced by a large woman into rubber. I don't just mean that was her predilection; she was literally poured into it. "You bi?" She came right to the point, her greeting a growl.

"No." It was a lie, but it seemed the best way to cut her short.

"Too bad," she said as she left.

Two young fellows moved in on my other side. They were East Village types, long-bearded and hairy, three degrees past casual in threadbare jeans and worn-out flannel shirts. One was white, the other black. There were little brown dots where the pupils of their eyes should have been.

"Hey, man." They hovered over me. "You waiting for us?"

I wasn't sure. "I was supposed to meet two fellows," I admitted cautiously.

"You got the goods, man?"

"The goods?"

"Come on, man! Come on now! We strung out enough without you jivin' us."

"I think you're making a mistake."

"You don't think we got the green, man? We got it!" A handful of bills appeared. "Now snow on us, man."

"You really have made a mistake."

"Hey!" A voice from the gloom behind me untangled

the situation. "Back here, you dim bulbs. Mama's waiting for you with the sugar-tit."

Shaking their heads and moving in three-quarter time, they left me. I sat back and nursed my beer. Not for long, though. Two macho truck drivers, company badges on their caps, broke my brief solitude.

"We been looking for you," the first one told me.

"Oh?" I was cautious, but hopeful.

"You was looking for us, too. Right?" the second one insisted.

"I'm not sure."

"Be sure," the first one demanded, patting my hand. They sat down on either side of me.

"You won't be sorry," the second chimed in, also patting my knee under the table.

"I'm the buyer, not the victim." I removed his hand.

"Whatever you say." The first one shrugged.

"Two beers," the second one told the waitress.

"You are the rapists, aren't you?" It seemed wise to make sure.

They looked at each other. "Whatever turns you on," the first one grinned.

"Which one of you is going to actually do it?" I inquired.

"Take your pick, lady."

"It's not up to me. It depends which one of you is the gay one."

"Gay?" Each of them inched away from me. "Back off, lady. Just look at us! Do we look gay? Hell, anybody could see that ain't our lifestyle." Quite insulted, they got up and left my table.

*They'll find you!* That's what Pogo the Player had told me. What he hadn't anticipated was that everybody else in the place would find me, too!

"Is it you that we seek, Mam'selle?"

*Here we go again!* I told myself. "Probably not," I replied. "I'm not looking for action. I'm not dealing drugs and I'm not in the market for any, either."

"*Oui.* Then it seems *très* likely that you shall be the one."

"Did Pogo the Player send you?"

"*Oui.*" He raised a questioning eyebrow toward the chair beside me and I nodded that he might sit down. His companion, remaining silent, took the opposite chair. "We have come to discuss the matter of the ravishment," the one who seemed to be doing all the talking informed me.

He was of medium height, slight and dark, quite good looking in an utterly French way. His jacket was double-breasted, deep maroon, watered silk cut in the narrow Italian mode. A white silk scarf filled the narrow V to a point halfway up his neck. He wore his black beret at a rakish tilt over long, girlishly curly hair. The dimple in his cheek and the cleft in his chin forecast a *boulevardier*'s future. At the moment, however, he was too young for that (about my age, perhaps even a year or two younger), and was better suited to the role of gigolo. Nervous hands said that role might work for him with either men or women. If there was one thing that he most definitely did not look like, it was a rapist.

The other man, however, did look the part. He was stocky and blond with a square face and a livid scar which ran from the corner of his right eye all the way down to his anvil jaw. His lips were thin, his mouth cruel. Subzero temperatures deadened his blue eyes. Hard muscles suggested themselves through his black leather jacket and black leather pants. Even his gold tooth looked like its sheen came from chewing nails to buff it.

"I don't want her hurt," I said. I looked at the one I assumed to be the rapist.

However, it was the other one who answered. "But of course not, Mam'selle . . ." He paused, waiting for me to supply the name.

"Just call me Christina."

"*Enchanté*," he said, kissing the back of my hand. "I am Lucien." He gestured toward his companion. "And this is Gunther."

"How do you do?" I acknowledged the introduction.

Gunther grunted—nothing more.

"M'sieur Pogo has given us only the sketchiest idea of what is wanted," Lucien told me. "Perhaps if you could go into the matter in more detail, Mam'selle Christina—?"

"Of course." I explained about Stephanie McCall's obsession and how I felt it was leading her into more and more dangerous attempts to get herself raped. "And so," I concluded, "I want to arrange to have her fantasy satisfied without her coming to any harm. That's where you come in." I looked at Gunther. It was easy to picture him raping Stephanie. He seemed just the sort of brute she'd had in mind.

But again it was Lucien who answered me. "Before we get into the specifics of how this is to be accomplished, Mam'selle Christina, there is the matter of the fee to be discussed." He lowered his eyes as if somewhat abashed at himself for having brought up such a delicate subject.

"How much did you have in mind?"

He named a figure.

"That seems rather high," I reacted.

"It is because ravishment does not provide one with steady work," he told me. "There are long periods of layoff between jobs. *Très* long." Lucien sighed.

"Even so."

"And there are no—how do you Americans say it?— fringing benefits."

"Then again, perhaps there are." I fished around in my

pocketbook and came up with the photograph of Stephanie I had brought along. "The victim." I handed it to Gunther.

He glanced at it coldly and passed it to Lucien.

"*Voilà!*" Lucien approved. "Your point is most well taken, Mam'selle Christina. Perhaps a compromise figure." He named it.

"All right," I agreed.

"It is permissible that I keep this picture?" Lucien asked. "To be sure there are no mistakes in the ravishment."

"Yes. You may keep it." I looked at Lucien. He really did seem quite slender, even boyish. "Are you sure you'll be able to hold her while Gunther does it?" I wondered. "Stephanie may not look it from her picture, but she's in a rather strenuous daily exercise program and I suspect she's really quite strong."

"But your view, it is the topsy-turvy one, Mam'selle Christina. It is Gunther who will do the holding. I think he will not have any trouble."

Gunther flexed his leather as if to drive home the point.

"You mean that he's gay and you're the rapist?" I asked, my tone betraying my doubts to Lucien.

"*Oui,* Mam'selle."

"I don't know." I spoke my thoughts aloud. "I really don't think you're going to live up to Stephanie's fantasy. You see, what she visualizes is some terribly macho brute."

"Have no fear, Mam'selle. She will be gratified."

"But I do have qualms. I don't think—"

"Give me your hand, *chère* Christina." He took it without waiting for me to comply.

"What—?"

Lucien carried my hand to his lap. He had unzipped his fly. His penis, flaccid and exposed, was lying extended down the length of one thigh. He arranged my hand into a fist to circle it. The girth was such that I could not make my fingers meet. "Now look quickly." He raised one corner of his double-breasted jacket.

I looked. His naked penis stretched almost to his knee. It was easily eight inches long, and it wasn't even erect!

"Are you satisfied that your friend will be gratified?"

I nodded mutely, overawed.

"Will there be, do you think, any other reassurances I can offer you, Mam'selle Christina?"

"Just that you won't really hurt Stephanie."

"You have my word."

"I'm more worried about him," I said, nodding at Gunther. "He looks so vicious! And why has he not said anything?"

"He is from Heidelberg."

"So? Do you mean he doesn't speak English?"

"I do not really know." Lucien shrugged a Gallic shrug. "He was once a famous duellist there."

"But no more?" I sensed that Lucien was driving at something.

"No more. He does not duel and he does not speak. Not English, Mam'selle Christina. Not French. Not even German."

"Why not?"

"A duel! *Voilà*! His tongue, it was cut out!"

I stared at Lucien in surprise. A duel! In this day and age! "By Jove!" I stole a line from Lord Alfred. It seemed peculiarly apropos to express my astonishment. "By Jove!"

"And now if there is nothing else, Mam'selle Christina—" Lucien started to stand.

"Just one thing. Your clothes. Stephanie really visualizes being raped by thugs. Gunther looks all right in his leather, but you are far too debonair."

"*Merci*. My tailor will be most gratified to have your approval."

"If I give you a little extra money, perhaps you might pick up some more suitable clothing—more ragged and beat up, more representative of the street, I mean—at one of the local thrift shops."

"But of course." Lucien quickly accepted the extra bills I offered him.

"Remember, she must be convinced that both of you are savage brutes while she is being raped," I reminded them as they got up to leave. "She must feel that she is at your mercy."

"So you have said, Mam'selle Christina, and you may rest assured that I have taken it to *le coeur*." Gunther was already out the door, but Lucien turned one last time before he reached it. "Do not worry, *chère Mam'selle*. I will ravish your friend with irresistible violins!"

Ah, the French!


Three days later, via Pogo the Player I received a full written report on the rape of Stephanie McCall from Lucien. The French are always meticulous as to details when it comes to matters of an erotic nature, and Lucien was no exception. He left out nothing, and the lasciviousness of his eye was worthy of Rabelais.

He and Gunther had picked up Stephanie's trail when she left the office where she worked as an advertising copywriter. She had gone straight home. An hour or two later, as night was beginning to fall, she had emerged again.

Her appearance was quite transformed, according to Lucien. Going into her apartment building in her low-heeled work shoes and tailored suit, she had looked stylish enough, but in the manner of a career woman dressed for her job—chic, but not particularly erotic. When she emerged, however, she was "*très* sexy" in high heels and miniskirt, half-buttoned silk blouse and *"sans* brassiere." Her garb was obviously calculated to display all of her considerable charms.

Lucien couldn't resist describing these charms. To his mind, I suppose, it was intrinsic to setting the scene. I thought it extraneous, but read the description anyway.

Stephanie McCall (as Lucien saw her) was a classic brunette with the high coloring one usually associates with women of the Mediterranean region. Her features were aristocratic, the cheekbones high, the nose generous, although by no means overly so. Her mouth was a trifle large, perhaps, but the lips were full and sensual, and her chin quite sweetly rounded. Her eyes were a very deep and smouldering shade of brown. There was much warmth in them, and much passion as well.

This was stressed by the way the outfit she had chosen showed off her body. It was a slim body and her dignified carriage might have offset its sensuality if she had chosen to let it. But she didn't. While she walked with true upper class poise, she also allowed her hips to sway and her unfettered bosom to jiggle in such a way as to draw attention. The body language Stephanie spoke was sending out diametrically opposed messages. The arrogant tilt of her classically molded head said she was unapproachable, but the stiff nipples bouncing under the silk of her blouse were an unmistakable invitation. Long-waisted and sleek, she might have rated a pedestal, but the saucy swing of her derriere was like a finger beckoning to the haystack. Her long legs may have carried her about the office efficiently enough, but as revealed by the miniskirt, it was all too easy to envision them curving around a man's hips in the act of love.

She looked like a young woman who wanted sex, wanted it badly, wanted it soon, and would have not the slightest trouble finding it. Indeed, Lucien reflected, he could not see why she should have any problem getting herself raped, for that matter. Certainly, now that he'd seen her, Lucien was in no way loath to fulfill the task he had undertaken.

When she came out of her building, Stephanie McCall had the doorman hail a taxi for her. Lucien and Gunther followed it in the car they had rented. Their route took them down Second Avenue and over the Queensboro Bridge.

Stephanie got out of the cab in front of a club in Sunnyside, Queens. Gunther followed her into the place while Lucien discreetly parked the car in a deserted lot a few blocks away. The moon was already up in the sky as Lucien started to walk back to the bar. It was a full moon, opulent, well suited to the warm spring night.

Approaching the bistro, Lucien slowed down to appraise it. As a one-word description, "garish" would have been an understatement. The neon was stark, the colors harsh, the psychedelic blinking of the bulbs relentless. "TOPLESS!" was topped by "BOTTOMLESS!" which in turn was rendered ironic by not one, but two announcements of "LADIES WELCOME!" Lucien wondered momentarily if that meant only naked ladies. Stephanie, however, had been dressed when she went in, and so he discarded the notion. In any case, from the outside the establishment was as rough and tough looking—indeed, rougher and tougher! —than any Lucien had ever seen in Montmartre. Its blatancy shocked the rapist's fine French sensibilities—but then he had never been to Sunnyside, Queens, before.

He entered. Immediately his eardrums were assailed by high-decibel rock music. Mirrors and strobe lights played havoc with his vision. Packed bodies—male and female— blinked lewdly on a postage-stamp dance floor. Naked women in waitress caps carried trays of drinks from the crowded bar to the tables in the back. Lucien spotted Gunther at the bar and elbowed his way to him.

"Where is she?" he asked.

Gunther gestured toward a spot further down the bar. Stephanie was perched on a barstool there, flashing quite a bit of thigh from under her miniskirt. The sight had attracted a burly-looking young man wearing tight jeans and a street-wise look of lechery. He was asking if he might buy her a drink and she was nodding yes.

Lucien worked his way to within earshot of them. "I haven't seen you around here before," the barrel-chested young man was saying. "What's your name?"

"Stephanie."

"I'm Tony. Here's our drinks, Stephanie." He handed her a martini and lifted his beer to his lips.

"Thanks, Tony." Stephanie drained the drink at one gulp. She turned her back to Tony and smiled warmly at the man seated on her other side. "Got a match?" She held a cigarette to her lips and leaned in toward him so that her unbuttoned blouse gaped open for him to catch a glimpse of her naked breasts.

"I've got a match." Behind her, Tony fumbled one from his pocket.

Stephanie ignored him and accepted a light from the other man. He looked older than Tony, but he was just as husky, and just as tough-looking. "My name is Stephanie." Her smile was an invitation. "What's yours?"

"Mike."

"Going to buy me a drink, Mike?" The silk blouse brushed his arm just below the rolled-up sleeves.

Mike flinched as if the dark nipple outline was a red-hot dagger. "Sure," he said hoarsely.

Stephanie drained the second martini. "Thanks, Mike." She swiveled around on the barstool and cocked her head at Tony, who was grumbling to himself over his beer. "Aren't you going to ask me to dance, Tony?"

"Sure." His eyes lit up.

Stephanie linked her arm through his and rubbed against him as they made their way to the dance floor. "Save our seats, Mike," she called back over her shoulder.

Watching her in the strobe lights, Lucien saw her hands lock low down on Tony's hips as they started to dance. Her blood-red fingernails reached around to dig into his buttocks. Her movements, jerky in the fast, multicolored flicker of the lights, were both primal and provocative. Her knees were bent, her legs wide apart, the tight mini-skirt riding high on her thighs, the V of her position pointing to the target of her exposed panty-crotch which the powerful lights rendered intermittently transparent. Tony's eyes never left her groin, her revealed bush, her pouting, swollen pussy lips. His own swollen organ seemed to be literally thumping to the beat of the music.

Lucien wasn't the only one watching them. Mike hadn't taken his eyes off Stephanie's pert and bouncing bottom. There was a cynical look on his face as he watched her, the look of a man who knew a cock-teaser when he saw one. But there was naked lust in his eyes as well.

The dance ended and Stephanie and Tony returned to their seats at the bar. "Miss me?" she asked, then turned to Mike and kissed him on the lips. Lucien spied her tongue making a quick invasion of his mouth. Tony stood awkwardly behind her, once again ignored.

That was the pattern. It continued for a couple of hours, with Lucien observing and Gunther patiently waiting further down the bar. Stephanie would squeeze Tony's thigh intimately and then desert him to dance belly-to-belly with Mike. She would hold Mike's hand against the silk over her breast and then drop it to lick Tony's ear as she whispered into it. She would straddle Tony's lap, rubbing up and down on it so that he couldn't help feeling the wet openness of her pussy, and then she would hop down abruptly, turn from him, and clutch Mike's erection through his pants.

"I'd like to be alone with you," she whispered to Tony at one point. "But I don't want to hurt Mike's feelings." And she took his hand and squeezed it briefly between her naked thighs to be sure he understood.

"I wish we could get away by ourselves," she whispered to Mike. "But it wouldn't be right to desert Tony." And she sneaked his hand inside her blouse so he might feel how hot and hard and ready her bare nipple was.

Both men were bulging at the seams of their pants crotches when Stephanie ran her fingers through her long blue-black hair and informed them that it was really time for her to leave. Of course both of them offered to see her home. "You can walk me to the subway." She linked arms with both of them, her breasts bobbling. "Both of you."

Motioning to Gunther to join him, Lucien waited a discreet interval and then followed the threesome out of the bar. The street was quite deserted. It was a factory district and everything was closed. There wasn't a soul in sight in the dim streetlight except for Stephanie and the two men.

They had halted in front of a deserted machine supply shop doorway. "I must have had too much to drink," Stephanie announced loudly to Mike and Tony. "I don't seem to have any inhibitions left at all. You know what I'd like to do?"

"No, what?" they asked in tandem.

"See which one of you has the largest equipment." Her Bryn Mawr accent was much in evidence as she spoke these words.

The two men looked at each other, confused.

"Show me."

Tony and Mike looked around them. Lucien and Gunther

shrank back in the shadows where they were sure they couldn't be seen. The men shrugged and unzipped their flies and took out their penises. They were both hard.

Stephanie hefted the erections, one in each hand. Then she dropped them and took a step back. "How disappointing!" she said coldly, her tone very bitchy, very upper class. "How very disappointing!"

"Huh?" Tony was floored.

"What is this?" Mike asked, the first to get angry.

"You two gentlemen simply do not have what I am looking for!" Abruptly Stephanie giggled. " 'Bye now." And she turned and started back in the direction from which she'd come, jogging, but not really running. The way she loped was like a challenge to them to chase and catch her.

"Fuck you, lady!" Mike yelled after her.

"You don't have the guts!" she called back.

"Let's show her!" Now Tony was angry.

"And have her start screaming rape? She's not worth it," Mike told him. "She doesn't want to make out. She's the type gets her kicks turning guys on and then spitting in their faces."

Stephanie was loitering at the far end of the block from them. "Chicken!" she taunted them. "Dumb clods!"

But Mike and Tony had decided not to involve themselves any further with her. They walked back to the club and went inside. Except for Stephanie's reeling a little drunkenly in the pool of light surrounding one of the lampposts and Lucien and Gunther hidden in the shadows of a doorway, the street was once again deserted.

Never had Lucien seen an attractive woman go to such lengths to provoke men to assault her. He had thought that she would surely succeed in getting herself ravished by amateurs before he and Gunther had an opportunity to victimize her themselves. Now with that opportunity at hand, Lucien acted to make sure that it would not slip away from them.

Stephanie, not walking quite so tipsily anymore, had deliberately set off on a roundabout route to the elevated station where the train for Manhattan stopped. She walked down deserted factory streets where half the streetlight bulbs were out. The overhead el blocked out the brightness of the full moon. Shadows merged with shadows. The entrances to empty parking lots and deserted alleyways led to pools of blackness. Nothing stirred.

There was a pervading smell of rotting refuse over the area. The sidewalks were embedded with cinders and spiderwebbed with the cracks of time. The cobblestones under the el structure were worn smooth. The silence was eerie.

Lucien dispatched Gunther on a roundabout route to intercept her before she might reach the stairway leading up to the station. Meanwhile, Lucien moved with catlike tread to close the distance between himself and Stephanie. Unwittingly (except perhaps on some subconscious Freudian level), she moved with breasts bobbling and hips swaying into a cul-de-sac defined by her two entrappers. Gunther stepped out in front of her where a garbage spill marked the entrance to a narrow alley. Lucien moved up quickly behind her.

"What do you want?!" she screamed when she saw them. Out to get herself raped though she might have been, Stephanie nevertheless reacted fearfully to the large, leather-clad brute of a man who loomed up in front of her so suddenly.

Of course Gunther didn't answer; tongueless, he couldn't. But his cold eyes moved to a point somewhere over Stephanie's shoulder. Instinctively, she whirled around.

Lucien was coming up on her quickly. He looked quite scroungy in a pair of beat-up corduroy work pants and a greasy T-shirt torn at the shoulder. When Stephanie whirled to face him, he pulled a switchblade knife from his pocket and pressed its button. Its sharp tip and blade gleamed in a stray beam of station light which shone through a striation in the overhead el tracks. Lucien let his tongue loll witlessly from his mouth—a nice touch, he thought.

Stephanie sucked in a deep, panicky breath and started to let it out in a scream. Gunther shut it off with a large hand clapped over her mouth. His large arms encircled her, crushing the silk over her breasts. Half-lifting her from the platform of her high-heeled shoes, he dragged her into the darkness of the garbage-strewn alley. Lucien followed with the threatening switchblade.

"Not a sound!" Lucien said, pressing the flat of the blade against her throat as he spoke. "You understand?"

Stephanie nodded and Gunther removed his hand from her mouth. A cloud moved in the sky and full moonlight brightly lit the scene in the alley. Lucien read in Stephanie's eyes that she found him rather small and slight and insufficient to be terrorizing her in spite of his powerful companion and his knife.

He decided she must be disabused of that notion immediately if he was going to earn his fee. Moving the knife away from her face, he slapped her. It was a light enough slap, but he repeated it several times until her cheeks were flushed with the rapid back-and-forth punishment. "Nothing personal, *chérie*." And then he kissed her, his three-day growth of beard further abrading her already sore face.

It was a deliberately insulting kiss. With Gunther holding Stephanie from behind, Lucien was free to use her as he wished. While his tongue probed her mouth and deliberately stabbed deep down her throat, he ran his filthy hands over the front of her body, leaving smudges on the silk blouse and the miniskirt. He squeezed her panting breasts hard and laughed jeeringly at the stiffness of the nipples. He twisted the flesh of her slender, shapely thighs and then reached between them with both hands to maul the derriere that was writhing so frantically as she struggled.

"Relax, *ma petite*," he told her. "I'm not going to hurt you." His laugh was nasty.

As if to make the point, Gunther twisted Stephanie's arm cruelly behind her.

"Oh!" she cried, tears streaming down her cheeks.

Lucien licked his lips as if the sight of the tears aroused him. With elaborate delicacy, he pulled the silk blouse out from where it was tucked into her skirt, and undid the two or three buttons which were still buttoned. Then he folded the blouse away from her breasts and tucked it under the arm Gunther was pinning behind her. He stood back and studied the naked breasts heaving in the moonlight. The bright red nipples were very long and hard. With each new pressure on her arm by Gunther, the firm mounds bobbled more enticingly.

"Doves!" Lucien exclaimed, tweaking one of the nipples sadistically. "Shall I kiss it, *chère Mademoiselle,* and make it better?"

Stephanie stared at him, not knowing how to reply.

"Shall I?" He made a motion as if to pinch her nipple again.

"If you like," Stephanie gasped.

"I like." He bent his neck, extended his tongue, and licked the deep cleavage between her trembling breasts from her belly to her neck. "I like," he repeated. He cupped one breast in a filthy palm and ran his tongue over it. *"Très bien."* He opened his mouth and sucked the breast into it. He licked the nipple, then kissed it, then sucked at it furiously.

As frightened as she was, Stephanie could not keep from squirming with the thrills his mouth was sending through her body. The other man, the one who had made no sexual overtures to her, held her so tightly that her visible reaction was limited. Nevertheless, Lucien could not miss it.

"That arouses you?" he asked, raising his mouth from her breast.

"Yes." Stephanie's voice was hoarse.

"Let me see." Lucien reached under her miniskirt and between her legs. Stephanie's sopping cunt had swallowed up her panties. "It is the truth." He kept two of his fingers there, stroking the silk between the throbbing lips of her pussy. "But I have something here, *chérie*, which will arouse you even more." He took her hand and ran it down the inside of his leg where his stiffening cock was hanging. He moved her warm fingers up and down the full length.

Stephanie's eyes widened with awe.

"What do you think?" Lucien asked her softly.

"You must have something in your pocket!" Stephanie blurted out.

"And what would that be, Mam'selle?" He squeezed her honeyed pussy.

"Another weapon, perhaps?" Her naked breasts filled with air and her fingers tightened over the shaft.

"A weapon?" He quickly bit into the fleshiness of her upper breast. *"Oui!"* He patted the hand between his legs. "A *formidable* weapon!" He pronounced it in the French fashion. "Shall I unsheath it for you, Mam'selle?" Without waiting for Stephanie to answer, he unzipped his corduroy pants and fished out his giant, semihard prick.

"Oh! . . . My! . . . God!" Stephanie stared. She slumped against Gunther behind her. The entrance to her pussy widened either in anticipation, or for self-preservation, she couldn't have said which.

*"Formidable!"* he exclaimed, patting Stephanie's cheek,

wiping some of the honey from her pussy on it in the process. "Is it not so?"

"*Magnifique!*" she agreed wholeheartedly, her Bryn Mawr French springing automatically to Stephanie's lips.

"*Merci, Mam'selle.* And now you will get on your knees and suck it!"

"That's not possible! I'll choke!"

"Gunther!"

The brute leaned on Stephanie's shoulders until she sank to a kneeling position. One of her knees squished down on a banana peel, but she was so apprehensive that she didn't even notice. Lucien approached her. In one hand he held the switchblade knife. The lethal tip gleamed in the moonlight. In the other hand he held the plus-eight-inch-long club which was his cock. Considering what he intended, it must have struck Stephanie as potentially more brutal than the knife.

"Smell it!" He pressed it against her upper lip, under her nostrils.

Keeping her lips tightly clenched, Stephanie inhaled deeply through her nose.

"The perfume is pleasing, yes *chérie*?"

"Yes."

"Now kiss it."

Stephanie pursed her lips and kissed the large, heart-shaped crest of his prick.

"Use your tongue!"

She kissed it again, inserting her tongue in the hole at the tip.

"Lick it!"

She licked the ruby head.

"The shaft too!"

She licked the shaft from the crest to the base and back.

"Do my balls, *chérie*!"

Stephanie kissed his balls. They were large and hairy. She licked them.

"Underneath!"

She licked and sucked underneath his balls. His huge donkey-cock slapped against the top of her head.

"Eat out my asshole, Mam'selle."

"No!" Stephanie pulled back.

His huge hands then pushed her head forward as Lucien turned around and dropped his pants and bent over. Stephanie kissed the bony cheeks of his ass. She licked them. Her tongue went to the cleft between them. Gunther's hand was like iron at the back of her neck. She stuck her tongue deep up Lucien's ass and sucked.

After a moment he turned around. He put a hand on either side of her cheeks and forced her mouth open. He thrust a third of his cock inside it. "Now suck my cock, *chérie*," he purred.

Stephanie started sucking as hard as she could. Slowly, quarter inch by quarter inch, more and more of the monster prick forced its way between her wide-stretched lips and down her throat. She sucked harder to keep from gagging.

Lucien reached down with both hands and played with her naked, heaving breasts while she sucked him. He began moving in and out of her mouth, his balls bouncing against her chin. He debated with himself whether or not to come in her mouth. It would be very satisfying, doubtless, but he decided against it. He shoved his huge cock all the way down her throat just so Stephanie could really feel how it choked her, and then he withdrew. "I'm going to fuck you now, *ma petite*," he told her. "Over here," he then instructed Gunther. He upended a garbage pail and sat down on top of it. His cock stuck up like some obscenely phallic totem pole in the moonlight.

Stephanie, her jaws numb, stared at it fearfully. She

could only guess what he had in mind. But whatever it was, she was afraid that huge prick would split her in two if he put it inside of her.

Gunther dragged her over in front of where Lucien was perched. Lucien reached out and lifted the miniskirt with the tip of the switchblade knife. Then he stretched out his other hand, twisted the fingers around the waistband of her panties, and tore them from her body. Gunther inserted his knee from behind and forced her thighs wide apart. Her hot, wet pussy spread itself out in front of Lucien like a feast.

"Pick her up and put her down on my lap." Lucien's gigantic organ quivered an invitation to the impalement.

"No!" Stephanie screamed. "You'll tear me apart inside! You'll kill me!"

"Do it, Gunther!" Lucien commanded, ignoring her pleas.

Gunther hoisted her from behind with an arm under the back of each knee. Her gaping quim hung down between his arms. The sharp red tips of her banana-curved oblong breasts strained toward the full moon as he held her suspended over Lucien's giant and beastly hard-on. Slowly he lowered her.

Lucien reached with his dirty fingers and drew the lips of Stephanie's dangling pussy still further apart. When the wet, trembling meat of her inner cunt was exposed, he inserted the heart-shaped wedge of his cock in the mouth of her pussy. Stephanie gasped and wept with apprehension. "Slowly," Lucien instructed Gunther. "Lower her slowly." He worked his prick up her tight shaft one inch and then two as Gunther obeyed his instructions. Then, feeling her clitty growing hard against it, he began moving it in small, tight, tantalizing circles. Soon he had four inches inside her, and then five.

"Ohh!" Stephanie moaned. "Ahh . . . Easy! . . . Don't

rip me! . . . There! . . . There! . . .'' Her hand dropped
under her as if with a will of its own and began to fondle
Lucien's big, hairy balls as Gunther slid her up and down
Lucien's huge, steel-hard prick. "Yes! . . . Yes! . . ."
Tears were still streaming from her eyes now, but they
were squeezed shut.

"Fuck you, American bitch!" Lucien snarled. "Fuck!"

"Fuck!" Stephanie echoed. "Fuck!" and she pressed
against the alley wall with her feet to move up and down
on Lucien's cock. Soon she was contriving for Lucien's
cock to penetrate her more deeply than Gunther's raisings
and lowerings had allowed.

"You're enjoying it too much!" Lucien's tone became
even more vicious. "Gunther, drop her!"

Gunther removed his support from under Stephanie's
haunches. She settled sharply and fully on to the impalement. The huge cock was buried all the way up her,
battering at the entrance to her womb—breaching it. Stephanie screamed. At the same time, she began to come with
deep, painful, grinding movements that were out of her
control. Gunther clapped his hand over her mouth, but she
kept screaming into it as she came.

"Pull her off!" Lucien told Gunther.

Gunther obeyed. He held her in front of Lucien with her
legs spread again. Her poor, swollen, tormented pussy was
still jerking wildly in an orgasm that was beyond her
power to stop. Her eyes opened and she stared at Lucien's
glistening tower of flesh as she continued to come . . .
and come . . . and come . . .

"On her hands and knees in the garbage," Lucien
ordered.

In this position, the last of her climax vibrating her ass,
her head forced down by Gunther in a pile of rotting
debris, her long, down-hanging breasts arching toward her
shoulders, Stephanie peered between her legs and watched

Lucien approach. He had left his pants on top of the garbage can. He had flat hips and a very small behind and from the waist down his physique was more that of an adolescent than a full-grown man. The exception, of course, was his gigantic erection.

He walked up behind the crouching Stephanie and grasped her by the hips. He slowly pushed his prick into her pussy once again. She was very sore and it was very painful, but she stifled her scream. She didn't want Gunther to put his hand over her mouth again. She discovered that if she wiggled her ass from side to side it relieved the pain as Lucien forced his way in deeper and deeper.

The orgasm had left her exhausted and she just prayed that she could survive his shooting his load up her without any further damage. It never occurred to her that she could be aroused once again. She was wrong.

When his cock was three-quarters of the way up her, Lucien wet his fingertip with his tongue and inserted it in her anus. Slowly, expertly, he manipulated her quim. Gasping, Stephanie started moving backwards against him. His balls bounced against her ass as he moved with her. Panting, grinding, in agony, in ecstasy, like some female animal of the field in heat, Stephanie fucked.

"Come inside me!" she sobbed after a little while. "If you must rape me, do it right! Come inside me!"

"*Merde!*" Lucien growled as he grabbed her by the hips and thrust home. A powerful geyser erupted from his huge prick.

Stephanie brayed like a mare and came with him as hot gushes of cream filled her and then ran down the insides of her thighs. She wrenched his huge cock back and forth with her exploding cunt.

When it was over, Gunther held her in the alley while Lucien went for the car. Then Gunther drove and Lucien got in the back with her, and he made her suck his cock as they drove back over the Queensboro Bridge. A few blocks from her apartment building, in the shadows of the overhead viaduct of the East River Drive, Lucien raped Stephanie one last time. Then they dumped her out of the car, threw her clothes out after her and drove away.

Lucien's report had aroused me. Lying in bed and going over it in my mind, my fingers strayed inevitably between my legs. My clitty was sticking out—red, stiff, aroused. I was just starting to stroke it when the telephone rang.

"Christina?" The voice in my ear was Stephanie's.

"Yes?"

"Christina, I've been raped!"

"Of course, darling. But the important thing is, did you enjoy it?"

# CHAPTER SIX

The next meeting of our consciousness-raising group was
unusually subdued. Amanda Briggs was still absent without explanation and the rest of us seemed each to have
fallen prisoner to her own introversion. Helen Willis had
never been too outgoing, of course, but Melinda Holloway,
whose rather sumptuous Great Neck, Long Island, home
was our gathering place this week, was uncharacteristically
withdrawn. "Post-divorce depression" was her explanation, and she showed no inclination to expand on it.
Stephanie McCall seemed loath to bring up her rape and I
would not have felt right mentioning it in defiance of her
silence. Joyce Dell, opting for the stereotype of snarly
adolescent, did little to help us in reestablishing group
solidarity.

Yes, young Joyce was back, leggy in the latest off-the-
rack miniskirt fashion, sharp-nippled in stretchy cotton,
smoldering with the desire—the unscratchable itch—of
her tender years. She offered no explanation for her sudden return. I knew something of her experiences from
Lady Vi's letters, but the others had to remain in ignorance,
since Joyce turned aside all their questions with a sullen

shrug. She had left on a crest of bubbling enthusiasm and now she was back with a cynical sneer and a monosyllabic summation of all that had transpired in California. No boon to sisterhood, our Joycie. No boon at all!

"What will you do about work and school now that you're back?" Melinda asked her.

"I'll make out."

"I'm sure you will, but do you have any money?"

"I managed to hold onto a little. Not much."

"I guess if you live at home and watch the pennies . . ." Helen said, making an effort to look on the bright side.

"I'm not gonna live at home. I'm moving in with this guy I know."

"An older man." Helen nodded as if understanding now how Joyce had solved her problem.

"Nope. A guy my own age. He's just starting college, same as me."

"But I thought you were into older men," Stephanie said, speaking for the first time.

"Not any more!"

"Did something happen in California to alter your preference?" I asked gently. I knew more about Joyce's situation than the others, but as with Stephanie, I didn't want to breach her privacy.

"California is California." Joyce shrugged her insolent shrug. And that was all she would say about it.

"A change of fantasy," Stephanie guessed. "It's called maturing." There was bitterness in her tone. "Speaking of fantasy," she added, "we have some unfinished business, don't we?"

"What do you mean?" Melinda asked.

"Christina."

I looked at her, caught off balance.

"We've all spilled our guts," Stephanie said, the words

jarring in her Bryn Mawr accent. "We've revealed our most secret, innermost fantasies, no matter how embarrassing. We've all done this except Christina."

All eyes were on me, causing me to flush. There was an air of expectation. They were waiting for me to respond.

My reaction was instinctive. I don't like being pressured, not even in the name of sisterhood. I don't like being put on the spot. "I don't really have anything to tell you," I said evenly.

A palpable resentment greeted my reticence. It hardened my noncommunicative position. The night my sisters had confessed their secret fantasies had been relaxed and easy and filled with concern and trust. I felt none of this now. Instead I felt myself cornered by my peers.

I had nothing to hide. Not really. But in the developing situation there was a principle at stake. I found the words to express it.

"We have certain ground rules," I reminded my sisters. "We are obliged to be supportive of one another. We have also agreed that everybody shall be given an equal opportunity to speak. And to remain silent," I added pointedly. "Nobody is to be forced to speak on any subject if she don't want to. There is no quid pro quo regarding fantasies or anything else."

There was agreement—albeit grudging—with my reminder, and I was left to ponder my reluctance privately. Truly, I was not sure I understood it myself. My fantasy—my *mystery* fantasy—was unusual perhaps, but certainly not so bizarre as to justify my silence on a topic which usually elicited a happy wagging of my tongue. As a rule I was far from reticent when it came to discussing sex—real or imagined. Perhaps it was just that I enjoyed frustrating the others, piquing their curiosity, impressing them with my air of mystery.

Still, my attitude may have been responsible for the fact

that this was not one of our more successful meetings. It wasn't so much that my reticence was contagious as that it justified the others in their own silence. We broke up early. I was home and in bed before midnight.

Nevertheless I slept quite late the next morning. Marie, my housekeeper, brought me breakfast in bed. As I balanced the tray, she drew the drapes and Park Avenue penthouse sunshine cascaded into the boudoir. The mail had already come and there was a letter on the tray. Between sips of my coffee I opened it. The sender was identified immediately by Lady Violet Smythe-Turnbull's meticulously British handwriting.

Dear Christina,

By the time you receive this, I judge that young Joyce will be back in New York. I have no way of knowing whether she will confide in you or not. In any case, old friends that we are, I do myself feel the need to unburden myself to you.

Ahh, Christina, as Bobby Burns might well have said, the best planned lays of mice and men gang aft a-gley. Just when things seemed to be going so swimmingly (in a urinary sense, I mean) between Alfie and young Joyce, cruel reality intruded on their idyll. And now it is an idyll smashed to smithereens. To sum up in the American idiom: it's a pisser!

But I'm getting ahead of myself. You will remember that in my last letter I detailed their initial contact— splashingly passionate—as secretly viewed by me through Buzzy Armbruster's high-powered, zoom lens telescope. Naturally, since I am an incorrigible voyeur, I made the effort to follow up on my husband's affair with my maid via Buzzy's other gadgets. This led me, a few nights later, to tune in his closed-circuit

TV on the bathroom in the East Wing. It was here
that Alfie and Joyce had arranged a tryst.

Sure that such a meeting was in the offing, I had
been fishing with the in-house video setup to locate it.
I felt no compunction whatsoever in doing this. En-
tranced by his nubile nymph with her predilection for
dampening dunes, Alfie had been neglecting his hus-
bandly duties towards me. I understood of course; I
have been caught up in extra-marital affairs myself
and have neglected Alfie in similar fashion; nevertheless, given the remoteness of Buzzy Armbruster's
habitat and the lack of alternative masculine succor, I
had no recourse but to get my jollies vicariously.
Alfie might do as he liked with no word of recrimina-
tion from me, but it was my prerogative to watch and
to obtain what joy from the watching that I could. It
was the least I was entitled to by virtue of my married
state. And so I fine-tuned the picture of Joyce in the
East Wing bathroom as she awaited my scruffy old
darling, Alfie.

Ahh, youth! How the flesh doth glow! Such health!
Such moist and shimmering allure! Yes, watching
young Joyce as she awaited Lord Alfred, I could in
no way fault her steamy, petulant allure.

The bathroon was lavish, tiled in the Roman style,
the tub sunken, the handles of the faucets pure gold.
Ormolu Cupids chased each other around the borders
of the floor-to-ceiling wall mirrors as well. They were
lewd, these Cupids, their penises plump with more
than a hint of tumescence, naughtiness twisting their
red lips, impertinent buttocks atilt with expectations
of sodomy. A crystal chandelier hung from the ceiling, glittering and tinkly, too majestic really for a
bathroom lacking an orgy in progress. The ceiling
itself was domed and also mirrored, but in dark glass

to cut down the glow of the chandelier. It was a setting worthy of the most precious jewel. Joyce filled that designation admirably.

She entered wearing a simple skirt and blouse with a tweed jacket over the outfit. Taking off the jacket, she stretched, a slender reed with unexpectedly voluptuous curves. Her lithe body rippled with the gesture, her provocative buns tilted roundly under the thin summer skirt, her hips jutted sassily, her breasts strained against the flimsy blouse. She ran her hands over her body, an indulgent caress which savoured the erogenous response of breasts and hips, *derriere* and thighs. Then she sat down on a stool and removed her sandals.

Joyce's skirt shifted as she crossed and re-crossed her legs to unbuckle the straps. She wasn't wearing any stockings and the flesh of her thighs, pink and appealing, flashed and re-flashed. Watching on the full-color video screen, I was quite stirred by the innocent exposure.

Standing again, she removed her skirt and laid it aside with the jacket. In the briefest of bikini panties, her legs seemed even more those of a chorine. They were lightly muscled and there was a discernible and inevitably erotic flexing visible at each inner thigh as she rocked idly on the balls of her feet and admired her full-length reflection in the wall mirror.

Now Joyce took off her blouse. Her breasts bobbled free of all confinement. They were glorious! Ahh, Christina, adolescent breasts in the first flush of womanhood! How could they be other than glorious? The uptilted mounds contrived to appear both soft and firm at the same time. The nipples were long and hard and bright red.

Cupping her bosom with her hands, Joyce turned this way and that in front of the mirror. She pirouetted, slowly, admiring herself from every angle. Once again she ran her hands up and down her body. She stroked her hips, and then stroked her *derriere* through the silk of her panties. Her hands strayed over her silk-covered Mound of Venus, pronounced and brazenly tilted, but she quickly restrained herself. She brought them to her breasts again as if striking a compromise with her libido.

She weighed the bosom mounds in the cup of her palms, one at a time. She stroked the sides with her fingertips, following the arc, the sweet curve. She spread them, tilting them outward, tracing the cleavage. She traced the faint pink aureole with the tip of her middle finger. She toyed with the elongated, blood-filled nipple. She tweaked it. She pulled on its twin gently. Her chest filled with air; she gasped as she pinched and tickled her breasts, tantalized and tormented them.

These nymphet self-fondlings were making my own breasts tingle as I observed them. It was a warm night and as I glanced down at the decolletage of my dressing gown I saw that the plump half-moons of my bosom were shiny with a film of perspiration. Emulating young Joyce, I allowed my trembling fingers to caress my nipples. My heart pounding more wildly now, I continued playing with them as I watched my husband's inamorata.

Joyce lifted one breast, straining to tilt it as far upward as she could. Her tongue—slender, wet, lascivious—snaked out and licked the nipple. The tip dueled with it, and then she took a long, lingering lick which brought the entire length of the tongue surface in contact with the sensitive breast-tip. Finally she pursed her lips and kissed the nipple, managing to force it between her lips a little and to suck it.

She was moaning now, deep in her throat. Her thighs were clenched and she was dancing on her bare feet, rubbing them together. Her silk panties, damp and crumpled, were sawing between the swollen lips of her spreading pussy. Watching her sucking her nipple and rocking back and forth, I could see that Joyce was very close to coming. My hands were rubbing my own *mons veneris* through the dressing gown now and my bottom was grinding against the velvet of the soft armchair in which I was seated. When Joyce came, it would trigger my orgasm. I was content to have it so.

Alas, both our climaxes were aborted—Joyce's deliberately, mine by example. She simply stopped cold, doubtless recalling that she was soon to be joined by her sex partner. She pulled off her panties—sopping now—and stepped into the bathtub of Carrara marble. Tilting her pussy with its cinnamon brown curls, she turned on the shower and directed the spray so that it struck her quim directly. From her reaction I could tell that the water was icy. It was Joyce's way of cooling herself off. She reached behind her, pulled the rubber band from her ponytail and shook her auburn hair loose. She kept it clear of the shower as she did the rest of her body, with the exception of the cunt she wished to cool. Finally she took a bar of soap in her hands, worked up a lather, and washed her privates. I could tell she was taking pains as she did this so as not to re-arouse herself.

The door to the bathroom opened. Lord Alfred— my Alfie—entered. He was wearing a dressing gown and pajamas. He peered at his naked young hoyden with her lathered cunt through his monocle. "By Jove!" he said, chewing on the end of his drooping old moustache. "By Jove!"

"Hello, Lord Alfred. I've been waiting for you." Our Joycie looked at him with eyes that were aglow with desire. "You've got too many clothes on," she added, observant wench that she was.

"By Jove!" Alfie took off the dressing gown. "By Jove!" He doffed the pajama tops. "By Jove!" He stepped out of the bottoms. "By Jove!" Staring at the wriggling Joyce, his randy old pecker stood at attention and he had to rub the steam from his monocle with a corner of towel. "By Jove!"

Joyce turned off the shower. "Come sit in the tub between my legs," she invited Alfie.

He scrambled to comply, leaning back on his bony elbows, his weight on his sparse haunches, his gnarled and weather-beaten old lance sticking up obscenely from the forest of pubic hair over his rather scrawny belly. He looked up and into the soapy pussy squirming over him. "By Jove!"

"Would you like a Golden Shower?" Joyce purred.

"By Jove!" It was unmistakably an affirmative answer.

Joyce spread her legs and bent them at the knees so that she was positioned in a slight, but distinct squat. The lips of her lathered cunt parted. A stream of golden fluid poured out between them. It washed an initial puff of soapsuds over Lord Alfred's upturned face.

He sneezed violently. A second sneeze followed immediately, and then a third. "By Jove!" he gasped. It didn't help. A parade of sneezes followed, one on the heels of the other.

"What's the matter?" Joyce said, bewildered, before she ceased urinating.

But Alfie was sneezing too hard to be able to answer her.

I could have answered for him. But of course I wasn't there, and in any case I was laughing too hard to have gotten the words out. It was poor old Alfie's hay fever, of course. Soapsuds always activated it. Mixing them with the hot pee of a sweet young thing in no way ameliorated the effect.

"Eat me," Joyce wheedled when his sneezing fit was over.

Well, of course he tried, poor old dear. But it was no use. Every time his nose came within range of the soapsuds still clinging to the lips of Joycie's tender, eager young cunt, Alfie would start sneezing again.

"By Jove!" Finally he stood up and bent his neck so that his head hung back over his aristocratically scrawny shoulders. In this manner he managed to bring his sneezing fit under control.

Joyce stood in front of him with her hands on her supple adolescent hips. One foot was tapping and—as if attached by a puppet string—one breast was jiggling. Her eyes were smouldering as she stared down at Alfie's long and crusty old limpo. Taking it in her hand, she slid to the floor in front of Alfie and tilted the cup of her pussy upwards. "Pee over my quim," she wheedled.

Alfie strained to comply. Joyce tugged on his over-cooked asparagus of an organ with gusto, but to no avail. He even danced up and down on his toes and thrust from the buttocks. Nothing helped. Nary a drop was forthcoming. Both urination and erection seemed beyond the power of His Lordship.

"What's the matter?" our Joyce asked, frustrated. "Why don't you do it? Would you rather fuck me?" she inquired—a sudden inspiration.

"By Jove!" There were beads of perspiration on Alfie's forehead.

"Come on, then!" Maintaining her grip on his limpo, Joyce balanced on her knees and licked at it. When signs of tumescence appeared, she slid to her back and tugged. "Put it in me quick," she urged.

Even as she was speaking, poor Alfie was going limp again. Irritated, Joyce yanked as if to claim his cock for her cunt before every last vestige of stiffness vanished. Alas! Her tug was counter-productive!

"By Jove!" Alfie said again, his voice moving up the scale as he toppled forwards. There was a slick of water, possibly of soap, on the marble floor of the tub, you see. He fell like a stone dropped from the White Cliffs of Dover. His arthritic limbs splayed out in every direction as he landed on Joyce like the proverbial ton of bricks, knocking the wind out of her in the manner of a deflated balloon.

It took awhile for Joyce to find the breath to untangle herself. When she did, poor Alfie was left behind in a mass of his own rusty hinges. Bursitis, arthritis— whatever! His elbows and knees, his knuckles and toes were all in need of oil. On top of the hay fever and the prostate trouble, the old darling was at the lowest Smythe-Turnbull ebb since the signing of the Magna Carta took away the family's right to buy and sell Saxons.

Ah well, as you know, Christina, I do adore the old fool. And so I have taken him in hand as it were and set about restoring the wreckage. Cortisone and anti-histamines for the joints and the nasal passages; a nip and a tuck to stiffen up the old prostate and open the urethra. He goes under the knife next Tuesday and the doctor assures me he'll be good as new and twice as randy.

Joyce, however, will not be here to enjoy the results. Typical of her generation, she rejected Alfie the first time he proved unable to offer her instant gratification. Ah, where will the world be if youth does not learn to develop patience? With everything at thirty-three and a third, they will never find out what they may have missed at seventy-eight. Already I am looking forward to substituting for Joyce in the aftermath of Alfie's recovery. If the child had only waited, she might have found joys that went beyond her fantasies.

But she has not chosen to give Alfie another chance. She has left California and is probably back in New York by now. Too bad for her. But too bad for me as well. Where am I going to find myself another lady's maid?

Have you any suggestions, *chère* Christina? Any at all?

> Desperately yours,
> Vi
> (Lady Violet Smythe-Turnbull)

I had nothing to offer by way of solving Lady Violet's problem. Indeed, when I finished reading the letter, I was more concerned with how my efforts to help Joyce fulfill her fantasy had backfired. Obviously a sneezing, arthritic lover with prostate trouble must have fallen far short of her dreams, even if he was a mature British aristocrat sophisticated in the techniques of the Golden Shower. Reality had driven Joyce into the arms of a lad her own age. Ah well, perhaps it was for the best.

It did not, however, enhance my self-image as a Fairy Godmother. I gave serious consideration to scrapping the whole project. But then coincidence once again pushed me into the role of deus ex machina. This time the fantasy to be actualized was that of Helen Willis.

Helen, slender and overbosomed, mother of two toddlers, wife of the insensitive Bruno, appeared unexpectedly at my office a few days after I received the letter from Lady Violet. Shy and nervous as always, it took her awhile to stammer out why she had come. Something had happened and she had to talk to someone, someone with understanding and experience, someone who could give her advice and guidance. She had chosen me. Flattered, I arranged to leave the office for an early lunch with Helen.

A martini loosened her tongue and she blurted out her problem. The previous day Helen had stopped by the garage where Bruno worked because he had left her without any money for the day's shopping. "He does that once in a while," she told me bitterly, "just to remind me who controls the purse strings."

Helen found Bruno in a storeroom at the back of the garage. His pants were down around his ankles and he was fucking a young girl spread out over a pile of used tires. "The worst thing was," Helen said with quiet fury, "that just as I came in he was asking her was she ready to come yet. All the years we've been married he never asked me that. He never gave a damn!"

"Oh, Helen!" I squeezed her hand. "The bastard!"

"Should I leave him, Christina? What do you think?"

"For being unfaithful? Absolutely not, darling! But you should certainly leave him for being such an inconsiderate lover all these years!"

"I don't know. The kids—"

"Where are the kids?" I asked.

"With my mother. She'll keep them for a few days. As long as I want, actually. She adores them, and since she spoils them rotten, they adore her back."

"Good. I think you need some time to yourself."

"To myself? Not really. I mean, Bruno will keep coming home at night. It's his house, too."

"Even after what happened?" I shook my head angrily. "He certainly is an unfeeling clod."

"The way he looks at it, it's no big deal and I should just accept it."

"Oh, I agree with that. Just as long as it works both ways."

"It doesn't." Helen laughed ruefully. "Bruno believes that the only proper way to deal with a cheating wife is to blow her away."

"Maybe somebody should blow Bruno away," I said, really angry for Helen.

"Don't think I haven't considered it!"

I was startled by the depth of violence in her tone. "You really mean that, don't you?" I said.

"I do. I think I actually do mean it."

"You'd better not go home for a while," I advised. "Not until you cool down. The bastard isn't worth capital punishment."

"But where—?"

"With me. You'll stay with me."

"Oh, I couldn't do that, Christina. The imposition—"

"No imposition. I've got a guest room. We're friends and that's all there is to it. It's settled."

Of course it wasn't that simple. It never is. Two nights later, when Malcolm Gold dropped in on me as he did every so often, both Helen and I realized that.

She was such a quiet guest, so undemanding, so mousy almost, that I had half forgotten she was there. I had given her one of my sleazier nighties—a green silk shorty with a deep-dip Greek bodice that Claude Montana had designed especially for me—to buck up her spirits. In spite of it, she had gone to bed with a self-help book. I was in the living room having a solitary nightcap when Malcolm let himself in with the key I had provided him.

"Oysters," he greeted me. "I had oysters for dinner. They energize the libido like a shot of adrenaline. I am in need of immediate relief. You are my friend. Naturally I came straight here." He unzipped his fly and took out his penis. "Can you help me?"

"You maniac!" I waved him toward the bar. "Help yourself to a brandy and calm down."

He filled the bottom of a wide goblet with cognac and dipped his penis in it. "I do feel a little calmer," he said.

"Try drinking some of it," I advised him drily. "That will really do wonders for your nerves."

"I did not come for serenity. I came for succor." He waved his long, slender semi-erection under my nose. "Suck."

"Will you simmer down?"

"An excellent year." He thrust it at me again. "Just taste it."

To pacify him I stuck out my tongue and licked. He was right. It was a good year. The brandy was excellent. But then I had known that. It was the same brandy I'd been sipping when he arrived. "A little bitter, darling," I teased Malcolm. "Where were you before dipping into my spirits?"

"Only here." He snapped the elastic of his jockey shorts. "It must be the aftertaste of the carrot sticks you've been nibbling. Have another lick and you'll see that's what it is."

I sighed, but I did what he wanted. I licked his hot, now slightly throbbing penis again. I took the crest in my mouth and sucked the brandy from it with my pursed lips. That, naturally, was the moment that Helen Willis chose for her entrance.

"Oh, my!" Her exclamation was loud.

"Oops!" Malcolm is unflappable, but he had the grace to react. He quickly stuffed his stiff penis back into his pants and zipped them up. "You didn't mention that you had company, Christina."

"I'm so sorry!" Helen was brick red. "I didn't mean to—I mean, your privacy—" she floundered.

Malcolm, libertine that he is, focused on her with obvious interest. Her oversized bosom was truly spectacular in the Montana creation. The silk clung to her in a way that made her slender body seem quite voluptuous. "Hello." He crossed the room and held out his hand to her. "I'm Malcolm Gold."

"I'm Helen Willis." Nervousness made her pump his hand energetically.

"Helen Willis?" A knowing look spread over Malcolm's face, curling his petulant mouth. "Oh, yes. You're in Christina's women's group, aren't you?"

"How did you know that?"

"She's mentioned you." Malcolm flashed me a secret wink, a reminder that I'd invented that ridiculous story for him, the one about Helen being raped by the auto mechanic. "But she never conveyed just how attractive you really are."

"Thank you." Helen blushed. "I'm not used to compliments," she added.

"Nor I to giving them," Malcolm lied. "But you are a special case."

"Would you like a brandy, Helen?" I asked her.

"Oh, no. I'm intruding. I'm really sorry. I just heard voices and— Well, I'll just go back to my room."

"You're not intruding." Malcolm said, holding her hand so she couldn't leave. "Is she, Christina?"

"Of course not. Malcolm's just an old friend. He drops in sometimes."

"An intimate friend," Helen couldn't help observing. She giggled nervously, a confirmation that she'd seen me licking his aroused penis.

"I suppose. Anyway, do join us for a nightcap." I went over to the bar and poured one for her.

"I'm sorry if I embarrassed you," Malcolm apologized to Helen.

"I wasn't embarrassed." The first swallow of liqueur brought a flush to her cheeks. Her gaze was uncharacteristically bold as she answered Malcolm.

"Oh, really?"

"Really." She looked him straight in the eye and took another healthy sip from the brandy goblet.

"Well, in that case—" Malcolm was incorrigible. He opened his pants, took out his organ and offered it to me once again.

"You are being quite exhibitionistic, darling," I reproved him. "Now stop it. Helen doesn't know your playful ways as I do. You're upsetting her."

"I'm not upset," Helen said, her soft brown eyes glittering.

I looked at her carefully. She meant what she said. "All right, then." I took the head of Malcolm's penis back between my lips.

"Are you sure I'm not intruding?" Helen asked after a moment. Her breasts were rising and falling very quickly under the green silk.

"I'm sure," Malcolm told her, his balls bouncing against my chin, though he had not taken his eyes off her.

I simply shook my head, Malcolm's cock half in my mouth.

Helen squirmed and sipped her brandy. The muscles of her slender thighs were flexed where the shorty nightgown revealed them. Her nipples stood out against the tight-stretched green silk.

"Don't sit over there all by yourself," Malcolm suggested, his voice hoarse, his breathing quick. "Come over here and join us. You can see better," he added.

Helen looked at me questioningly. I nodded that it was all right. She went to the bar and poured herself some more brandy and then came over and sat down next to me on the couch.

After a moment I pulled my mouth away from Malcolm's groin. "It's hot in here," I declared. I unbuttoned the top of the black lounging pajamas I was wearing and took it off. My blond hair cascaded over my naked breasts.

Malcolm bent and caught them in his hands. He rubbed his balls over the nipples, making them tingle and harden. My thighs clenched without my willing them to do so. He put his long cock between my breasts and rubbed them up and down in the cleavage, bumping and throbbing against the softness of their inside surfaces. I began to pant, quite aroused.

"You're so uninhibited," Helen blurted the words out. "Both of you." Her long, slender neck was arched toward the action between my breasts and Malcolm's penis. There was a film of perspiration over her delicate features. The second snifter of brandy had completely banished her customary shyness. "Are you very excited, Christina?" Nevertheless, her voice trembled.

"Yes. My nipples have always been very sensitive," I told her. "When Malcolm touches them with his cock— his hot, naked, stiff prick—I'm really turned on."

"His hot, naked, stiff rapier," Helen said, giggling, though she was nervous, excited. "Rapier," she repeated. "I know just what you mean," she added. "My nipples are very sensitive, too."

"I can see that, darling." I shot a knowing look at the way the tips of her breasts were pushing out against the green silk. Quick breathing had made the half-moon tops overflow the bodice.

"I've been neglecting you," Malcolm said as he swiveled toward Helen and his hard-on grazed the revealed tops of the mounds of flesh.

"Oh, no." Helen drew back. "I've really intruded too much already." The sudden movement, however, betrayed her intent. The nightie slipped away from her bosom and one of her large breasts tumbled out completely. The nipple, aroused and cherry-red, was as long and hard as any I'd ever seen. It was so erect as to be almost obscene.

"Jesus!" Malcolm's eyes widened. One of his hands closed over Helen's shoulder to hold her in place as he rubbed the tip of his hard cock around the wide pink aureole.

"Oh!" Helen melted. Her thighs parted. Her hand fluttered to the hem of the green nightgown. She pushed it up over her flat belly. The silky brown hair of her pussy appeared. One long finger found its cleft.

Watching Helen play with herself as Malcolm's long cock rolled over her oversized, plump breast, I became even more excited. I stood up, pushed down my pajama pants, and stepped out of them. I came up behind Malcolm and rubbed my golden bush up and down between his buttocks. "Lick his cock, angel," I suggested to Helen.

For an instant, Helen pulled back. There was no mistaking the look of reluctance which spread over her face. It was replaced by a look of conscious resolve. "All right," she agreed, before her small mouth encircled Malcolm's hard-on. Her cheeks hollowed as she sucked it deep into her throat.

I knelt behind Malcolm and licked his balls from under his ass. His entire gangly frame began to tremble from head to toe. Finally, gently, he pulled his cock out of Helen's mouth. "A moment," he said. "We don't want things to end prematurely."

"How was it?" I asked Helen, curious as to how the

reality of sucking Malcolm's prick had squared with her initial reluctance.

"Good," she said. "Much better than I expected. You see, the only man's cock I've ever had in my mouth before is Bruno's. It's always sort of sweaty and sour. And it's so thick, I gag on it. I dread sucking it. I always feel forced and degraded."

"I hope you don't think that I—" Malcolm was upset.

"No. Not at all. This was very different. Your rapier is so—so—*clean*! It's slender and shiny and it smells good. I really enjoyed licking it and sucking it. I never knew it could be like this."

"Well then—" Malcolm took his prick in his hand and held it out to Helen's lips again.

"No." She drew back. "Thank you. But I've already interfered too much between you and Christina. I want you to go on with what you were doing before I came in. I'll just sit here and watch. Or, if you prefer, I'll just leave."

"You don't have to do that," I assured her. "Neither Malcolm nor myself is inhibited by being observed."

"I wish I could be that loose," Helen sighed. "I was very conscious of you watching me, Christina, while I was sucking Malcolm's rapier." Her eyes drifted to it, and then up and down Malcolm's lanky, slender body. Then they returned to his crotch and lingered over its relative hairlessness.

I guessed that she must be making comparisons with the paunchy, hairy, apelike Bruno. Poor Helen! So deprived! I smiled at her reassuringly and pulled Malcolm over to the couch beside her. When, at my prodding, he sat down there, I perched on his knee. Helen reacted with a gasp which jutted out her one bared breast remarkably when Malcolm's taut cock twanged against my hip.

Fondling it in my hand, I kissed him. I licked his sensuous lips with my tongue and they parted obligingly, then let my tongue flutter into his mouth like a butterfly. When the tip touched the tip of his tongue, his prick throbbed in my fist. I opened it so that Helen might see the reaction in my palm.

"Oh!" she gasped. Her naked nipple trembled and her bush quivered even as her hand moved between her legs to steady it.

"Play with yourself," Malcolm told her. "That really turns me on."

She stared at him from very wide eyes and used the fingers of both hands to separate the lips of her pussy. The nub of her clitty stuck out—a hard, red button. "I never thought I could do anything like this," Helen murmured. She ran the tip of one finger back and forth over the clitoris.

I felt the warm honey bubbling inside my pussy. "Take off your trousers," I told Malcolm, afraid it would soil them. When he complied, I sat back down on his lap and rubbed gently back and forth with my wet, widespread quim. "I'm very hot," I told him. "I want you to put your prick inside my cunt. I want you to fuck me."

"Oh, God!" Helen cried, rubbing her cunt harder and bouncing up and down on the couch beside us. "Do it!" she urged Malcolm. "Do it to Christina!"

"Do what?" he teased. He shifted position casually and the tip of his cock once again bumped the nipple of her down-hanging breast.

"Fuck her!" Helen moaned. "I want to see you fuck her!"

"All right, then," Malcolm said. He pushed me off his lap, stood up, and bade me bend over and grasp the arm of the couch so that my ass and exposed quim jutted out behind. "Watch carefully," he told Helen. He reached in front of me and grasped my naked breasts for leverage. He squeezed them and fondled the nipples. An instant later I felt the wonder of his cock sliding between the inflamed lips of my pussy. It was so long! So long! He buried it to the hilt and his smooth-egg balls wedged into the bottom of the cleft of my ass. "Is this what you mean?" he asked Helen.

"Fuck her!" she pleaded. "Fuck her hard! Fuck her fast! Fuck Christina!"

I twirled my ass slowly, savoring the sensation of Malcolm's cock rotating against my aroused clitoris. Slowly he pulled it out and then pushed it back in. I reached between my legs and tickled his balls. He moved in and out more quickly, his pelvis slamming against my butt. The next time he pulled it out, I pushed backwards with my ass as he bore back into me. The thrill of the contact tore a peal of laughter from my lips.

Helen was kneeling beside us now, her small, delicate nose almost touching the juncture of Malcolm's cock and my cunt. Both her heavy breasts were hanging free, weighing down her slender figure, covered with perspiration. Her knees were wide apart and her hand was snaking into her widespread cunt from behind, the arm rubbing between her buttocks. Her tongue was half lolling from her mouth and her soft eyes were crazed.

I recognized the look. She was on the verge of coming, but deliberately delaying the orgasm to stay with us. I had done the same thing myself in a variety of situations. It was the most exquisite self-torture.

The sight aroused me to a frenzy. I began fucking as hard as I knew how, wrenching Malcolm's cock this way and that with all my might. At the same time I watched between my legs—upside-down—as his lancelike cock stabbed in and out of the wound—the gash!—of my hungry cunt. "I'm going to come!" I gasped. "Hold it all the way inside me while I come! Please, darling! Please!"

Malcolm grabbed my hips and buried his cock. I started to come with its tip pressed against the mouth of my womb. The vision of my golden-haired cunt and his dangling balls blurred with the rainbow colors of my orgasm. I dug my nails into the material of the couch arm, forced my ass backwards, clutched his cock with my glovefinger of a muscle-rippling quim and exploded. Dimly I felt Malcolm's answering explosion, the geyser of his clean white cream washing up the track of my pussy, its overflow, the coolness of it drenching my thighs and his balls as it began pouring out even as he was still shooting more jism deep up inside me.

"AAAHHH!!!" The scream was wordless as well as mindless. Helen fell back on her haunches and her shapely, slender legs stuck straight up in the air. Her naked breasts spilled over her rib cage and onto the carpet. Her ass bounced uncontrollably, both her hands clawing at her sopping pussy, tearing the orgasm from deep inside her. Even as Malcolm and I were coming, she came with us.

When it was over, the three of us fell back on the rug, exhausted. We stayed that way a long time. Helen was the first to sit up.

She looked at Malcolm's body. "You're so—so clean-cut," she exclaimed. "Your rapier is like ivory."

"Thanks." It was one of the few times I ever saw Malcolm on the verge of embarrassment.

"I want to thank you both for letting me watch," Helen said, her eyes continuing to yearn over him.

"It was our pleasure," Malcolm replied accurately enough.

Watching Helen as she continued to sneak secret glances at Malcolm, I remembered the fantasy she had confided to us at the consciousness-raising meeting. I remembered the dream lover she had described. Malcolm didn't quite live up to her fantasy, but his persona was surely close. And it was surely a welcome contrast to the animal Bruno. "Listen," I told them. "I've got an idea."

"What?" They both turned to me.

"A picnic," I suggested. "Why don't we go on a picnic tomorrow?"

# CHAPTER SEVEN

The repeated salary increases I had granted Malcolm Gold as *World*'s editor had decidedly given him a taste for the better things in life. Where once—around the time I first met him—his idea of a picnic would have meant a peanut butter sandwich in a brown paper bag, now it called for a hamper from "21" complete with cold lobster salad, truffles, caviar, a salmon in aspic, petit fours and Dom Perignon '68 complete with a silver bucket of ice and a wine steward's towel. It had also made Malcolm privy to an important truth, one he now passed on to Helen Willis. "Ants never bother the rich," he told her. "That's why their picnics are always successful."

"Are you rich?" Helen asked. Cute and relaxed in shorts and a cotton shirt stretched to the shredding point, Helen was bothering less and less to hide the fact that she was attracted to Malcolm.

"No, but Christina is. Besides, wealth isn't a matter of money. It's a matter of image. When the ants see champagne and caviar and a "21" imprint, they don't ask questions. They just turn around and scurry in the opposite direction. And they don't stop scurrying until they find jelly sandwiches and lukewarm lemonade.''

''If I'm so rich now, how come I'm in the Catskills?'' I asked Malcolm. ''This is where you used to take me when I was poor.''

''Some things are constant,'' he said. ''It was a great spot for making out then, and it's a great spot now.''

I laughed. In his lederhosen—Alpine hiking shorts, if you prefer—and bright red flannel shirt, Malcolm was the picture of a youth in one of those Bavarian hiking clubs. Given his Semitic ancestry, there was a certain amount of irony to this. The inconsistency, however, didn't bother Helen. She obviously found him amusing as well as sexy.

''I'm going to get some sun,'' I said, then lay face down on the blanket and undid the straps of my halter so that my tan would not be marred. I felt the rays nipping at my buttocks where my shorts had ridden up. The sensation was vaguely titillating.

We had found a clearing near a riverbank and spread out our picnic there. Sunlight striated by the tree branches speckled most of the area with light and shadow, but the spot where I stretched out was clear of intervening foliage and was bathed in a lambent warmth. I had nibbled at the food and quaffed two goblets of champagne. Now I felt lazy and a little sleepy. I half-dozed in the sunlight.

Time eased past on a fleecy, slow-moving cloud. It was very quiet here in the heart of the woods. Unusually so, considering that two other people were here with me. After a while I opened my eyes and glanced around for Malcolm and Helen.

They were propped side by side against the trunk of a large oak tree. One of Malcolm's arms was around Helen's thin shoulders, the hand trailing innocently over the straining hillock of her breast. Her head rested against his chest.

Both of them had their eyes closed. Their breathing was deep, content.

As I watched them lazily, my chin propped on my hands, my nipples digging into the picnic blanket, Malcolm's eyes blinked open. He looked down at Helen. He stretched his fingers to stroke the plump curve of her breast. A ray of sunlight played over his forehead and there was a hint of perspiration there. "Lovely," he decided, looking at Helen. "You're really quite lovely."

"Ahh, flattery will get you everywhere." Helen's eyes didn't open, but a slight blush suffused her aquiline cheeks.

"It's not flattery. I mean it. You're a very attractive lady."

"Not really," she said, the blush deepening. "It's the wine making you talk like that."

"Why do you reject compliments, Helen?"

"Because I don't believe them, I guess. I know what league I'm in. I'm not up there with Christina, for instance."

"Christina is Christina, and you are you. It's not a contest. It's perfectly logical for a man to find each of you attractive in her own way."

Helen started to protest again and then thought better of it. Her tongue, pink and sharp, appeared and licked her lips as if to confirm an acceptance of Malcolm's judgment. It was a very sexy gesture.

Malcolm bent toward her, his eyes questioning, his lips poised. Helen's nod was slight but definite. He kissed her.

How sweet! Watching, I reacted to the pastoral setting. Birdsong trilled from the surrounding tree bowers. Wildflowers flashed their colors from the grassy sward. The cool stream gurgled beyond the riverbank, its liquid murmur punctuated by the occasional deep croak of a frog hopscotching lily pads. And in front of me a young woman and a young man embraced, lips parting, tongues exploring, flesh warming in the speckled sunlight. How sweet!

The hardening nipples of Helen's too-large breasts demanded attention, and Malcolm's expertly caressing hand provided it. The first kiss melted into a second one. Their bodies turned toward each other. Their limbs entwined. Their breathing became harsh, excited.

Helen pulled slightly away from him. "Christina will wake up and see us."

"So what? After last night—"

"That was then. This is now."

"I don't see the difference." He stroked her hip, his fingertips sliding under her shorts to tease her behind.

"I was a lot drunker then. We all three were." Helen was in the throes of an approach-avoidance conflict. She was reaching behind and trying to push his hand away, and yet at the same time the uptilting mound of her pussy was rubbing against him through their clothing.

"Perhaps we should have some more champagne, then." With his free hand he groped for the ice bucket with the second bottle in it.

"A better idea would be if we cooled off a little." Helen sat up, disentangling herself from him.

"Okay. Let's go for a swim." Malcolm stood. His erection distended his lederhosen.

"I didn't bring a bathing suit."

"You're kidding." Malcolm laughed. "Haven't you ever heard of skinny-dipping?"

"Sure. When I was a kid. But I'm not a kid anymore. I'm a married lady with two kids of my own."

"And still well on the sunny side of thirty," Malcolm reminded her. "Listen, when you become mature, the first thing you'll learn is that there's no great virtue in behaving maturely. All it does is stop you from having fun. Come on now." He took her hand. "Let's get out of these clothes and into the water."

"Well, all right." She pulled her hand away. "You go behind that bush to undress and I'll go behind this one."

"You're incredible!" Malcolm's head wagged at the irony.

"Last one in is a rotten egg!" Helen teased as she scampered to the opposite side of the clearing.

They reappeared simultaneously, both naked. Helen put a finger to her lips, an unwitting tribute to my sleeper's pose. Little did she guess with what dedication I was observing them through the slitted eyes behind the curl of my outflung arm.

Malcolm's eyes were fulfilling one of the fine points of Helen's fantasy. They were fixed with admiration on her heavy breasts, and shone with wonderment at the way they stood out from her slender frame. The nipples grew under the caress of his stare, emerging from their berrylike aureole settings like twin lipsticks being extended. Helen blushed when Malcolm's cock started rising from between his legs. To cover her embarrassment, she ran toward the bank of the river. Following the pronounced bouncing of her marvelous breasts as she ran, Malcolm's cock hardened and slapped back against his flat belly. As he followed after her at a trot, it did indeed have the length and slight curve of a rapier twanging for action.

I heard the first splash while he was still in sight. Then he vanished and I heard the second one. Cautiously, I got up and made my way to the riverbank, positioning myself behind a copse of bushes where I could observe them without myself being seen.

The river at this point was more like a pond. Further upstream it had narrowed and the natural dam which had been created slowed the flow to a trickle. Further down, it widened and ran free once again, its dancing sparkle polishing the rocks. But here it was a sun-warmed pool, shoulder high at its deepest point, a mirror for clouds and willows.

Helen was lying on her back and floating, the softest of breezes rippling the surface of the water around her. Her magnificent breasts floated free of her body, nipples pointing arrogantly upward at the sky. The clear water magnified the silken triangle at the base of her almost boyishly shallow belly. Her eyes were closed, her features tranquil, her body quite still.

Near the opposite bank Malcolm stood and looked at her. The water was only up to his hips and the tip of his penis was visible against the flat of his belly. Obviously he still had an erection. Staring at Helen in her role of bosomy water nymph was in no way relaxing it. His sigh of desire was almost audible as he started to swim toward her.

His well-formed ass flitted in the sunlight like polished ivory as he moved through the water. His golden tan had not touched his buns. Slender and lithe, his strokes were as effortless as the progress of some exotic fish. But in place of a bottom fin he had his swollen-balled erection to guide him to the bait which had attracted him.

Just before he reached Helen, Malcolm dived. He came up under her and there was an orgy of splashing. When it was over, he was cradling her in the shallow water, one arm supporting her back, the other under her knees. His prick lay over her belly, tangling in the soft brown hair at its base. As Helen's breasts rose and fell very quickly, Malcolm bent his head to kiss the nipple of one of them.

"Oh!" Helen's reaction was a sigh on the soft summer breeze. Her nails clawed at the back of his neck, urging his lips to suck in more of her breast, prodding his tongue to lick harder at the nipple.

Carrying her, Malcolm started moving toward the shore. Halfway there he paused and released her breast to kiss her on the lips. Moaning audibly, Helen grabbed his cock and rolled it back and forth over the exposed cleft of her pussy. Once again the water erupted with splashing.

Watching them, I began to perspire. I had left my halter back on the blanket and now my naked breasts were reaching for the sun like budding flowers. I was aroused, my shorts quite damp. I removed them, and my underpants as well. When Malcolm and Helen came out of the water, I decided, I would have a swim to cool off both my libido and my flesh. Voyeurism is hot work, darlings, is it not?

For the moment, however, the amorous pair had been stayed in their progress toward the shore. It was desire, of course, which halted them. They had changed position and were both standing now, facing each other, the level of the water not quite reaching their groins, their sex organs exposed, hungry and aroused and exposed. Mouths open wide, they were kissing, devouring each other.

Helen's breasts were crushed against Malcolm's smooth chest. Her nipples dug into him hotly. The overflow of flesh, slightly flattened by the pressure between them, surrounded his ribs. Their hands were clutching frenziedly at each other's bottoms. Their thighs were pressed together. Malcolm's hard-on was flat against Helen's belly. The lips of her open cunt were nipping at his swollen balls.

Malcolm's hands reached lower and he picked her up. She hung free of the water, her hands clasped around his neck, her body supported by his hands under her thighs. Her cunt, sparkling with water and with honey, tilted invitingly just under his groin. Licking her lips, Helen removed one hand from Malcolm's neck and reached down. She forced his cock down from his belly and wedged the tip into the entrance of her pussy. They both looked down at the juncture of their organs. Obviously the sight excited them still further.

Of course it affected me as well. Watching as Helen's

fantasy began to come true, I was torn between letting it proceed and the risk of spoiling it by joining them. Hot as I was, my more restrained nature won out. I contented myself with inserting a finger up my pussy and stroking my clitoris while I continued to watch. You see, darlings, I really do put a high value on acting in the best interests of friendship.

They had moved to deeper water now. Helen's legs were locked around Malcolm's buttocks, and both of their asses were thrashing wildly. It was obvious to me that they were fucking—fucking deeply, and hotly, and very, very hard!

Helen's oversized breasts were a blur of motion as they bounced against Malcolm's chest. Her face was buried against his shoulder, her teeth sunk into the flesh there. His hand was under her, a finger in her anus, its movements a counterpoint to the thrusts of his long, hard prick deep inside her pussy under the surface of the water.

Their sudden loss of balance told me that they had arrived at a mutual orgasm. They splashed the water with abandon, Malcolm's long saber stabbing in and out of the wet, red cunt-gash, Helen's heavy breasts flailing every which way as she clung to her impalement. They slid beneath the surface and came up with Helen screaming, "Don't stop! Don't stop!" and went under again, limbs slipping and sliding and kicking. "Take this!" Malcolm's balls went splat against the lips of her pussy. "And this!" His spurting cock buried itself deep inside her wrenching, clutching quim. And once again they rolled in the water, gasping and sputtering, coming . . . and coming . . .

*Oh, Malcolm!* I was with them in every way but the joining of our flesh. *Oh, Helen!* Their heat was my heat, their frenzy my frenzy, their coming mine as well. A thorn pricked my nipple and it was but an added titillation to the onset of my climax. My hand dug between my legs; it was drenched with syrup. I pounded my clitty with mindless brutality. I had felt Malcolm's cock in my cunt fucking me so many times. I could feel it now as it fucked Helen in the water. I could feel it fucking me. I stuffed my mouth with knuckles to keep from braying aloud as I joined Helen and Malcolm in their coming . . .

When my head cleared enough to look again, they were walking side by side toward the shore, their arms around each other's waists, their hands trailing over each other's naked bottoms. I scrambled to get out of sight. They headed back toward the clearing. When I was sure it was safe, I came out of hiding and slid from the bank into the river. The water was cool, crystal balm to my sex-scalded skin. I swam for a long time, letting the water wash the ache from my nipples, enjoying the gentle douche of the current, calming down emotionally as well as physically.

After my swim, on silent bare feet, not putting on my shorts but holding them until the sun should dry me, I made my way back to the clearing. Malcolm and Helen had evidently not been bothered too much by my absence. They were stretched out on the blanket and were playing lazily with each other. I squatted behind a bush and settled down to watching them once again.

Beads of water glittered over the surfaces of their bodies, adding to the eroticism of the picture their entwinement presented. The sun was drying the water on Malcolm's body; the moisture seemed to become absorbed into his flesh, deepening his tan. He was patting at Helen's wetness with the towel from the champagne bucket. When most of it was sopped up, he produced a tube of suntan lotion. She had not started out with a tan, as he had, and now the delicate whiteness of her body was turning pink. "I don't want to make love to a lobster the next time," he told her. He rubbed in the lotion, starting at her shoulders and working his way down.

"Oh, goody!" She patted his sandy-haired groin. "Then there *is* going to be a next time."

"Sure," he said, his hand moving in small, knowing circles as he rubbed the suntan lotion into the bulging fleshy tops of her remarkable breasts.

"When?" She kissed his thigh and then licked her way up its inner surface with her tongue.

"Soon." His fingertips, shiny with lotion, grazed her risen nipples. "Whenever you say."

"I say now." She nibbled at his balls. "Right now."

"Let me finish putting this stuff on you. You can burn just as easily balling as not, you know."

"I know." Helen's bosom inflated with a voluptuous sigh. "Oh, how I know!"

"Lie back so I can do your belly."

"Mmm! Don't forget to do my pussy." She wriggled.

"The sun doesn't shine there," he teased her, his hands kneading her belly, one finger in her navel.

"When I'm excited, it does. It opens all up. You wouldn't want my clitty to get all blistered, would you?" She spread her legs as if to demonstrate.

"Oh, no! We can't have that." Crouching over her, Malcolm's long penis was once again sticking straight out between his legs. He put a dab of lotion on one fingertip and ran it gently around the lips of her pussy.

"That tickles!" Helen gasped.

"Sorry."

"I didn't mean for you to stop. I *like* the way it tickles." She put her hand over his and brought it back to her juicily gaping cunt.

"I have to do your legs, Helen."

"They can wait." Her ass moved in circles as she rubbed against his hand.

"Just be patient a couple of minutes longer," he said,

pulling his hand away before he started smearing the lotion over her thighs.

"I don't like being patient. I like being fucked!" Helen pouted.

My, my! I was having trouble reconciling this brazen voluptuary with the shy, withdrawn Helen I knew from the consciousness-raising group. The Helen who was married to Bruno and the mother of two children, the Helen who was a pillar of the PTA and who was always telling the rest of us to watch our language, the Helen who only submitted to sex because it was expected of her and who valued gentleness above all other qualities in her fantasy lover—that Helen was a far cry from this squirming hussy pulling demandingly at Malcolm's erect prick. Yes, he had really turned her on. And once turned on, it seemed, there was no turning our Helen off!

"Turn over," Malcolm told her.

"Are you going to stick it in my behind?" she inquired as she complied. "Nobody's ever done that before. Bruno tried, but I screamed so loud that he stopped. He has this big, thick sausage and no finesse whatsoever. I could throw up just thinking about him doing that to me. But your cock is so slender and elegant, I don't mind if you want to try it. I know how delicate and gentle you can be, how subtle."

"We'll see," Malcolm said, straddling her hips and then laying his hard-on in the cleft between the pert cheeks of her small ass. "First I want to finish your back." He moved forward and then back on the balls of his hands as he creamed her back. His long cock slid up and down the crack of her behind. "How does that feel?" he inquired.

"Glorious!" She was leaning on her elbows and her heavy, swaying, pendulous breasts were all agasp with the thrill of his prick moving up and down the sensitive cleft.

I empathized as I watched Malcolm's shiny pink balls

bouncing against the soft, tender flesh of her behind. My nipples were hard again, my pussy squirming. I reached underneath and found my anus, and I groaned with the excitement of the touch and squeezed my thighs together to catch the spurt of hot honey washing over their inner surfaces. I thought of all the times Malcolm had fucked me. I remembered how it felt when he fucked me in the ass with that long, slender, clever prick of his. I wished he was fucking me there now! I groped for the quick high up in my bottom once again.

Finished, Malcolm laid the suntan lotion aside. He moved backwards and when Helen widened the spread of her legs, he settled to his knees between them. He put his hands on her naked buttocks and squeezed them. Impulsively, he bent and kissed one sun-pinkened cheek.

"Bite me there!" Helen writhed. "Let me feel your teeth! But don't hurt me," she added, sudden fear in her voice. "Be gentle, darling." She reached behind her with a twisted arm, stretching, finding his naked balls and tickling them with her fingertips. It was an exquisitely delicate caress.

Malcolm's head swooped downward again. His tongue uncoiled—long and red—and licked lightly up the cleft between her buttocks. Then it licked down to the base again. His small, sharp, white teeth flashed in the sunlight as they nipped at the tender skin separating Helen's anus from her pussy. She moaned and writhed and pushed down for him to nibble her again.

"I like that!" she panted. "Nobody's ever done that to me before. The sensation—it's indescribable! Your tongue! Your mouth! Your teeth!"

"Shall I lick your ass again?" Malcolm teased, but his cock was very hard and stabbing at the air as he rocked on his heels between her legs.

"Yes! Oh, yes!"

"Shall I kiss your pussy?"

"Ahh!" The answer was wordless but profoundly affirmative.

"Would you like me to suck your cunt? To eat it?"

Surprisingly, Helen found her voice and her words were quite explicit. "Put your cock in me first," she said. Malcolm couldn't see her face, but I could and it was brick red. "Fuck me just a little with it and be sure you stroke my clitty while you're fucking. Then take it out and lick up my pussy juices."

Bemused, Malcolm did what she said. He lay over her, the two of them face down, and when her ass raised up, he slid his long, thin cock into her quim. From where I was I could hear the liquid sound of his balls slapping between Helen's legs as he fucked her. She was raised up on her elbows and tearing at her huge breasts with her hands each time he slammed into her.

"That's it!" she gasped. "Fuck me! . . . Harder! . . . Faster! . . . No, wait! I don't want to come! Take it out! Take it out! I want to come with you eating me! I want to come in your mouth!"

But I couldn't wait while Helen followed her fantasy. My fist was between my legs, grinding there, demanding the dizzying climax the spectacle had built in the furnace of my cunt. Even as Malcolm did what Helen wanted, my naked flesh, bathed in sweat, erupted with my own orgasm. The bush concealing me shook as in a high wind with the force of my coming.

They were too occupied to notice, of course. When Malcolm pulled his glistening cock from her raw, open cunt, Helen twisted around and grabbed it and pulled him to her. "I want to lick it," she said. "I want to lick *my* juices from *your* prick."

Yes, I realized dimly as I came to my senses, Helen was indeed taking pains to follow the scenario of her fantasy.

And Malcolm, always sensitive to his sex partners, knew instinctively how to heighten her pleasure. "Does your honey taste as good when you lick it off my prick as it does to me when I suck it out of your burning slit?" he asked her.

"Mmm!" Her mouth was too filled with his prick for words.

"You like to talk about it, don't you?"

"Mmm."

"I like the way it feels when you lick my cock at the base where my balls are. I like feeling my hard-on sliding around in your throat. But do you know what I like best of all?"

"Mmm?" It was a question, meaning "No. What?"

"Using my tongue on your clitoris to make you squirm. Watching your ass writhe with hot excitement while I eat you. Feeling your cunt under my mouth—in my mouth—all hot and wet with sweet-tasting honey."

"Oh, God!" she said, pulling her mouth away from his prick. "Do it! Do it!"

I had just come, and yet the intensity of their interaction now hardened my nipples once again and sent a fresh spurt of hot syrup through my orgasm-clenched pussy. There are times, darlings—erotic times—when my body surprises me. I would have said that masturbatory orgasm had banished lust and replaced it with fatigue. I would have said that any further interest on my part in the lovemaking of Helen and Malcolm would have been strictly clinical. I would have been wrong. My cunt was once again on fire as I watched them. My flesh was willing even when I would have said that my spirit had lost interest.

Helen was in a crouch. Her large, long-nippled breasts were resting lightly on the grass. Her small butt was thrust pertly upward toward the azure sky, her neck twisted impossibly; she was determined to watch Malcolm's head between her legs. "Put your tongue all the way up," she begged as she rocked back and forth with her plump little ass squirming.

"Like this?" Malcolm deliberately misunderstood and thrust his tongue deep between the quivering cheeks.

"OH! . . . No! That's the wrong— Wait! . . . It feels so—! Leave it! . . . Put it—!" Helen's turmoil was acute.

Malcolm compounded it by slipping his fingers into her sopping pussy and manipulating her clitty while he prolonged the forbidden anal kiss. My own heart was pounding wildly as I watched this. My bodily apertures yawned and yearned and my fingers scrambled haphazardly to fill them. "Ohhh! Ahhh!" My own moans softly echoed Helen's in my ears.

"Or maybe this is better." Abruptly Malcolm switched targets. His tongue snaked up under Helen's spread pussy and licked the raw, pink flesh. He stiffened his tongue and pushed it in slowly, rubbing her clitty, straining toward the entrance to her womb. His hands were busy playing inside the crack of her ass as he did this. His slender cock was extended a good half inch above his bellybutton.

"GOD!" Helen shrieked. "OH! GOD!" The sudden explosion of her orgasm was too much for her and she collapsed, falling forward as she came. Malcolm grabbed her hips and held them up to hold her hard-jerking quim in place as he continued to eat it through the waves of her orgasm. "OH! GOD ALMIGHTY!" Her large breasts twisted cruelly under her as she seemed to be trying to burrow into the earth in reaction to the unbearable thrills being provided by Malcolm's mouth.

She was still coming—a series of quakes, each one more violent than the last—when Malcolm abruptly removed his honey-smeared mouth from her quim and his fingers from her writhing ass. Standing behind her, he pulled her up by the hips until she was virtually standing in a doubled-over position on her hands and toes. Then he stepped in behind her and brutally stabbed into the raw gash of her cunt with his inflamed hard-on. His ass moved like a corkscrew as he fucked deep inside her. She screamed and began yet another series of orgasms which made of their balling an extremely violent combat.

It was too much for me. I was beside myself. As I heard Helen screaming over and over again that she was coming . . . and coming again . . . and still coming, I could restrain myself no longer. I bolted from concealment and crossed the clearing to where they were. Panting and perspiring, I flung myself on them so that Helen was propelled to the ground with Malcolm on top of her, his prick still inside her climaxing cunt, still fucking her brutally. I stood in front of Malcolm as he fucked Helen. My cunt was on a level with his straining face. "Eat me!" I begged him, squeezing my nipples and rolling my hips to tempt him. "Eat me while you fuck her!"

"All right!" he gasped. One outflung arm circled my hot behind. An instant later his face was buried in the moist, blond curls of my pussy. And then his mouth—his wonderful, sensual mouth!—was kissing the swollen lips of my cunt, sucking the syrup into his throat, drinking at my fountain of honey with a skill that had me shrieking every bit as mindlessly as Helen. When his tongue touched my clitoris, my hands twisted in the hair on top of his head and I held him fast so that my cunt could spread itself over his mouth as I started to come.

"You're coming!" I heard Helen exclaim, and I realized dimly that Malcolm was shooting his thick white cream deep up her exploding pussy. I let myself go then and slapped wet and hard over Malcolm's face with my own orgasm. "You're coming!" she babbled. "So clean and sweet! I never felt a man come inside me like this before! So clean! So clean!'' And she was off again, and so was I, and I cannot really say which of the three of us was the first to stop climaxing.

Later as we drove back to the city from our Catskill picnic, I could not help feeling a little guilty for having crashed the party of their final orgasms. Although it was true that Malcolm had been my lover first, he was pretty much available to me whenever I wanted him. On the other hand, Helen's fantasy had been very important to her, and it had *not* included another woman. In a way I felt as if I'd betrayed my own Fairy Godmotherhood.

I suppose I was overreacting. Helen was very quiet but said nothing on the return trip to confirm my fear that I might have spoiled the realization of her fantasy for her. As for Malcolm—that smug male!—he hummed all the way home with the contentment of a pussycat gorged on canary feathers.

''How about if I take the three of us out for some thick steaks,'' he suggested as we were crossing the Tappan Zee Bridge.

''That sounds marvelous!'' Helen's eyes lit up and her contented weariness seemed to dissolve.

''Take Helen,'' I said. ''I don't want to be bothered having to dress and go out again.''

''Gee, I didn't think of that,'' Helen agreed with a sigh. ''With this traffic it'll be midnight before we can change and eat.''

''Okay. Alternate plan, then.'' Malcolm was at his most debonair with two attractive women to appreciate his charms. ''Nobody changes. We go to my place, I take three choice New York–cut fillets out of the freezer, and we eat them in the rough.''

''Terrific!'' Helen said, impressed.

"I need a bath," I told him. "You two have your steaks, if that's what you feel like. You can drop me on the way."

"You can shower at my place."

"I want to soak. I don't want to wait, and I don't want to feel like anybody else is waiting for me to get through. Drop me first."

"Are you sure you don't mind if I go up to Malcolm's?" There was that old shy unsureness in Helen's tone.

"Don't be silly." I kissed her. "You go along and enjoy yourself. Malcolm's at his best after he's had some red meat."

"Thank you kindly, ma'am. It's always nice to be tossed a bone, too."

But his nose wasn't seriously out of joint. I knew Malcolm quite well enough to know that. And Helen was trying very hard not to glow at the prospect of being alone with him. Her husband Bruno, I reflected, was in the future going to have some hard times living up to the comparisons she would now be able to make.

Traffic thinned out after the bridge, and it was less than an hour later when Malcolm dropped me in front of my building on Park Avenue. The doorman ushered me into the ornate lobby and the elevator operator—new to the job and obsequious—sped me by express to my penthouse. As I fumbled for my keys, I could hear both my telephones ringing on the other side of the door.

It was my sleep-in French housekeeper's day off. Because of the picnic, however, I had left the apartment early that morning, while Marie was still dressing. The last thing I had shouted out to her over my shoulder was to be sure to turn on the telephone answering machine before she left.

Alas, the French! She was both a superb housekeeper

and an accomplished lady's maid. My penthouse apartment always gleamed, my clothes were ironed and pleated to perfection, the temperature of my bath was perfect to the fraction of a degree. But my telephone and its accessories were beyond her. When she answered my calls, her responses were incomprehensible to the callers. When she took messages, they were incomprehensible to me. And when I tried to solve this dilemma with an answering machine, she neglected to activate it. That's what had happened this morning. And now, as I came through the door to my apartment, both my numbers were ringing at the same time.

The phone was on a small table at the end of the foyer just before the drop to the sunken living room. I dived for it and ended up on my hands and knees with the wire wrapped around me. "Hell! Hello!" I babbled into the mouthpiece without waiting for an answer. "Hold on. I've got another call." I pushed the hold button and then picked up on my other number. "Hello! I'm on another line," I said. "I'll be right with you." I switched back to the first line. "Hello?"

"Christina. It's Diana. Diana Coltrane."

"You're back!" I exclaimed.

"I'm back. The producers insisted. They said they'd close the show if I didn't return right away. No matter how big a star you think you are, there's always some white cat just waiting to push you around."

"I wondered what happened to you. And to Amanda."

"I have to talk to you about that."

"I want to talk to you, too. But listen, hang on a minute, will you? I have another call. I'll get rid of whoever it is and then we can talk."

"Okay."

I put Diana Coltrane on hold and switched to the other line. "Hello?"

"I thought you'd forgotten about me," Amanda Briggs said.

"Amanda! How are you? *Where* are you?"

"Oh, I'm back in New York. I just got in."

"Did you come back with Diana?"

There was what seemed like a long pause. "No. We didn't come back together. We took separate flights." Her voice sounded odd—strained.

"Is something wrong, Amanda?"

"I have to talk to you, Christina." Amanda, who was usually the calm one—our group's earth mother—sounded suspiciously close to tears.

"All right. But hold on a second. There's someone on the other line." My instinct told me not to tell Amanda Briggs that the someone was Diana Coltrane. "I'll tell them I'll call them back."

"I'll hold on."

I switched back to Diana. "Listen, Diana," I said, "something's sort of come up, darling. I wonder if I can get back to you?"

"You can't, Christina. I have to be at the theater in less than an hour. And I really do have to talk to you."

"It's that urgent, hunh?"

"It concerns your friend Amanda Briggs." The way Diana said the name there was acid leaking through the earpiece of the telephone.

"Did you and she have a fight or something?"

"A fight? Oh, no. Why would we have a fight?" Her voice dripped sarcasm.

"What happened, Diana?"

"Listen, I don't want to be interrupted while I'm telling you about this. Get rid of your other call first."

"I'll see what I can do." I switched back to Amanda Briggs. "Listen, Amanda," I said. "How about if I get back to you, angel?"

"Oh, sure. Why not. I know you have more important people to talk to than me." There was no mistaking the bitterness in her voice.

"Now, you know that's not it, Amanda. I want to talk to you. I want to know where you've been, what happened, why you sound so down."

"Diana Coltrane is the answer to all three questions!" Amanda blurted out. "But why should you want to hear what I have to say about a friend of yours? Go ahead and take your other call—your important call!" The line went dead in my ear as she slammed down the phone.

Sighing, I switched back to Diana. "What is it that you want to tell me about Amanda?" I asked her.

"That bitch!" The words exploded out of Diana.

"Don't call her that, Diana. She's a friend of mine," I reminded her.

"That's right! You are both white, aren't you? And friendship is for *white* women!" Again there was a sudden harsh click and a buzzing. Diana Coltrane had hung up on me, too.

Obviously something had gone wrong at the ball. The glass slipper, it seemed, was in smithereens. And as far as my lesbian Prince Charming and Cinderella were concerned, Fairy Godmother's magic wand had definitely lost its pizzazz!

# CHAPTER EIGHT

It would all be sorted out at the next meeting of our women's group. That's what I told myself. Bolstered by the supportive atmosphere of the group, Amanda Briggs would bring her bitterness under control and purge herself of it by revealing what had happened between her and Diana Coltrane. We would deal with young Joyce Dell's California-inspired disillusionment with mature men. Stephanie McCall would come to grips with the actualization of her rape fantasy. Our support, following her idyll with Malcolm, would enable Helen Willis to confront the reality of her marriage to the sexually insensitive Bruno.

Yes, sisterhood would ease all our problems. It might even elicit from me—at long last—the revelation of my own withheld sex fantasy. It could be a relief to get it off my bosom. Yes, the next meeting would surely be a watershed for all of us. That's what I thought, but—

"The meeting is canceled."

My caller was Melinda Holloway, the voluptuous redhead who at thirty-eight was the senior member of our little band of sisters. The next meeting was to have been at her house, and now she went on to explain to me why it had been called off. It added up to the fact that each of the others seemed to have a reason for not coming.

Helen Willis had explained to Melinda that Bruno was very suspicious since she had returned from her unexplained, weeklong absence. Unimaginative as he was, he still knew he had been caught by her with another woman, and Bruno dimly perceived the possibility that she just might have reacted by seeking solace in the arms of another man. He hadn't pushed the question (perhaps he was afraid to hear the answer), but he had taken to crossexamining her regarding her comings and goings. He accepted the fact that she was going to her women's meeting because it fit into her past pattern. Therefore, Helen told Melinda, that's where she said she was going on the evening of the meeting. However, she confided, she was actually going to the apartment of her lover.

*Malcolm!* I shook my head to myself ruefully. *No wonder I hadn't been seeing much of him lately!*

"She sounded quite wicked," Melinda told me. "For Helen, that is."

"But did she sound happy?" I wanted the perception of someone else.

"Happy? I don't know. Involved, though. Definitely involved. Very deeply, I would guess."

"Oh." *That was too bad,* I thought to myself. I knew Malcolm. He was a wonderful lover, just the man for a fling, but there was no future with him. He thrived on variety. Once he had proposed that he and I should be sexually faithful to each other, but I had disabused him of that notion quickly and firmly. Since that time, Malcolm had come to value a multiplicity of relationships as much as I do. If Helen's involvement was a search for stability outside her marriage, then she was going to be disappointed.

"It's funny," Melinda said, almost as if she'd been reading my mind. "Helen's getting all serious over what should probably be just a casual fling, while Joyce Dell is quite casual about entering into a relationship which ought to call for commitment. I mean, after all, she's moving in with this boy. She'll be living with him and that will be a first for her. Yet she treats it as if it wasn't at all important. I guess I'm getting old, Christina. I just don't understand young people today.''

''Oh, come on now, Melinda. You're not that old.''

''I'm thirty-eight.''

''You look ten years younger. Lots of women who are ten years younger would envy you that amazon body of yours. Not to mention that gorgeous red hair. Not many women, regardless of age, can lay claim to being as voluptuous as you are.''

''Thanks, darling. That's really nice of you. But the thing is I can't get over having wasted all of that on a man with the sex drive of a caterpillar. All those wasted years of marriage! And all that erotic yearning is still bottled up inside of me!''

''Well, we're just going to have to figure out how to unbottle it, angel,'' I assured her. ''I promise you, I'm going to work on it. After all, what are friends for?''

''To solve the problems of The Great Unfucked.'' Melinda laughed. ''What else?''

''How come Joyce can't make the meeting?'' I returned to our original topic.

''It's moving day for her and the new boyfriend.''

''I see. And Stephanie?''

''Said she had a business dinner. I don't know if that's really true, Christina. She sounded—well—peculiar. These past few weeks she's been seeming more and more that way to me. Oh, well, maybe it's my imagination.''

''No it's not.'' Stephanie McCall had been acting differently ever since the rape. ''What about Amanda?'' I asked. I'd been too afraid of rejection to try calling her myself since the night she'd hung up on me. "Why isn't she coming?"

"Search me. She's back from wherever she was."

"I know that."

"But she isn't taking my calls. All I get is her damn answering service. I leave messages, but she never phones back. Do you think something happened to sour her on the group?"

"I hope not," I said. I felt really bad about Amanda Briggs. I made a mental note to myself to make an effort to contact her, and Diana Coltrane as well. It was important to sort out the situation, to smooth over whatever had happened.

Before I had a chance to do that, however, I received an invitation that directed my attention elsewhere. It came in the form of a long distance telephone call. After I hung up, I immediately thought of Melinda Holloway and called her.

"How would you like to go to a party?" I asked her.

"Sure. When is it?"

"Next Friday, Saturday, and Sunday."

"That sounds like some party," Melinda chuckled.

"It will be."

"Where is it?"

"In Morocco."

"Morocco! Christina, are you serious?"

"Never more so, darling. It's being thrown by Idris Arafa, an old and very dear friend of mine. He's leased the Concorde to fly guests from New York to Casablanca. From there we'll be flown by his fleet of private planes to Fez."

"Fez?"

"That's where he has his villa. High up in the Middle Atlas Mountains, overlooking the city."

"I thought Morocco was in the desert," Melinda said, confused.

"Part of it is in the Sahara. That's the part that's in dispute. There's a revolution being fought there right now. But most of Morocco is in the mountains. High mountains. Even in summer you'll see snow on some of the crests around Fez. In winter there are very popular ski areas nearby."

"Is this friend of yours an oil sheik or something? I mean, after all—leasing the Concorde, a fleet of private planes, a villa in the mountains—I've only read about people with that kind of money, Christina."

"Idris is not a sheik, angel. He prefers to be known simply as Monsieur Arafa."

"Is he French?" Now Melinda was totally confused.

"Oh, no," I explained. "Morocco was ruled by the French for so long that the French influence has stuck. Not in Fez particularly, where the Berber influence is heavy and the Spanish were the occupiers. But on the Mediterranean coast, around Casablanca and Tangier. These are very European, very French cities. Idris came from Casablanca originally. His father made the family fortune there during the war. Believe it or not, his business was camels. They were an important part of the army's supply lines."

"Which army?"

"First the French. Then the Vichy French. Then the Germans. Then the English. Then the Italians. Then the British again. Then the Germans again. And finally the Americans—who proved to be the most profitable of all for that wily old camel hustler, Idris's father."

"And does the son still deal in camels?"

"Oh, no. Too much mechanization has come, even to Morocco, for camels to be profitable anymore."

"Is he in oil?"

"Who knows? He dabbles. He isn't in any one business. He invests. And he spends a great deal of his time at leisure. As you surmised, Melinda darling, he is disgustingly wealthy."

"Why does he live in Fez if he came from Casablanca?"

"Humphrey Bogart," I told her. "And high-rises," I added.

"I beg your pardon?"

"The movie. You know."

"Before my time, Christina. I may not be as young as you, but I'm not that old."

"Well, that flick has turned Casablanca into a Mecca for European and American tourists. And this influx drew in a whole population from the desert and mountains to service them. The tourists needed hotels and the people who served them needed housing. It was boom time in the building industry. High-rises everywhere. Idris's daddy really increased his camel fortune putting them up. But today you couldn't pay Idris to live in Casablanca. He hates everything his father's investments helped build. It's too European for him. He's very proud of being Moroccan even though everything about him demonstrates how much influence French culture had on his developement. Who knows? Maybe that's what he's rebelling against. In any case, he prefers to live in Fez, which is the most traditionally Moroccan of Morocco's big cities. But all the same he lives like a wealthy European libertine."

"He sounds like a very complicated man."

"He is."

"Is he good-looking?"

"Attractive. That is, if you find Omar Sharif attractive."

"I most certainly do!" Melinda exclaimed.

"Of course he's younger than Omar. He doesn't have that gray at the temples."

"How young?"

"I'm not sure. Somewhere between my age and yours," I told Melinda. "But from what I've observed," I added, "Idris seems to prefer women closer to your age than mine."

"You're just saying that to whet my appetite." Melinda laughed excitedly.

"Then you'll come?"

"If you're sure I won't be crashing his party."

"It's not a problem. He explicitly told me to include any friends I might care to bring along."

"Just what kind of party is this, Christina?"

"Precisely the kind you're looking for," I told Melinda. "That is, if I remember your fantasy rightly, and I'm sure I do." I added this last so that Melinda would clearly understand the opportunity I was offering her.

"I see." She spoke her next words very slowly and thoughtfully. "Well then, I wouldn't miss it for the world."

I slept over at Melinda's house in Great Neck Thursday night and we drove to Kennedy Airport where the Concorde was waiting for us very early Friday morning. The same plane flew us back from Casablanca very late the following Sunday night. What transpired between those two flights is really much more Melinda Holloway's story than mine. She told it at a subsequent meeting of our women's group which, after a good deal of pleading and arm-twisting, was attended by all the members. Here, in her own words, is the story of Melinda Holloway's Moroccan adventure.


*It really began on the flight from Kennedy to Casablanca. Despite its large seating capacity, there were only about two dozen passengers aboard the chartered Concorde, all guests of Christina's Moroccan friend, Mon-*

*sieur Idris Arafa. In addition to the personnel flying the aircraft, there were another fourteen or so attendants charged with catering to our every desire. Everything on the flight was champagne class and we were wined and dined and entertained in royal Moroccan fashion. These servants (truly there is no other way to categorize them) were dressed in the finest Islamic Empire livery and overseen by a major-domo more resplendent than a Romanov Archduke turned doorman at a Las Vegas casino.*

*We snacked on caviar fresh from the Black Sea and dined on grouse and venison just slain in Scotland. The cuisine, like the wine, was French in style. The chef had been borrowed by our host from a famous Paris restaurant and would be flown directly back to Paris at the end of our flight. Gypsy violinists from Andalusia alternated with a jazz pianist from Greenwich Village to entertain us as we supped in the spacious Concorde restaurant lounge.*

*The food and wine made Christina sleepy. After dinner she excused herself, pushed up the arms between the seats in one of the rows, stretched out with a blanket, and took a nap. With lots of room at our disposal, I took a window seat in another row and made an attempt to read a paperback I'd brought along with me. It was no use. I was too excited at the prospect of Morocco to keep my mind on the novel. Nor could I sleep. I shut my eyes and allowed free reign to the fantasies chasing around inside my head. Under the circumstances—with all that Christina had implied about the party—it was only natural, I suppose, that these fantasies should become quite erotic.*

*Well, married to the man I was married to for so many frustrating years, fantasies have long been the most active and satisfying part of my sex life. Sadly, nothing since my divorce has altered that very much. It has become a pattern with me—my mind turning me on, my body following.*

*So it was now, on the supersonic jet. I was wearing*

slacks and a blouse (following Christina's advice to wear casual clothes for travel) and I could feel that my fantasies were stretching the silk over my nipples and dampening my crotch. I opened my eyes to find a blanket with which to cover myself so that I might pursue my sensual vision without embarrassment.

"Cold?" a man's voice asked me. He had taken a seat in the same row, leaving one vacant seat between us.

"Yes. A little," I said, wondering uncomfortably if he had observed my earlier writhings in my seat.

"Lemme help." He took the blanket, shook it out, and spread it over me. When he sat back down, it was in the seat next to mine.

I smiled at him. We were too small a group for me to show the little bit of annoyance I was feeling. "Thanks," I told him.

"If I'm distoibin' ya, say so and I'll go."

"Not at all," I told him. Distoibin'? The pronunciation echoed in my head. His accent was pure Lower East Side New York. I looked at him, wondering at his presence in this company of Beautiful People.

He was a short man in his twenties with very wide shoulders and a broad chest that was barrellike. Even seated I could see that he was bandy-legged. Yet somehow I sensed that he would be a good dancer, light on his feet. His most striking feature was the shock of Brillo-curled red hair on top of his head. I'm a redhead myself, but my tresses are copper toned, a sort of golden red, and they both contrast and blend with the creaminess of my complexion. His red thatch was more the orange color of scraped-down battleships and it added to the pugnacity of his densely freckled face. The face itself was sort of squinched up like a pug dog, narrow of eye and harsh at the mouth and jaw. It had a built-in belligerence even when he smiled at me, as he did now.

*"We ain't met, have we?"* He stood up, an attempt at formally introducing himself. *"I'm Kid Killarney."*

I didn't have to stand myself to see that if I did he would reach only to the top of my breast. *"Melinda Holloway,"* I told him. *"Is that really your name? Kid Killarney?"*

*"Nah. My real monicker is Laszlo Csokonai. My folks was Hungarian. Ain't no ring fans gonna buy a name like that, though. By the time they yell for you to belt the other guy with a label like that, it's all over. So on accounta the red hair my owners changed it to Kid Killarney, everybody should think I'm Irish."*

*"You're a boxer,"* I realized.

*"Yeah. Lightweight. Maybe someday Middle if I can make the weight. I just been sold, case you're wonderin' how I come to be here with all these fancy people."*

*"Sold?"* I looked at him blankly.

*"Yeah. To this Mister Arafa."*

*"I'd heard that there was an Arab slave market, but I didn't think it reached into America,"* I said, shocked.

*"You got it wrong. I ain't no Arab's slave. I was sold like American style. A lotta people, they each owned a piece of me, which means they put up money so's I could train to fight and whatever. This Mister Arafa, he bought 'em all out, so now I'm consolidated with the one owner which is him. I talked to him on the phone and he's gonna bring me along real slow and careful right up to the title. He's set up a training camp for me at this Fez we're going to. He says I gotta promise to train real strict, but before I start, I should get all the wild oats or whatever outa my system. So he says I should come to this party and do it while I'm young, 'cause afterwards it's all gonna be work building toward the title."*

*"Just how old are you, Kid?"* I asked him.

*"Twenty-two."*

I hadn't thought he was quite that young. Now I saw

*that the weather-beaten look on his face came from scar tissue. It made him look both older and harder than he probably really was.*

*"I forgot to duck." His grin said he'd been reading my mind.*

*"I'm thirty-eight." Now why did I say that? It just seemed to pop out. Maybe it was that I could see that Kid Killarney was attracted to me and I was so unsure of myself that I had to test if the attraction would hold true once he knew my real age.*

*"Yeah? Older women turn me on," he told me without much finesse, but with unmistakable honesty. "You're in really good shape for your age," he added candidly. "Do you work out?"*

*"Not nearly as much as I'd like to." The double entendre was deliberate. "And I've never worked out with a professional boxer," I added. (Well, why not? Presumably we both understood the kind of party to which we'd been invited.)*

*"I guess maybe I could show you a few things."*

*It was hard to know if he was matching my banter, or being ingenuous. I let my eyes roam down his short, powerful body. They lingered on the lump distending his trousers. "Perhaps you're chilly too," I suggested. "Perhaps we should share the blanket."*

*"Yeah. Pa'haps." He raised the seat arm between us and moved closer, spreading the blanket so that it covered both our bodies. "Ya wanna play a little?" he asked bluntly.*

*I didn't answer him. I just took his hand in mine and held it to my breast. His palm was very calloused, the knuckles hairy. When the hair brushed my nipples through the silk of my blouse, it felt the way it looked—like rusty barbed wire. He slipped his hand inside the blouse and played somewhat roughly with the nipple.*

*"You sure ya thirty-eight years old?"* Kid asked. *"I thought women's breasts was supposed to sag when they get older. Yours are firm and hard like a kid."*

*"Thank you."* My voice came out a moan.

He slid up in the seat and kissed me then. His tongue was thick and pushy and street-wise. *"It really turns me on you being such a tall lady,"* he told me when the kiss was over. *"Big women, they're like a challenge to me. Satisfying them, I mean."*

Twenty-two years old! *I had a flickering, bitter memory of my ex-husband. He'd been over forty when we split. And in all the years we'd been together, he'd never shown the slightest interest in my satisfaction. Kid Killarney, at twenty-two, understood without words that his joy and mine were intertwined, that the better he could make it for me, the better I would make it for him.*

*"You're the biggest man I ever met,"* I murmured to him. *And to be sure he understood, I reached down between his legs and squeezed his hard-on through his pants.*

*Kid undid the waistband of my slacks and pushed them down. He pushed down my panties with them. Then, under cover of the blanket, he caressed my naked buttocks.* *"You got a great ass."* He licked my ear.

*"It's too big."* I writhed under his touch.

*"It's just perfect for the way you're built."* He ducked under the blanket, kissed it quickly but deeply, and then surfaced again. *"It sure is hot."* He grinned his tough newsboy grin, one side of his mouth going up at the corner.

*"So am I!"* I panted. I found the zipper to his pants and opened it. He wasn't wearing any underwear. His stiff cock came twanging out. It was much bigger than I'd expected it to be considering his small build.

*I made a fist. I have large hands. It circled his cock*

comfortably, but there wasn't a whole lot of finger length left over.

Kid's hand traced the cleft of my buttocks and moved in on my pussy from behind. Soon his hand was coated with the honey between my legs. He spread the raw flesh and found my clitty and rubbed it. "Jesus, I'm hot!" he snarled. His cock throbbed rhythmically in my hand, thick with juice.

"So am I!" My wet pussy squirmed over his hairy knuckles.

"I wanna stick it in ya!" He moved to mount me under cover of the blanket.

"Someone will see us." I stopped him.

"So what? Who cares?" His hot balls slid down my belly and over the soft silk of my cunt hair.

"Wait!" Again I stopped him. "I don't have my diaphragm in. Do you have any—?"

"No. Shit, no!"

"I can't take the chance!" In my frustration, I half sobbed the words.

"Skin a cat," he said, stroking my belly, my thighs, the opened petals of my pussy.

"What?" I squeezed his prick and tickled his balls with my other hand.

"More than one way," Kid explained. He used both his hands to open my legs wide under the blanket. My seat was in the reclining position, and now he pushed against my buttocks until I had my weight on my back and my ass was raised and spread. His knuckles pushed into the crack between the cheeks, moved down to my pussy, and then back up again.

"What are you doing?" I moaned. The inside of my fist was sweaty as it moved up and down his hard, throbbing cock.

*"Keep jerking me off!"* The little boxer didn't answer my question. *"I gotta come!"*

*"So do I!"* I squeezed his wire-haired balls and milked the jism up the shaft of his cock.

Kid's knuckles were deep inside me now, in my ass and in my pussy by turn. He clenched his hand and made a fist inside me and moved it. I almost screamed, but clenched my teeth over the blanket instead. I wouldn't have believed it, but his fist moved up my ass and then inside my pussy. I stretched wide to accommodate it.

*"You ain't never been fist-fucked before, huh?"* Kid's mouth was at my ear, his cock straining in my hand.

*"No! Never!"*

*"How do ya like it?"* He began pumping from the elbow, his fist deep inside my widespread cunt, his wrist rubbing the lips of my pussy as he moved.

*"It's excruciating! It hurts! It's driving me crazy! The sensation—! I never felt anything like it before."*

*"You want me to stop?"* He twisted his fist viciously.

*"Yes! . . . No! Don't stop!"* I was half-hysterical. *"Don't stop! Deeper! Harder!"*

He began punching inside me now, real jabs. I could feel his knuckles, his fist bruising me, his wrist. When he twisted his wrist and punched again, my stiff clitty was the target. Then, quickly, he delivered an uppercut all the way up my ass and just as quickly was back in my pussy again, punching out my stiff, inflamed clitty.

*"Oh, God! I'm coming!"* I bleated through the blanket in my teeth. *"I'm coming!"* And with the words, I automatically yanked viciously at his prick.

It spurted over my belly and thighs. In my blind orgasm I tugged on it still harder and was rewarded by Kid's fist grinding against the very mouth of my womb. My head spun then with the intensity of my climax, and the last *excruciating sensations of the fist-fucking propelled me into a blackout.*

*When I came to, Kid Killarney smiled his relief. He excused himself and went to the bathroom to clean up. When he came back, I went. We dozed in each other's arms under the blanket after that. We only really came awake when the Concorde was making its approach to land at Casablanca.*

*There were limousines waiting to take us to a very swanky hotel on the beach. It was near a private airport owned by Idris Arafa, our host. A fleet of planes was waiting there to take us to Fez. Most of us, however, would have a couple of hours to clean up at the hotel. The landing strip was limited and only one plane could take off at a time.*

*Kid Killarney, however, was to leave on the first plane. Monsieur Arafa, it seemed, was eager to meet the boxer he had acquired. "How do you feel?" Kid asked me just before we parted.*

*"Sore. I'm very sore."*

*"That'll pass. It's bound to happen with fist-fucking."*

*"It was quite an experience."*

*"Did you like it?"*

*"I'm not sure," I replied honestly. "It hurt, but it was fantastically thrilling, too."*

*"Only a boxer knows how to do it right." He winked at me. "You get the technique down on the small punching bag." He kissed me quickly. "See you in Fez."*

*"See you in Fez." I waved goodbye to him.*

*Christina and I each had our own suite at the hotel. Mine was on the ground floor and had French doors leading out to a lanai—a private garden shaded by four high date palms and fenced off by trellises thick with voluptuously climbing red and white roses. After I'd show-*

ered, I went out to the lanai and lay down naked on a chaise lounge so that the sun might dry me off.

Morocco! I couldn't believe I was there! Casablanca! That I, Melinda Holloway, until very recently a suburban matron, should be in this romantic setting was in itself a turn-on. I felt young and strong and I admired my Junoesque body in the sunlight.

Yes, Kid Killarney had told the truth. My breasts were quite firm for my years. My legs were as long and shapely as a Rockette's. My hips were wide and sensually curved. My bottom was plump, but as Kid said, it was none too big for my torso. And my pussy, with its silky red covering, was a wondrous throb-box of pleasure.

I ran my hands down my body, my fingertips trailing over the sun-hardened nipples, the slight curve of the belly, the moist cleft of the cunt. I twisted the tendrils of my long red hair around one of my erect nipples and laughed. I raised one knee so that my thighs could rub together and then lowered it and raised the other. I remembered the battering of Kid Killarney's fist in my ass and cunt and there was a spurt of honey between my legs.

I parted my thighs and put my hand between them. I was suddenly very horny again. I found my straining clitty and rolled my own knuckles over it.

A sound behind the rose trellis distracted me. I peered in the direction from which it had come. I saw nothing. I reached for my clitty again. As I did so, I turned to one side and inadvertently found myself looking into the mirror on the inside of the opened closet door in the sitting room of my suite. Through some trick of refraction, it revealed the spot behind the trellis from which the sound had come. In the mirror I could clearly see a Moroccan man standing there watching me naked on the chaise lounge. He had raised the hem of his burnoose all the way up over his belly and was pulling on his tumescent prick.

*Although the hood of his robe was raised, I could make out his face clearly. He had a heavily bearded face and his skin was very dark, almost black. His eyes were like smouldering coals as they stared at my naked body. The tendons of his legs stood out like ropes from sexual tension. His belly was covered with thick black hair, and so was his groin. The hair almost concealed the sizable heft of his swollen black balls. His lips were curled in a snarl and his hand was moving like a piston over his circumcised cock.*

*He had no way of knowing that I could see him spying on me. Watching me play with myself had inspired him to start jerking off. Now, watching him pulling on his swarthy pecker so excited me that it never occurred to me to go inside and draw the curtain and bring myself off in privacy. On the contrary, the knowledge that it was my body that was inspiring him in turn inspired me to exhibit myself in raunchy ways designed to enable me to watch the cream shooting from his big cock when his orgasm exploded.*

*Watching him carefully in the mirror, I lifted a breast to my mouth and licked the nipple slowly and sensually. Using both hands, I parted the lips of my pussy and exposed the glistening pink meat inside the swollen purple lips. I stretched the bright red clitty between my fingers so he could see it.*

*Even in the mirror I could see the sweat on his face now. I dipped one middle finger into my pussy and writhed around it. He rocked back and forth on his heels and the hood fell away from his face and revealed a tangle of shiny, curly black hair. I bounced up and down on the chaise lounge and frigged myself and never took my eyes off him in the mirror.*

*He had both hands around his shaft now and there was ecstasy on his face as he stared through the rose vines at my horny, hot, naked, squirming body. I watched the wedge-shaped tip of his cock carefully. It became tomato red in contrast to the darkness of the shaft. The little hole widened. It drew back. And then the cream was spurting from it and over the roses and the thorns indiscriminately.*

*It was my doing. I took my reward. Squealing, I jammed fingers into my cunt, found my clitty, and dived into my own multicolored orgasm. Dimly, I heard the peals of my own laughter trilling out over the lanai.*

*When I recovered enough to look in the mirror, he was gone. About twenty minutes later, as I was finishing dressing, there was a knock at my door. When I opened it, the masturbator was standing there. I could only stare at him with my mouth open.*

*"I am Riffi," he announced. "In the employ of Monsieur Arafa. I will take your bags to the plane."*

*"Are you going to Fez, too?" I blurted out.*

*"Oui." Riffi picked up my bags and departed. In no way did he betray having played the peeping Tom with me. Still, there was that in his arrogant stride as he departed that told me I hadn't seen the last of Riffi.*

*It was late afternoon when we arrived at the villa of Idris Arafa. "Villa" does not begin to describe the sprawling mansion, with its mountainside acres overlooking the twelve-century-old city of Fez. Everything about the residence was lavish. Everywhere there were inlaid tile walls and inlaid gold ceilings and spectacular electrified chandeliers crusted with precious gems. Ancient tapestries and hand-woven Moroccan rugs abounded, as did the most modern conveniences for the comfort of the guests. In keeping with Moslem law there were only abstract paintings and sculptures, since representation of the human face and form is forbidden. Nevertheless, this stricture permitted a spectacular representation of avant-garde art which seemed to fit right in with the work of the ancient and anonymous Moroccan masters. Rich, deep colors created an ambience of opulence (perhaps even decadence) which had its own built-in sensuality.*

*Monsieur Arafa had sent his apologies that he could not personally greet us; he had been detained by business. Each of us was conducted to his or her private room by a servant garbed (male and female alike) in a colorful caftan. It was late afternoon, and so I did not yet change for dinner but rather had a quick wash, combed my hair, and went looking for Christina.*

*She was having a drink on the east patio of the villa. A small group of people had congregated there and were chatting and laughing. Christina seemed to know them well, and they her, and there was a decided aura of intimacy about the scene. I would have felt awkward intruding on it. Instead, I decided to go for a walk around the grounds.*

*My ramblings took me to an overlook obviously designed to take advantage of the spectacular view of Fez it afforded. From it one could see, like a snake crawling in and out of the city, the road which was the caravan route between the Sahara and Tangier. The ruins of old Moorish forts and castles fringed the city. They marked the Tour de Fès road—The Corniche Route—which encircles some ten miles of the Fez perimeter.*

*In the concrete of the overlook there was a stand embedded with a telescope on it. I looked through it. The focus had been set on that part of the city known as Fas el-Bali—the ancient city, or Medina—an impenetrable maze of palaces, mosques, souks (native marketplaces), national monuments, and medrassas (Moslem colleges). The sight was labyrinthine, impossibly narrow alleyways rendered sunless by high, steep buildings. It was a gloomy scene, and yet behind some of the crumbling facades there were wide courtyards and sumptuous residences.*

*This was in contrast to the turmoil of such areas as the Tanner's Quarter where men, naked save for breechcloths, immersed themselves in vats of dye to stain the hides of freshly slaughtered animals. The hides were stretched out on rooftops for miles, and looking down on the scene it seemed one impossible patchwork quilt. The stench, I would learn later, was horrendous, and yet the hordes of children scattering before the ever-stampeding burros in the twisting corridors seemed as unaware of it as they were of the droppings of the live beasts.*

*The tortuous maze of Fas el-Bali seemed symbolic of the trap of overpopulation which holds Morocco (indeed, most of Africa and Asia and South America as well) in its grip. Peering through the telescope, I observed a universal irony as time after time the movement of goods by burro took precedence over the safety and welfare of the little laboring children in their way. An exclusively Moroccan phenomenon? Not at all. Just take a jaunt through Mississippi and observe the ten-year-old stoop laborers picking cotton in the fields.*

"Fez is quite beautiful with the sunlight on its spires and ramparts, is it not?"

*I had not heard the man coming up behind me. Now I wheeled around to face him.* "I wasn't looking at the domes and minarets," *I told him.* "I was observing the Medina."

"Ahh. Well, that is perhaps not so beautiful."

"No. Not beautiful at all." *I looked at him.* "Sad." *He was a young man, blond, Scandinavian looking with his Viking haircut and pale blue eyes. He was tall and muscular in riding clothes. There was a drawn, almost cruel quality to the angular planes of his face. His nervous manner with the riding crop he held somehow seemed to confirm this vague air of violence.* "Where's your horse?" *I blurted out.*

*"I've already stabled him."* There was no accent, only a lilt, but the edges were harsh, the tone precise with a sort of northern coldness. *"You have just arrived to take part in the orgy?"* he asked me bluntly.

*"I've just arrived."* My face very red, I answered carefully, neither confirming nor denying the second assumption of his question.

*"You are a big woman, a strong woman. I shall look forward to being with you."* He snapped the riding crop hard against the side of his thigh.

*"You're fairly large yourself."* I didn't know what else to answer.

*"Then we are well matched."* There was a steely glint in his pale blue eyes. *"I am Par Virstrom."* He clicked his heels and before I knew what he was doing, he bent and kissed the back of my hand.

I laughed out loud. (Nervousness? Because his nose had tickled? A response to how old-fashioned and ridiculous it seemed?) *"I'm happy to meet you."* I tried in vain to cover my reaction. I told him my name.

*"I amuse you?"* He seemed offended.

*"Not at all."* Nervously I sought a topic which would not vex him further. *"Do you like to ride?"* I asked, the best I could do on the spur of the moment.

*"But of course!"* he responded, whipping his riding crop viciously at the trunk of a cedar tree as if to underline his contempt for such an obvious question.

*"I do hope you don't whip your horse like that!"* I blurted out. *"I have very strong feelings about the mistreatment of animals."*

*"Horses enjoy being beaten. It is in their nature."*

*"I doubt that,"* I told him coldly. *"I don't think enjoyment of pain is in any living creature's nature."*

*"Not any. All."* He struck his leg hard with the riding

*crop again.* "All living creatures have the capacity to enjoy pain. Particularly man. And," he added, "woman."

"Not this woman!" I was firm.

"You don't enjoy pain?"

"Absolutely not!"

"Feeling it, you mean?" There was a sudden, intense gleam in the bland blue eyes.

"Why . . . yes . . ." I wondered what he was driving at.

His next words were a clarification of sorts. "You might feel differently about bestowing it, however."

"You mean striking somebody else? Well, I suppose I would feel better about that than about being struck by them."

"Yes. Of course you would." The gleam was a positive sparkle now. "You might even find it exciting, don't you think?"

"I don't know." But the shiver which ran up my spine told me that there was more than a little something in what Par Virstrom was saying.

"Exciting," he echoed. "Like this." He pulled his jodhpurs free of one boot, bared his shin and struck it violently with the riding crop. A red welt appeared. When he struck it a second time, a thin stream of blood trickled into his boot. "Try it and see," he said, handing me the riding crop.

I hesitated. I had heard about S&M, but I had never thought about becoming involved in it myself. Until my divorce I had led a rather cloistered sex life. Since then, opportunities to widen my range of experience had been limited. There was a challenge in that trickle of blood running down Par Virstrom's leg. Even if I couldn't justify it intellectually, I could feel it quite deeply. It was a sexual challenge—so testified the trembling in my groin. Even *so, I had always assumed there was something sick about this sort of thing.*

*"Just once," he urged. "Try it just once."*

*My hand was shaking as I took the riding crop from him. He braced his leg against a tree, then pulled the jodhpurs as high up over his knee as he could. The muscles of his upper thigh stood out against his pale skin. "Strike here." He indicated the virgin flesh.*

*I slashed his thigh with the riding crop. My nipples hardened at the sight of his skin turning pink. Immediately he urged me to strike again, and I did so. When his face contorted with the pain of a third blow, my doubts were banished. His reaction to the pain filled me with excitement and I laid on the blows again and again without waiting for encouragement from him.*

*"Wait!" he panted finally. He sprang away from me and his fingers went to the leather belt at the waistband of his jodhpurs. He opened it and pushed down the riding pants and his underwear as well. His hairless belly—flat, white, muscular—framed a rather small but very stiff cock. "Let's do it right," he panted. He got down on his hands and knees, his modest hard-on flat against his stomach. He stuck his behind out toward me and wriggled it provocatively. The cheeks were surprisingly plump—almost girlish. They were crisscrossed with the fading scars of former beatings. "Whip me!" he moaned.*

*I laid on with a vengeance. Each blow I struck heightened my own excitement. Each welt that appeared sent a thrill through me; each moan found its echo in the hardening of my clitoris.*

*The blue sky of afternoon was deepening into the pearl-gray and vermilion of early dusk. It was Friday and from the city below us rose the chant of the muezzins summoning the Moslem faithful to the mosques. Soon their prayers rose like the humming of a swarm of bees to provide the background to the bizarre scene of cruelty that Par and I were acting out.*

*"Harder!" He squirmed, his cock jerking against his belly, his swollen balls straining against the tight skin of the sac which held them. "Again! Again!"*

*Despite the cooling of the fireball which was the setting sun, my exertions were such that I was bathed in perspiration. I took off my blouse and resumed beating Par with the riding crop, my firm, long-nippled breasts swinging hard away from my rib cage with each new downstroke.*

*"You are a Valkyrie, Melinda Holloway!" he bleated. "An American amazon. Your skirt," he moaned. "Please! . . . Please! . . . Take off your skirt. I want to see the way your body moves when you strike me!" He rocked back and forth on his hands and knees as he spoke, his stiff cock stabbing into his navel now.*

*Breasts heaving, I took off my skirt and stood before him for a moment in my panties. They were flimsy, the material gauzy and quite transparent. Also they were embarrassingly drenched with the honey of my arousal.*

*Par stared at what had been revealed, his white face shiny with lust. He licked his lips as he appraised the muscles standing out in my thighs, the syrup glistening on the red, silken curls at the base of my belly, the arrogant thrust of my mons veneris with its swollen purple lips and exposed pink, wet cleft. My excitement lay open and exposed in my crotch for him to see. His breathing became hoarse. "Strike again!" he snapped, the words half a command and half a moan.*

*"Be patient." Deliberately, I teased him. I slid the hilt of the riding crop into the waistband of my panties and pushed them down from my hips. Wriggling provocatively, I worked my way out of them. I spread the lips of my*

*pussy in front of his face and stroked my clitty so he could see. Then I moved behind his kneeling figure and struck his plump, lightly bleeding butt with the riding crop as hard as I could.*

*"God!" he screamed. "Again!"*

*I struck again and again, now as worked up as he. So vigorous were my movements that my breasts slapped painfully against my body. My thigh muscles were sore from straining. My cunt was raw with hunger.*

*"Now!" Suddenly Par screamed again. His whole body shot forward spasmodically except for his high, girlish ass which rose in the air, demanding the lash. "Now!"*

*My cunt on fire, I brought the riding crop down hard on the cleft between his bottom cheeks. He fell forward with his chin in the dirt, both hands clutching for his hard little cock as it began to spurt. The sight was too much for me. I flung the riding crop aside and straddled him. I pushed his hands aside and grabbed his geysering prick. I rubbed my burning, yawning cunt over the thick, bleeding flesh of his ass. In this position, half riding him, my legs spread wide to force one cheek of his plump ass up my pussy where I might feel it against my clitty, I came with him . . .*

*Below us the intonations of the faithful of Fez rose in chorus to the fiery gray and purple sky. A sudden gust of wind swept over the mountainside on which we strained toward our own version of Heaven. And somewhere a Moroccan dervish danced a mime describing yet one more of the endless possibilities of erotic satisfaction . . .*

*After our orgasms, we parted quickly, Par Virstrom and I. He muttered something about seeing me later at the orgy and hurried off, presumably to apply balm to his wounds. I put on my clothes, went back to my room, and took a long hot bath before dressing for dinner.*

*The evening gown I chose to wear was a new one. I had picked it up at B. Altman's before I left New York with Christina. It cost more than any dress I had ever bought before in my life.*

*It was a two-piece ensemble designed by Kaspar and made of silk crepe de chine edged with a delicate picot trim. It was a rich green, contrasting with my red-gold hair, and the large, widely spaced abstract pattern was in off-white. The top consisted of a V which met at my belly and was held in place by thin straps. It covered my breasts head-on—concealing the nipples—but displayed them provocatively from either side. Much of their ripe, fleshy curve was visible due to the wide cleavage of the decolletage. The skirt started low on my hips, revealed the twin mounds of my rising derriere in back, and hugged my legs very tightly as it fell to my ankles. A slit ran up one side all the way to the waistband. In order to move, I had to move first one naked leg and then the other outside the slit. Because I didn't want to ruin the drape of the gown, I didn't wear any panties. I worried that when I moved my pussy might blink into view. Ah, well, I told myself, it is supposed to be an orgy.*

*All eyes turned as I descended the broad staircase to the predinner cocktail party below. I gloried in my reflection in the men's eyes. It said that I was a long-legged, large-breasted, red-haired, sensual Venus. When I let my hips sway slightly near the bottom of the staircase, an almost audible murmur seemed to sweep the room.*

*"Not bad for an old bag, hey?" I winked at Christina as she walked up to greet me.*

*"You look terrific, Melinda."*

*"So do you."*

*It was true. Christina's gown was as different from mine as it could be. It was gold chiffon, tantalizingly see-through, designed especially for her by Bill Blass. It had full, flowing sleeves and a slim skirt which reached only half-way to her knees. She wore gold slippers with it. I was sure that like me she hadn't worn any panties. Indeed, the flesh of her beautifully molded and sassy bottom, and of her high, uptilted, perky breasts, was intermittently visible as she moved under the playful lighting of the ornate chandeliers.*

*"Come meet our host," she said as she slipped her arm through mine and led me through the crowd. Its very parting was a tribute to the sensual picture we made as we moved together.*

*Idris Arafa rose and bowed deeply from the waist when Christina introduced us. He was a handsome man in his early thirties with a pencil-line mustache and a complexion of olive-gold. Quite slender, he was the kind of man who could—and did—wear evening clothes splendidly. His white dinner jacket, narrow-cut, silk-striped black trousers and scarlet sash were perfectly tailored to his aristocratic figure. Even the scarlet fez, which matched the sash and had a little gold tassel grazing one of his high Moroccan cheekbones, seemed no less than a rakish accent to his elegance. How did he keep it from falling when he bowed? I wondered. And then I stopped wondering as our eyes met and held.*

*Yes, from that very first moment there was an undeniable attraction between us. It was palpable and sensual. Christina recognized it and smiled. "I can see you two are going to be great friends," she said.*

*"I shall not leave your side," Monsieur Arafa assured me.*

*"How possessive," Christina teased him.*

*"The prerogative of a host."*

*"You see," she said to me. "A little bit of patience and then— Well, you'll see."*

"*Patience?*" *I looked at her blankly.*

"*It has been pretty dull and uneventful up until now.*"

"*Not for me it hasn't,*" *I murmured.*

"*Oh?*" *Christina looked at me quizzically. "Do tell all.*"

"*Later.*" *Monsieur Arafa offered each of us an arm. "I believe we are going in to dinner now.*"

*He used his host's prerogative to seat Christina on his left and me on his right. It was a long banquet table and there were many guests. About halfway down its length I spied Kid Killarney looking like he was strangling in his evening clothes. Beyond him Par Virstrom perched gingerly between two brunettes. He took out a monocle, screwed it into his eye, spied me, smiled briefly and humorlessly, and then put it away again. A moment later, at my elbow, the servant Riffi served me soup harrira, a Moroccan delicacy. Our eyes met, but he gave no indication of remembering his voyeur's view of my nude horniness in Casablanca. "A fine servant," Monsieur Arafa commented as Riffi continued on down the table with the large, sculpted, traditionally free-form silver tureen and ladle. "He really knows how to give service.*"

In more ways than one! *But I did not, of course, speak the words aloud.*

*Instead of having brandy after dinner, the entire assemblage—women as well as men—retired to a large drawing room where we were served the traditional mint tea in glasses lined with the mint leaves, and* kif *in long slender clay pipes that were passed around among us. "What is it?" I whispered to Christina. I've never been into drugs very much and I was concerned.*

"*Just a form of concentrated raw-leaf marijuana,*" *she told me. "It won't hurt you.*" *She took a deep puff and passed the pipe to me.*

*I took a deep breath. I was not there, after all, to deny myself new experiences. I expelled the breath, put the mouthpiece of the pipe to my lips and inhaled deeply once again. The smoke was harsh, but it seemed to mellow out as it spread through my lungs. I sort of liked the way it made me feel—relaxed, cozy. The next time the pipe came my way, I sucked at it eagerly. The scene before me took on soft edges. Everybody seemed so friendly, so loose. This perception seemed very important to me, and I turned to share it with Christina.*

*My voluptuous young friend was otherwise occupied. She was being kissed by a young man who—through my haze—seemed to have at least a dozen hands. They were all over her, tangling in the blond hair over her see-through bodice, squeezing the delectable bare flesh of her bottom under her short skirt, prying her flushed thighs apart. Nor were her hands circumspect either. They had unbuttoned his shirt so that she might caress his bare chest while they kissed. It seemed I was not the only one the kif had loosened up.*

*"Everyone seems to be feeling quite friendly," Monsieur Arafa smiled down at me. He had discarded his dinner jacket and unbuttoned his ruffled shirt to the waist. With his red sash and firm, olive-skinned chest, he looked quite dashing.*

*"Yes." I smiled up at him encouragingly.*

*"You are my guest," he said, "and I would not want you to feel neglected."*

*"Well then," I said, made bold by the kif, "perhaps you had better not neglect me."*

*He bent and kissed the little pulse at the base of my neck. His pencil-line mustache proved surprisingly ticklish. The tip of his tongue enhanced the sensation.*

*"Why don't you sit down," I suggested, my voice husky.*

*Even as he sat, he reached for me with both hands. My half-exposed breasts were crushed against his hard chest. His kiss was fierce, demanding. His tongue played in my mouth with virtuoso expertise. The kiss left me breathless and panting.*

*"Your gown is very becoming," he told me, staring down at my breasts struggling to escape the crepe de chine.*

*"Thank you, Monsieur Arafa." I lowered my eyes with false modesty.*

*"Call me Idris."*

*"All right. Idris." Feeling as relaxed as I'd ever felt, I licked my lips voluptuously. At least I hoped it was voluptuously.*

*It must have been, since it inspired him to kiss me again. This time his hands moved over my breasts, searching out the nipples under the flimsy material, testing their firmness and finding it good. I responded by caressing his chest with my hands. His heart was beating very fast. It excited me to realize the effect I was having on him.*

*When I opened my eyes, it was to focus on Christina's pertly naked behind. She was on her hands and knees kissing her young man with her derriere sticking out at me. A man's head blotted it out as he bent to bestow a juicy kiss on it.*

*"Shall I lower the lights?" The servant Riffi was standing over us. Although his pants were traditionally baggy, there was no mistaking the erection distorting one leg of them. His eyes burned in his swarthy face with its heavy beard.*

*"Yes, Riffi. Do that," Idris told him.*

*With the lights dim, the cloud of* kif *smoke hanging over the scene became more noticeable. It seemed to emphasize the naughtiness of the writhing bodies lost in its* swirls. *Discarded clothes were starting to litter the ancient carpets and bare flesh was becoming predominant.*

"*It's warm.*" *Idris removed his ruffled shirt, and the maroon sash. Then, without asking, he removed the sparse V top of my gown. My breasts bobbled free, shiny with a soft film of perspiration, the nipples erect and straining. Idris bent his neck and licked a drop of perspiration from the tip of one nipple with his long tongue.* "*Delicious!*" *he pronounced.*

"*I'm to your taste then.*"

"*Indeed.*" *He reached into the slit of my gown and stroked my naked thigh.* "*Like satin.*" *He bent again and kissed the flesh.*

"*Higher,*" *I teased, still stoned, still bold.*

*His mouth moved higher.* "*What a delightful surprise,*" *he breathed as he discovered I wasn't wearing panties. His lips found the lips of my pussy and bestowed a deep, intense, lingering kiss.*

"*Ahh!*" *My nails dug into his shoulders as I held him there.*

"*Hey, Melinda. How's it goin'?*" *Kid Killarney materialized in front of me. He was wearing a jock strap—nothing else. His balls bulged out on either side of it.*

"*Hello, darling.*" *I smiled up at him. I loved him. I loved Idris. I loved everybody.* "*Don't I get a kiss?*"

"*Looks like you're already getting one.*" *Kid nodded down at Idris sucking at the lips of my pussy.*

"*If one's good, two is better.*" *I raised my mouth to him.*

*His kiss was a reminder of how he'd fist-fucked me on the plane. The memory excited me. I reached inside his jock and squeezed his balls.*

"*Jesus!*" *Kid whipped out his cock and shoved it in my mouth without asking permission.*

*I found myself terribly excited to be sucking it while Idris licked my cunt. I closed my eyes and let the sensations carry me along for a while. Then I opened them and saw Riffi staring at us and rubbing his crotch in the corner of the room.*

*Pushing Kid's cock from my mouth, I picked a strand of red barbed-wire groin hair from between my teeth. Then I eased Idris's head out from between my legs and closed my quivering thighs. I stood up and crossed the room to Riffi. "Do you always enjoy yourself alone?" I asked him forthrightly. "Don't you ever do anything but watch? Don't you ever participate?"*

*"I am a servant," he stammered. "It is not permitted."*

*"Nonsense." I beckoned to Idris to join us. "I want him to fuck me," I told him, indicating Riffi.*

*"Of course. Your wish is his command." Idris nodded to Riffi that it was all right.*

*"Wait," I said, then removed my dress so that I was naked. Then I got down on my hands and knees. "For being so nice about it, I'm going to be nice to you while he does it." I unzipped Idris's fly and took out his prick. "You put it up my pussy from behind," I told Riffi. "And you put it in my mouth," I instructed Idris.*

*"What about me?" Kid Killarney was back, his pug face screwed up with the hurt of having been rejected.*

*"More than one way to skin a cat," I reminded him. I arranged things so that the ferociously bearded Riffi was on his back with his black cock sticking straight up in the air. I impaled myself on it and then bent forward to take Idris in my mouth. I wiggled my ass to let Kid know that it was all right to put his prick where his fist had been. A moment later I felt him shoving it up my ass and then there was the glorious sensation of the two pricks—the black one and the white one—rubbing against each other through the delicate partition of skin separating my cunt from my anus.*

*I felt depraved, I felt glorious. Impaled on Riffi's perpendicular cock, I was bent in such a way that my breasts dangled over his swarthy face. His thick black beard tickled them maddeningly as he sucked at the nipples by turn. His muscular butt jerked up and down as he drove his prick in and out of my tight, wet, clutching pussy. I gloried in the way its rigid length and breadth overstuffed my tingling cunt.*

*Riffi was built powerfully, and that was good since Kid Killarney, although sprawled over my ass, was actually pounding into me in such a way as to put the strain on the swarthy servant. Kid's strong, calloused boxer hands clutched my hips, but his weight was on the determined hard-on corkscrewing in my anus. The red Brillo hairs of his groin tickled my nether cheeks excruciatingly, and his balls felt like hot coals bouncing against them.*

*The sensation prompted me to take Idris's balls in my mouth one at a time and lick them. He was kneeling at Riffi's head, his knees on either side of Riffi's cheeks, his cock sticking out over Riffi's face for me to kiss and lick and suck. As its throbbing prompted me to take it in my mouth again, a distraction caused me to glance sideways.*

*The first thing I saw was Christina, still in her see-through mini-gown, doubled over in a ball with her arms wrapped around her ankles. Her wide-spread cunt was completely exposed, raw and pink against the golden curls spilling over from the base of her belly. Some distance away from her, three young men were lined up with naked erections sticking out in front of them. One by one they charged her, thrust their cocks into her cunt, withdrew, and stepped aside for the next man. They kept lining up over and over again and the pitch of Christina's squeals became more and more hysterical with each new assault on her throbbing pussy.*

*Suddenly, unexpectedly, a new man charged her from the side. His plump, girlish behind shook like jelly as he thrust his smallish erection into Christina. Behind him, a naked Berber woman with a vicious-looking whip cracked it over his buttocks repeatedly. The flaying added to the fresh welts appearing there. It also inspired him to stab into the provocatively exposed cunt repeatedly. The way the behind moved identified Par Virstrom for me even before I saw his face.*

*One of the young men who'd been taking turns came up and pushed Par away from Christina. That's when his eyes lit on me. With the whiplash still snapping at his haunches, Par came over to our squirming little group.*

*"Doesn't that hurt?" I asked him as the Berber woman beat him virtually under my nose.*

*"Oh, yes. Deliciously!"*

*"Please!" Idris's abandoned cock stabbed impatiently at my cheek. "Resume."*

*"Sorry." I took it in my hand and put it back in my mouth. Then, on impulse, I seized Par's prick, sticky with Christina's pussy juice, and forced it in beside Idris's organ.*

*It felt small by comparison. But when the lash fell on Par's plump buttocks again, it jumped in such a way as to thrill and excite Idris as well as me. Kid's cock in my asshole rubbed up against the impalement of Riffi's prick in my cunt. There were now four pricks inside me. I stopped thinking and simply let the delirious feeling of approaching orgasm engulf me.*

*The two pricks fucked inside me as the four swollen balls bounced and rolled over my chin. I had a finger up both Par's and Idris's asses now. I felt crammed with hot, about-to-explode cock—my mouth, my cunt, my ass. I felt myself letting go with an orgasm that started at my toes and swirled the red-gold curls on top of my head. Idris came in my mouth, and with the jerk of a whiplash, Par came with him. Their combined jism washed down my gulping throat as Kid Killarney's cock in my ass erupted with a violence that abraded Riffi's prick up my cunt and brought it off as well. Jism was dripping from my mouth, my cunt, my ass as I kept on coming and coming and coming . . .*

*They say life begins at forty, but I was only thirty-eight years old. What wonders might the future hold? The possibilities seemed limitless.*

*After all, my fantasy had actually come true!*

# CHAPTER NINE

Such was Melinda Holloway's account of the first night of
the Fez orgy as related to the fully attended meeting of our
first women's consciousness-raising group following our
return from Morocco. After the cancellation of the previous month's meeting for the various reasons already described, it was no easy job to get everybody to agree on a
time and a place for us all to assemble. The general apathy
about such a meeting said that our group was in danger of
breaking apart permanently.

"Our esprit has sprung," was the way I put it to
Melinda when I called her a couple of weeks after we
came back.

"What's there to talk about?" she yawned.

"You're a perfect example. You're apathetic."

"I'm tired, Christina. When you're my age, orgies leave
you weary. I just don't have the energy to get all exercised
over the group the way you do."

"Don't you want to see it go on?"

"I suppose so."

"Will you come to a meeting next Thursday if I can set
it up?"

"Gee, Thursday. I don't know."

"Please, Melinda!" I wheedled.

"Oh, all right, Christina. If you can get the rest of them to come, I'll be there."

That wasn't easy. Helen Willis had found Malcolm too mercurial to hold onto as a lover, so she couldn't use him as an excuse not to attend. Nevertheless, she seemed reluctant. "Things have sort of settled down to okay with Bruno," she told me. "If I say I'm going to one of our meetings, it'll make waves."

"Make waves," I urged her. "Don't go back to being a doormat."

"I don't think I'm doing that, Christina."

There was just enough doubt in Helen's voice for me to work on. By pushing, I was finally able to get her to reluctantly agree to attend the meeting, if I could set it up. Counting myself, that made three of us that would be there.

"You're the only holdout," I lied to Joyce Dell.

"I just don't feel like I'm getting anything out of it. Maybe it's because the rest of you are older than I am."

"Not that much older. Besides, what do you want? Instant gratification? Youth doesn't entitle you to that any more than maturity does."

"Why not?" Joyce wanted to know. "Why doesn't it?"

It was not an argument I particularly wanted to get into. "I'm going to bring jellybeans from Woolworth's," I coaxed. Joyce was ape when it came to jellybeans.

In the end I persuaded her with the promise of a bonus of a quarter-pound bag for her alone. Jellybean freaks are like that.

Stephanie McCall was a tougher case. She was negative about the group. I suspected it had something to do with her rape, but if that was so, she wasn't verbalizing it. Instead, she was voicing a different sort of disillusionment.

"Nobody's really frank," Stephanie said, her tone bitter. "There's too much equivocation, too much ducking of feelings, particularly when it comes to sex."

"I thought we were starting to be pretty frank about that," I argued.

"Have you been frank, Christina? At least the rest of us have discussed our fantasies. You've even balked at doing that."

I had to admit the justice in what she said. "Listen, Stephanie," I told her earnestly. "I'll make you a promise. If you'll come to the meeting Thursday, I'll describe my sex fantasy in detail."

"You might not be so wise to do that, Christina." She laughed harshly. "Once you tell your fantasy, it has a way of coming true. And that can be devastating."

"Is that what happened to you, angel?"

"I'm not baring my libido any more," Stephanie said, neither confirming nor denying it.

"Will you come to the meeting if I do what I said?"

"I guess so, Christina. Curiosity always has been my weak point."

That left Amanda Briggs. There had been no contact between us since the night she had hung up the phone in my ear. I expected that if I called her she would be hostile.

"Christina van Bell!" Amanda answered, her tone a snarl set in ice.

"Don't hang up!" I exclaimed quickly. "Please!"

"What do you want?"

"Our group is meeting. I want you to come."

"I don't think so."

"Everybody will be there."

"And you need the token dyke?" Amanda was stubborn. "Is that it?"

"You know that's not it. Don't make out like you're

just a stereotype to us. You're not. We want you to be with us. We love you. We need you.''

"Just as long as you don't have to listen to me, right? After all, I might just say something you don't want to hear about a friend of yours. Sisterhood is one thing, but a friend—well now, that's really an important relationship.''

"Listen, Amanda, even if you did have an affair with Diana Coltrane and it ended badly, which it obviously must have, you're not going to make me feel guilty for remaining a friend of hers. Besides, even if you feel negatively toward me, what about the rest of our group? They're not involved. They care about you. How can you just turn your back on them out of pique?''

"They're all going to be there?'' Amanda weakened.

"Every one of us.''

"All right. I'll come.'' She didn't sound any friendlier, but at least she had made the concession, no matter how grudgingly.

The meeting was held at my Park Avenue penthouse apartment. I'd arranged for a lavish spread of caviar and champagne. With all of the negativism being harbored by the individuals who made up our group, I figured loosening everybody up was a must. The champagne had some effect, and then Melinda Holloway's detailed and raunchy account of how her orgy fantasy came true relaxed us all still more. Indeed, hints of the old togetherness were definitely in the air when Stephanie McCall shook out her blue-black hair like a lioness ruffing out her mane and firmly requested with Bryn Mawr arrogance that I deliver on the promise I had made her.

"Your fantasy, Christina,'' Stephanie demanded, one hand on an arrogantly jutting hip, oblong breasts firmly establishing their banana curve against the jacket of the expensive tweed suit she was wearing. "The time has come for you to tell it to us."

"All right. I just hope you're not all disappointed. You see, there's nothing that unusual or bizarre about it. As a matter of fact, darlings, I suspect that many women harbor a fantasy similar to mine." I hugged the tightly clinging silk caftan I'd purchased in the Fez medina to my bosom. "As you all may know, I am not entirely without erotic experience."

"That has got to be the understatement of the year!" Melinda Holloway interjected, doubtless remembering various views of me in the midst of the orgy at the Arafa villa.

"Nevertheless," I continued, "there is one experience which I have never had and which piques my sensual imagination."

"What's that?" Joyce Dell asked.

"It's the woman's version of sex without emotional involvement," Helen Willis answered for me. "And frankly, I don't think it's too realistic in terms of human behavior."

"Not to judge, darling," I reminded her. "It's my fantasy, after all. Besides, there's more to the concept than that. The thing is that what's envisioned is pure eroticism. The virile, handsome stranger arrives. His clothes melt away. Your clothes melt away. The two of you have sex. It's a peak experience. The stranger departs. No complications. No sweat. No body odors. No discovery of each other's shortcomings."

"In other words, no humanity involved," Helen said disapprovingly.

"Perhaps." I shrugged. "But that's not the point. Pure sex. That's the point."

"And that's your big fantasy? I think I read about that

somewhere." It was the first time Amanda Briggs had spoken to me all night and she was openly contemptuous.

"No. My fantasy goes a lot farther than that."

"Then get down to it, Christina." Stephanie was urgently curious. "Describe it to us."

"Well, there are a lot of different versions," I hedged.

"Pick one, dammit!" Amanda was still hostile.

"All right." I inhaled deeply. The silk of the caftan caressed the nipples of my breasts. There was inspiration in this self-titillation. "In my version I have just arrived at the latest 'in' disco to dance, when suddenly there is a blackout. The entire city has been plunged into darkness. I am in the center of a milling crowd on the dance floor of this posh club. My escort had gone to fetch us drinks and now he is lost in the blackness. I am totally alone among strangers. I am vulnerable."

"A blackout?" Amanda jeered. "That seems a bit much to base a fantasy on."

"It wouldn't have to be a blackout," I explained. "Any situation dark enough for anonymity in a crowd would do. An unlit New Orleans street during Mardis gras, for instance. A subway train with the lights out. Even a darkened movie theater."

"Go on with the disco scene," Melinda suggested. "Don't let Amanda intimidate you."

"The crowd is packed pretty tightly," I resumed. "And although the strobes are out, the disco music is still blaring out its pronounced, erotic beat."

"Where is the electricity coming from for that?" Amanda wouldn't let up.

"Batteries," young Joyce said, waving away the objection. "Who cares. This is supposed to be a fantasy."

"People push up against me," I continued. "I'm wearing a simple black sheath of pima cotton—light-weight for dancing. It's mini with a strapless top. I'm not wearing anything under it. The pressure of the crowd pushes it all the way up between my legs and crushes it against my breasts. It's very hot and the air conditioning's out and everybody's perspiring. The disco scene . . . all those bodies . . . not much clothes . . . The crowd excites me.''

"Crowds excite you?" Joyce Dell was puzzled.

"Yes."

"You must love rush hour." Young Joyce still didn't understand.

"It's not that." I tried to clarify. "It's the idea of sex with people all around and not knowing what you're doing. I suppose it's childish, but it's the getting away with something right in the middle of everybody. Pulling it off, if you will.''

"Pulling him off?" Now it was Helen who misunderstood.

"No. Or at least not necessarily."

"Let's stop interrogating Christina," Stephanie suggested. The chic brunette really did want to hear my fantasy. "Let's just be quiet and let her tell it in her own way. Now you're on the floor of this disco," she prompted me. "The lights have gone out. Your escort is lost somewhere in the darkness. Hot, perspiring bodies are pressing in all around you. The music is blaring and people are dancing. You're wearing this wisp of a dress and it's being pushed up into your pussy and crushed over your breasts. What happens then, Christina?''

"A hand circles my waist in the darkness. It's strong, a man's hand. It pulls me through the press of bodies until I'm up against the chest of the man to whom the hand belongs. I can't see him. I can only feel his chest against my breasts. He's taller than I am. His chest is very broad. He's wearing a silk disco shirt and it's unbuttoned in a deep V to the waist. There's a light matting of curly hair on his chest. It tickles my nipples through the cotton of my dress. 'Dance?' he asks, his voice very sure of itself. His hands are already holding me by the hips. 'All right,' I tell him, then clasp my hands around his invisible neck. He moves against me intimately, belly to belly, thigh to thigh. His pants are very tight and I can feel the ridge of muscles over his belly and the hard tendons of his legs.

"Behind me an anonymous man's behind is grinding against mine, forcing me to step in more closely, to rub more intimately against my unknown partner. I feel his prick climbing his belly. Soon it is a hard ridge crushed between us. We are standing on one spot now. It is too crowded to move. Hot, perspiring bodies push us this way and that and I cling to him for support. His hand moves up from my hip to lift my chin. The blackness deepens as I close my eyes while his mouth covers mine. There is laughter around us and some chattering. I hear it as we kiss. His tongue in my mouth excites me. My own tongue moves wildly in response. His hands are both over my breasts, squeezing them through the cotton. People bump against us. It excites me that they are so close and don't know what we're doing. I roll my belly voluptuously over his stiff, trouser-penned cock. 'Do you like the way that feels?' The kiss is over and his tongue is in my ear now as he speaks. There is no need for me to answer. The movements of my body against him are reply enough. His fingers are playing with my nipples through the cotton now. Our dance is a travesty, but in the pitch blackness, who is there to know?

"Indeed, the crowd is an ally to our eroticism. Each time it shifts, we are pressed into new intimacies. He rolls down the strapless top of my dress. My breasts swing free. Now I am really excited! Suppose someone bumps up against me and discerns my breasts' nakedness? The danger of being found out heightens my raunchiness. I slide my hand over his muscular belly and fondle his erection through his pants. His hands are firm over my ass now, crushing my miniskirt shamelessly, holding me tight against him. He bends and licks my nipples. Then he kisses them and sucks them. I moan, beyond caring that any of the dancers around us may hear.

"Somebody is pushing against my partner from behind, forcing his cock to jab into my belly. The insides of my thighs become slick with the honey this provokes. He covers my trembling hand with his own, then pushes it aside and opens the zipper of his pants. I encircle his hard-on with both my hands. It is huge, quite thick, and the hair of his groin is smooth and silky as gossamer. His balls burn in the palms of my hand. I am quite beside myself now. There are people all around us. The lights may go on at any moment. My escort may return with our drinks. Yet here I am squeezing the jism-tight balls of a total stranger while his strong hands reach between my legs from behind and separate the pulsing, inflamed lips of my pussy. I'm fondling his cock! He's working a finger up my tight, honeyed cunt! And nobody knows! Nobody knows! They're all around us, bumping against us, touching us, and they don't know what we're doing. I am as turned on as I have ever been.

" 'Fuck me!' I want to say into the invisible ear. 'Put your thick cock up my squirming cunt and fuck me right here in the middle of all these people! Fuck me!' But before I can find the courage to whisper the words, he breathes his own hot words into my ear. 'We're going to do it!' he says. It's a statement, not a question. He isn't asking me, he's telling me. 'Right here! Right now!' His hands go under my miniskirt and lock under my naked ass. My hands are already clasped around his neck. He lifts me. I feel the wedge-shaped head of his cock as it thrashes between my wide-spread thighs, seeking the entrance to my pussy. I take one hand from his neck just long enough to guide it.

Then I clasp my hands behind his neck again. I lock my ankles around his waist. His hands, still clasped under the miniskirt, support me. One of his fingers finds its way to my anus and thrusts deeply upward.

"In my down-hanging position, I am particularly vulnerable. The thrill propels me forward. My cunt slaps wetly against his pelvis and it sucks up all of his hard cock—deep inside itself. He contrives to lift one of my breasts to his mouth and to suck on it as he moves back and forth, fucking me. I moan, and then I groan. His panting is likewise audible. Both sounds are lost, however, in the blaring disco rhythms. And the people who are still constantly bumping against us—even against the naked, sticky-wet parts of our bodies—do not catch on to the fact that we are standing there in the middle of the crowd fucking each other as hard and hot and deep as we know how.

" 'I'm coming!' I blurt out finally, digging my nails into the back of his neck. My legs clench around his midsection and my bottom bounces in his hands. 'I'm coming!' I squish my quim up and down his cock, my clitty riding the shaft. 'I'm coming!' Suddenly he slams us back against a couple dancing behind us. They are still complaining goodnaturedly about the force of the collision as his cock erupts inside of me. I squeal and half cry as I feel the scalding cream filling my climaxing pussy. My cunt keeps squeezing his cock frantically and sucking up the geyser as one strong jet follows another. Finally we swing around in a last, mad, whirling prolongation of our ecstasy, and then it's over. He sets me on my feet. He releases me. He vanishes. My wonderful, invisible, anonymous lover is once again just another member of the unseen crowd."

There was a long silence after I stopped talking. Finally Joyce broke it. "What happens then?" she wondered.

"Nothing much." I shrugged. "I clean myself up as

best I can. The lights go back on. My date comes back with our drinks. We dance."

"But what about the guy?" Joyce exclaimed. "Don't you finally get to find out who he is?"

"How?" I smiled because she still didn't understand. "He's just part of the crowd now. He doesn't know who I am and I don't know who he is. That's what makes it so wonderful. It's the perfect fuck and it's carried off in a crowd and it's completely anonymous. That's the whole point of the fantasy!"

"Why rip it apart?" Melinda shrugged. "It's her fantasy. Let her enjoy it. The reality will wipe it out soon enough."

"That's right." All of the others nodded agreement. "That's what happens. That's the way it works out."

I looked at them in consternation. "What's this you're all saying?"

"That fantasies are only fantasies," Helen answered me. "Actual experience is something else."

"That's right." Joyce Dell stretched her coltish legs. "Something different."

"Very different!" Stephanie McCall shuddered.

"You can say that again!" Melinda's cynicism was repeated.

"In spades!" Amanda Briggs chimed in with her bitterness.

"Wait a minute! Wait a minute!" I shook my head to clear the cobwebs. I was appalled. "Be more specific. Explain yourselves. Helen—" I turned to my slender friend with the outsize breasts. "You described your sex life with Bruno as a disaster *sans* orgasm. Are you going to tell us now that the affair you had wasn't an improvement over it?"

"Sure it was an improvement over what used to be with

Bruno. I never said it wasn't. I only said that reality and fantasy are two very different things."

"Are you saying that when your fantasy turned into a reality with Malcolm you were disappointed?"

"That's hard to answer. It was a marvelous erotic experience, and yet in a way I suppose I was disappointed. You see, it didn't change the reality of my life."

"You never said you expected it to!" I protested.

"You're right. I didn't. I don't think I ever thought of it that way. But somewhere buried in my subconscious, I think that is what I was expecting. You see, with Malcolm at first it really was my fantasy come to life. He was a suave, sophisticated, considerate lover—just the opposite of my husband. But it was ephemeral, transient. There was no permanence to it."

"You wanted permanence?"

"Could there be any satisfaction without permanence?" Helen spread her hands.

"Yes!" I said emphatically.

"Not for me!" she said with equal strength.

"Different strokes," Melinda murmured, looking from one to the other of us. The other members of the group nodded agreement.

"Well, if it was permanence you were after, Malcolm certainly wasn't the man for you," I granted to Helen.

"No. He wasn't. He was the man for my fantasy, but not for my reality. And in the end my affair with him, hot as it was, destroyed the fantasy. The fact is I don't think I'll ever be able to enjoy the fantasy again."

"But where does that leave you, darling?" I asked, genuinely concerned.

"Stuck with commitment," she smiled wryly. "I've got two kids, don't forget. Not to mention Bruno."

"How are things with Bruno?" Joyce wondered. "Still the same?"

"Not quite," Helen said hesitantly, groping for the words. "Since Malcolm, I've been able to say right out what I want when Bruno and I make love. At first he was shocked. Bruno really is a throwback, you know. But now he seems to be getting over that and my speaking up turns him on. For the first time in a long time, I feel like I'm really holding his interest. I don't think he'll be looking for greener pastures for a while."

"What about you? Will you be seeing Malcolm again? Maybe somebody else?" I asked.

"If I get bored with Bruno." Her tone said Helen really had changed. "But basically I'm committed to making our marriage work, and to improving our sex life." She smiled impishly. "I had an orgasm with Bruno for the first time last night," she confessed.

"Then maybe the fantasy did accomplish something," I said, trying to reassure her.

"It accomplished a lot of things, Christina. But if you really want to know what spoiled it, it was you."

"You mean because I was there? Because I was a part of the sex scene with Malcolm?"

"No. I mean your manipulating. I mean my always being aware that you were contriving things."

"That's not fair!" I was defensive.

"Probably not," Helen sighed. "But it's true. People don't like being manipulated, Christina. It may make their fantasies come true, but it also ruins them."

"That's right," Joyce Dell chimed in. "When you feel like a puppet, it spoils things."

"Did you feel like a puppet in California with Lord Alfred?" I demanded.

"A lady's maid? Me? How else could I feel?"

"That was only your job. I'm talking about your fantasy. I wasn't even there. How can you accuse me of pulling the strings?"

"I suppose you really didn't," Joyce granted. "All the same, I have to agree with Helen. The reality sure shattered the fantasy. I mean, what it boiled down to was this creaky old man trying to piss all over me. He was urbane and sophisticated like in my fantasy, but the reality is he just plain couldn't cut the mustard. After the first time, it was a drag. It taught me that simple balling with a young, energetic stud is more satisfying."

"Then you agree with Helen," I sighed. "The reality shattered the fantasy."

"It sure as hell did for me!" Stephanie McCall piped up. "But I don't blame you, Christina. You had nothing to do with my being raped."

I winced and bit my tongue and listened.

"You were raped?" Melinda asked, shocked, as were the others.

"Yes," Stephanie said, then described what had happened. Her account pretty much agreed with Lucien's report. What was different was the tone of loathing with which she related the incident. "It's not the physical thing I'm talking about," she tried to explain. "A cock was forcibly rammed into my pussy. It aroused me. I had an orgasm. It was brutal and it hurt a little, but I suppose that's what I wanted. I mean, what did I have to complain about? I'd fantasized it a hundred times. I'd tried to provoke it I don't know how often. And finally I succeeded. So why do I feel so awful? About myself, I mean."

"You were forced, that's why!" Amanda Briggs's excess flesh was trembling with indignation as she spoke. "You were insulted—deeply and basically insulted. As a woman. And as a feminist, too."

"I'm some feminist," Stephanie confessed, shaking her head with self-disgust. "My fantasy wasn't bad enough when it came to confirming the stereotype macho men like to have of women. I had to go get myself raped and prove they were right.''

_''You didn't get yourself raped,'' I said, unable to stand by and watch Stephanie heap any more guilt on herself. "I did.''

"What do you mean, Christina?''

I confessed what I had done. I told about having gone to Pogo the Player. I described the meeting with Lucien and Gunther. I revealed how Stephanie's rape had been set up by me.

"But why?'' Stephanie stared at me with bewilderment and hurt.

"I was afraid that if you kept on the way you were going you'd get yourself raped by real rapists, maybe even killed.''

"In other words, Christina the manipulator did it for your own good, Stephanie,'' Amanda Briggs said bitterly to Stephanie. "Isn't that right, Christina?''

"I thought it was,'' I pleaded. "I really did.''

"Well, at least you cured her of her fantasy,'' Melinda said drily. Perhaps she was trying to make me feel better. If so, she didn't succeed.

"And did I cure you of yours, too?'' I inquired of Melinda, my ego plummeting.

"As a matter of fact, I think you did.''

"Now just a minute!'' I rallied. "I was at the orgy, too, remember?''

"How could I forget? You arranged it for me, didn't you?''

"No! I didn't!''

"Well, you certainly arranged for me to be there. And you did that so I could act out my fantasy of having four men at once, didn't you?''

"Well, it did all seem to come together,'' I admitted. "But what's wrong with that?''

"You manipulate so much you don't even know when you are manipulating!" Amanda Briggs interjected bitterly.

"Oh, I don't care about that," Melinda said, dismissing Amanda's comment. "And I enjoyed myself at the orgy— at least at first. I won't argue with Christina about that."

"Then in what way did it spoil your fantasy?" I wanted to know.

"By making me face my limitations." Melinda spread her hands ruefully. "I'm thirty-eight years old," she said. "My fantasy coming true made me realize what that means. You see, when I used to think about it—four studs all concentrating on me, down and dirty, pure raunch—it never occurred to me that there would come a point where fatigue might set in. But that's what happened. These guys were balling me and buggering me and I was sucking them, and I got so tired I couldn't wait for it to end. Also, I was bruised and sore. Worst of all, I became bored. Yes, bored with men who boiled down to nothing but pricks stuck in parts of me that were already sore. But you know what's really terrible? I'll never be able to fantasize that scene again without shuddering!"

"My efforts seem to have flopped all the way down the line." My voice rang bitter in my ears.

"It's a little late to be sorry!" Amanda said, seemingly unable to pass up an opportunity to zing me again.

It was too much. "Now you just listen to me, sweetie!" I turned on her, snarling. "Everybody else may have good reason to dump on me, but I'm damned if I know what your complaint is!"

"My complaint? Just that thanks to your meddling I had one of the worst times in my whole life!"

"Meddling? I didn't meddle. You were interested in Diana Coltrane. All I did was invite you to a dinner party where you could meet her."

"Of course it was just by accident that we were the only

two women at the party without male companions, and
that we both were open to lesbian experiences!''

"I hoped it would work out. You said you fantasized
sex with Diana as the aggressor. She'd mentioned she
would welcome a relationship with a white woman who
wouldn't mind being subservient. I didn't see any harm in
bringing you together.''

"No harm!'' Amanda snarled, beside herself. "No harm
indeed!''

"Why don't you tell us what happened?'' Melinda said,
trying to calm Amanda down. "You'll feel better if you
get it off your chest instead of generating all that hostility.
Really you will.''

"I suppose you're right.'' Amanda took a deep breath.
"I left Christina's dinner party with Diana Coltrane. I was
really star-struck. She was every bit as shining and black
and beautiful as I'd thought she would be. She liked me,
too, I could tell. Some people look at me and what I see in
their eyes is that I'm a little overweight, a little chunky—
pretty enough, but not dynamically attractive. But what I
saw in Diana's eyes was that my flesh was voluptuous,
that she wanted to wallow in it, in short, that she dug me.
We went back to her place. She asked me and I said okay.
It was that simple. Two days later Diana took a leave of
absence from her show and we left together for the Costa
del Sol in Spain.''

"Just like that?'' Helen was impressed.

"Just like that. We were in love, you see.'' Amanda's
tone softened in spite of herself, in spite of her bitterness.
"That first night sealed it. The nights that followed confirmed it.''

"What happened?'' Joyce asked.

"Christina. Christina happened.''

"What are you talking about?'' I exclaimed. "I wasn't
even there.''

"You might as well have been!"

"Will you kindly tell us just what it is that happened?" I demanded.

"All right. It was one night when we'd been in Spain about a week. Everything was going just the way I'd fantasized it. Diana was forceful and aggressive and domineering. I was soft and compliant, happy to cater to her whims. The Spanish moon smiled on the twinings of our black and white bodies."

"This one night we'd taken our mattress out on the walled-in terrace. The sky was splashed with stars and it was very bright out there. We lay down in each other's arms and we kissed. We were both very hot. Diana's long, sleek, ebony body writhed like a snake against me. My plump white flesh was slick with perspiration as it squirmed to envelop her.

"There are pictures in my mind—flashes of memory: Diana sucking on my breast, her pointy red tongue circling the wide aureole, her lips closing around the nipple . . . her slender, delicate hands kneading the baby fat of my thighs, parting them, reaching under me, wallowing in the flesh of my ass . . . her hand over mine then, taking it, guiding it to her wet, trembling pussy, pushing my fingers inside to where the stiff clitty was waiting . . . And finally her hand between my legs, the small fist she made, my fearful joy as it widened the lips of my pussy and sort of screwed up inside me . . .

"It was like nothing I'd ever felt before. I was frigging Diana, but all of my attention was on my pussy and her fist. I contrived to bend my knees and stretch my legs wide apart so that my hungry cunt sort of widened and popped up. Diana's knuckles went up higher, her fist turned and ground inside my pussy. The sensation was excruciating—ecstatic, painful, indescribable.

"Suddenly her other hand slid into the cleft between the

generous cheeks of my ass and clenched. Now there were two small black fists inside me. The tears streamed down my cheeks. My ass and cunt were both jerking violently. I was being thoroughly fist-fucked—up my anus, up my pussy—and there is nothing like it. I could see Diana's fist buried in my quim to the wrist, the swollen lips of my pussy clutching at its delicate bones. I could feel her other fist reaming me and I could visualize her very arm buried between the fleshy cheeks of my ass. I could see her cunt jerking violently against my hand with the excitement of what she was doing. I could see her nipples stabbing the air like small daggers. I could see the cruel way her expressive mouth twisted, the dominance shining from her eyes.

"It was what we wanted, what we both wanted—she to dominate, I to be the passive victim. But then, just as I was on the verge of coming—and perhaps Diana was, too—she went one step too far." Remembering, Amanda Briggs shuddered.

"What did she do?" Melinda asked gently.

"She slammed both fists into me at once. Hard! Very hard, so that it really hurt! And she said, 'How do you like that, Christina?' "

"She called you Christina?" I was beginning to understand.

"Yes! And she was using me to get even with you. You must have hurt Diana a lot, Christina. What did you do to her?"

"Made love to her. That was all. It upset her. I know that. I thought it was because we were both women. But later she told me it was because I was so aggressive and white and that reminded her that she was black and made her feel used."

"If you knew her problem," Amanda demanded, "how could you get me involved in a situation like that?"

"You aren't aggressive like me. You're passive. I thought that would work out all right for the two of you."

"She didn't want me. She wanted to get even with you. Maybe with all white people. After that night, the meeker I was, the more vicious she became. She went from being domineering to being downright sadistic. I was hooked on her and she knew it and she took advantage of it. She even got to calling me by your name to make me cry. Finally I couldn't take it anymore. I left."

"She didn't like that," I realized, remembering my short phone conversation with Diana the night she'd hung up on me. "If there's one thing Diana can't stand, it's rejection."

"It was the most miserable experience I ever had!" Amanda summed up.

"And you blame me for it?"

"Well—"

"That's okay. I guess I do have a large share of the responsibility. I guess I really have made a mess of things." I looked from one to another of the group. "Not one of your fantasies really worked out," I realized. "Not one!"

I was really disillusioned. Fantasies, it seems, must always be doomed to failure. The reality can never live up to the vision. It's always a disappointment.

Isn't it?

# CHAPTER TEN

As painful as it had been for me personally, for our group as a whole that meeting was cathartic. Purging themselves of the anger and disillusionment resulting from the actualization of their fantasies seemed to free the women to get back on the consciousness-raising track which had been the original purpose of our meetings. Sex receded as the focus. We no longer concentrated on eroticism, neither its frustrations nor its satisfactions. We realized once again what we had known instinctively when we first started to meet: Sexual desires and problems, imagined and real, are symptomatic of the deeper questions related to our functioning as women in a male-dominated world.

How disappointed Malcolm Gold would have been to learn that more important issues had eclipsed our pantings for coital fulfillment. I did not confide in him, of course. He was the wrong gender; it was really none of his business. Besides, I'm not sure he would have believed that a group of women would rather spend their time discussing political strategy for the passing of the ERA than techniques of cocksucking. Malcolm may have been modern enough to perceive that sex objects have brains, but he had not yet reached the point of realizing that they might rather use them than their pussies.

Such is male folklore regarding women. Such are the stereotypes to which we are expected to conform. Emotion—translation: sexual appetite—is supposed to rule us, to render our intellects ineffectual. To set aside our fluttery clitties in favor of feminist consciousness raising was an act of rebellion. And so we rebelled.

Because of the tenor of the meetings, the weeks which followed were a most satisfying period for me personally. I was able to get past my guilt, even to absolve myself to some extent. I was sorry I had been manipulative, and if being manipulative was a part of my nature, I would certainly make an effort to keep it in check in future. These meetings put it into perspective, reinforced other, perhaps more desirable, aspects of my character, defined me in more positive terms rather than by the flaw of being overcontrolling in relationship to my sisters and their fantasies. I came to terms with myself and my nature, and my love for my sisters grew because they helped me to do this.

Alas, I was less able to come to terms with my disappointment regarding the seeming impossibility of actualizing my own sex fantasies satisfactorily. I am, my dears, a romantic at heart. This strain runs deep in my character. I had been gored badly by the results of my meddling. To give up the dream that sex dreams can come true was to me as traumatic as a child's shattering realization that there is no Santa Claus. The loss of erotic anticipation is a major loss indeed.

Nevertheless, I accepted it. I filed my fantasy in the Inactive file. I resigned myself to the mundane and convinced myself of how much more mature it was to fuck with the body than with the mind. But I confess, like

O'Neill's characters in *The Iceman Cometh,* I was finding that my fantasyless beer seemed to have a lot less fizz.

Time passed. One month. Two. Three. I was as erotically active as I had ever been, which is very active indeed. I was growing quite accustomed to flat beer. Actually, I no longer noticed that the fizz was gone.

Malcolm discerned a change in me. "You're becoming quite mellow, Christina," he remarked one evening when we were having an after-work cocktail together.

Well, darlings, that was one way of viewing it. "I suppose I am." My answer was noncommittal.

"I miss the old spark, though," he added.

"I'm tired." I shrugged it off. "It's been a long day."

"I didn't just mean this evening."

"It's been a long summer."

"It's not over yet," he pointed out.

"I suppose not."

"Which reminds me, the DeVanders are having a Labor Day Eve party and we're invited. Would you like to go?"

"All right."

"You don't sound very enthusiastic," Malcolm said, peering at me over the rim of his martini glass.

"It's just that I'm tired, I told you. I *would* like to go."

"All right, then. It's settled. I'll accept for both of us."

The DeVanders were a young couple with new money and new morals. Their estate on the North Shore of Long Island was one of the showplaces of the region. They kept their own stables and riding trails crisscrossed their wooded, somewhat hilly acreage. Their pool was larger than the public one at Jones Beach; their gardens sculpted by a landscape architect hired away from the Bronx Botanical Gardens; their outdoor tennis courts shaded by stately, transplanted oaks; and their indoor courts air-conditioned and with easy access to saunas and steam room. There were separate showers at either end of their nine-hole golf course. Three masseurs and three masseuses were among the forty-two permanent members of their household staff. Their parties were large and not very intimate.

Ralph DeVander was of the order nouveau riche. He was all white teeth and suntan. His sun-bleached hair and his muscles testified to his prowess at just about every sport. He was an accomplished yachtsman, polo player, fox hunter and womanizer. He brought a similar expertise to all of these diverse activities—and a similar lack of emotional involvement. We had gone to bed together in the past and I had found Ralph expert, tireless, and finally rather boring. I would have liked him so much better, you see, darlings, if there had only been just one pimple on his ass.

Sissy DeVander, Ralph's wife, was more flesh and blood than he, but inhibited by a snobbishness intrinsic to her birth and breeding. She really couldn't help it. As much a libertine as her husband, and blessed with a pale, bosomy, Anglo body, long, supple, clutching legs, and a motorized libido, she was nevertheless hampered by her inability to feel at ease in the sack with anybody whose ancestors had come to America after the Revolution. While she had been known to fuck plebeians, she had not been known to admit enjoying it.

Their parties were not orgies. While guests were not required to refrain from erotic activity, they were expected always to be discreet. No balling in front of the servants. Particularly on Labor Day.

"Why a Labor Day party?" Lowell Delano was greeting Ralph DeVander as Malcolm and I emerged from our limousine. "Don't you think celebrating the damn day might be interpreted by the blighters as encouragement?" Lowell had been Ralph's roommate at Princeton. Now, not yet thirty, he was a tax consultant employed by one of the most prestigious law firms on Wall Street.

"I hadn't thought of it," Ralph admitted. "Sissy just picked it off the calendar because it was a holiday."

"Should be more careful in times like these, old buddy. If we don't protect class distinctions, who will?" Lowell turned to kiss Sissy on the cheek as Ralph came down the steps to greet us. Lowell squeezed Sissy's left buttock familiarly as soon as his "old buddy's" back was turned to him. The footman standing in the open doorway behind Sissy pretended not to notice. The trousers of his livery, however, were very tight. The sudden bulge which appeared at the crotch bespoke proletarian envy of the caress.

"Get Mr. Gold's and Miss van Bell's bags, Horace." Sissy, still wriggling under Lowell's fondling, issued the order to the footman without turning around. The bulge jutted sharply as Horace trotted down the steps to comply.

Lowell stood behind Sissy and continued to grope her as she kissed me on the cheek by way of greeting. Standing there in his gray pinstriped Brooks Brothers suit, he was the image of that respectability so treasured by the financial community. Only a trained observer's eye like mine would have discerned the naughtiness of his hands still investigating the hallowed succulence of Sissy DeVander's ass.

A sly and subtle operator! Such was Lowell Delano's Wall Street reputation. As dark as Ralph DeVander was fair, he was a brooding, wealthy young man who believed in the system and in his inalienable right to fondle any female of whatever station who happened to cross his path.

"Christina," he greeted me with a kiss, his close-clipped mustache a caterpillar investigating the terrain of my lips. At the same time he contrived to get one well-manicured hand between us to squeeze my breast.

"Don't do that!" I slapped his hand away sharply, making it very obvious why I was rebuking him.

Horace the footman squelched a snicker. He was a

young fellow, probably well-hung. There was a certain mirth lurking in his green eyes, a glimmering of a twist at the lips which seemed to say he found the cavortings of the wealthy quite amusing indeed.

Unfazed, Lowell turned from me back to Sissy. Covering his friend's gaffe, Ralph DeVander escorted me and Malcolm into the house. "The party's out back on the terrace," he told us, leading the way.

"Christina!" Lady Violet Smythe-Turnbull's shriek of recognition was unmistakable. She swooped down on me and engulfed me in her embrace.

"Darling!" I gasped. I had to gasp because of the way we were crushed together bosom-to-bosom. "I didn't know you were in New York."

"We just got in, angel."

"Then Lord Alfred is here, too? How is he?"

"Good as new and twice as randy." Lady Violet's laugh trilled out over the terrace. "See for yourself."

I looked over my shoulder to find Lord Alfred bearing down on me. "By Jove!" His mustache drooped over the bones on each side of my wrist as he tickle-kissed my hand. "By Jove!" His rheumy but appreciative blue eyes took in the turquoise silk sheath by Oscar de la Renta which I had chosen to wear to the party. "By Jove!" He missed neither the perk of my braless nipples, nor the smooth derriere attesting to my lack of panties. "By Jove!" He patted my naked thigh below the mini-hemline. "By Jove!" His caress, unlike Lowell Delano's, was the prerogative of an old friend and I made no objection to it. "By Jove!"

"Have you met Prince Feydor?" Lady Violet asked as she hooked her arm through Malcolm's, pulled me away from her husband, and led us over to a tall, slender man with a very curly black beard and brown eyes softer than a beagle's.

"Enchanted," the Prince said, clicking his heels, a gesture not too effective since his feet were bare. So was much of the rest of him. He had evidently just emerged from the swimming pool and droplets of water were clinging to his rather hirsute form.

"Balkan," Lady Violet told me sotto voce while Prince Feydor kissed the back of my hand and dripped onto the protruding bosom of my de la Renta silk. "I can't for the life of me get straight which country, though. Whichever it is, he's expatriated from it."

"Little while I dry," the Prince suggested to me. "We dance?"

"My pleasure," I told him, the wet stain spreading to distinctly reveal the aureoles around my nipples. "But do dry off first."

"Like Sahara," he promised. "Then disco." He rotated his brief lastex bikini trunks in a manner more suggestive of sex than dancing. Behind me I heard Ralph DeVander wince at the overt display.

"He's a foreigner," Lady Violet said, placating Ralph. "He doesn't understand our concept of discretion." Over his shoulder she quickly winked at me.

A band started to play across the patio. They had set up along one side of the swimming pool. Hidden, multicolored strobe lights played over them and over the area of the patio which had been set up as a dance floor. The music was loud, cacophonic, the beat strong and sensual. The flashing strobes gave the dancers a lot of leeway to respond without being open to observation.

"Dance?" The silver-haired, but youngish man who materialized in front of me was not anyone I had met before.

"All right." I responded to the aura of virility given off by his wide shoulders and broad chest. There was the kind of thick muscularity about him that one usually associates with a professional athlete.

"I don't believe we've been introduced," he said as he led me across the patio to the dancing area. "I'm Bryan Kennedy."

"Christina van Bell," I told him. "Are you any relation to the *Kennedy* Kennedys?"

"Interesting question." His eyes twinkled. "I get it a lot. The thing is I haven't figured out a snappy answer yet. Still, the Kennedys are a very large and varied family." He ran his eyes admiringly over my undulating figure as we started to dance.

We continued to dance in silence. The floor filled up and we were forced to move more closely to each other. Bryan put his hands on my hips and guided me lightly. I clasped my hands around the back of his neck. We started to move against each other now. I smiled. He grinned back. He had a very nice grin. I closed my eyes. We danced. Our bodies carried on the conversation.

When the number was over, Malcolm claimed me for the next dance. "Hey there, you with the stars in your eyes . . ." he hummed in my ear.

"That's not what they're playing," I pointed out. "And you're not very funny," I added.

"I'm observant," he told me. "And I know you long and well, Christina." His slender loins pressed hotly against mine as we danced, confirming his words. "I can tell when you've been turned on because it turns me on." His long, slender penis, semi-aroused, slid over my belly. My mons veneris reacted, pressing hotly against it. I was guilty as charged.

Yes, after knowing each other for more than five years, Malcolm could still make me react to him sexually. Also, he could make me blush. Flustered, I changed the subject. "I think it's going to rain." I looked up at the sky.

"Maybe," Malcolm said, following my gaze. Heavy

night clouds had blotted out stars and moon alike. The sky above us was pitch-black.

"Game time!" As our dance ended, Ralph DeVander stopped the orchestra from beginning another set. "Everybody follow me."

"Where are we going?" Lady Violet asked.

"The maze," our host said, pointing to an illuminated area of high hedges beyond the landscaped gardens.

"Where did that come from? It wasn't here the last time I was here," I remembered.

"We just had it installed," Ralph replied. "Just so we could all play this game. We had it electrified, too. It's bright as day, as you can see."

"Game?" Now it was Lady Violet who looked up at the sky. "I don't know, Ralph. It looks to me like we're in for a bit of a blow."

"It wouldn't dare rain." Sissy DeVander joined her husband. "Ralph wouldn't stand for it."

"By Jove!" Lord Alfred approved this firm stand by a member of the landed gentry even if Ralph was a colonial.

"Just what is this game that has to be played in a lit-up maze?" I wanted to know.

"At the very center of the maze there is a clearing," Ralph explained. "It is bisected by a tall trellis which has wide apertures but which is vine covered in such a way as to conceal them. A bar in the shape of a semicircle will be available to those on either side of the trellis. One of our footmen—Horace, I believe—will serve drinks to the players when they reach this area. Now, at the entrance to the maze there are a multiplicity of paths upon which one may set out. There are, of course, countless split-offs from these paths. Some are circular. Some lead to dead ends. Some lead to the center of the maze."

"What are we supposed to do when we get to the center?" Bryan Kennedy inquired.

"Have a drink," Sissy DeVander retorted, drawing a chuckle from the guests.

"That too, of course," Ralph agreed. "The first one who reaches the center will find that the last entryway through which he or she passes has a hedge door which may be closed behind him, therefore sealing off that half of the area. After closing that hedge door—which then, incidentally, will look from the outside like all of the other impenetrable hedges—the contestant will reach through the trellis with both hands. If his or her hands are not grasped, the contestant will withdraw them, have a drink and wait. As the first one there, he will be the Jailer."

"The plot thickens," Lady Violet murmured to Prince Feydor.

"This central area is the Jail, then?" Malcolm sought clarification.

"In a way, I suppose that's true. You could call it that."

"Ralphie, you haven't changed since prep school!" Lowell Delano said contemptuously. "You were always coming up with half-assed games nobody could figure out then, and you still are!"

"This isn't so very complicated!" Ralph was defensive.

"I've followed it so far," I supported him. "But what happens then, darling? What happens when the second contestant reaches the clearing?"

"Well, the second one to reach the clearing will come into it on the opposite side of the trellis from the Jailer."

"Suppose he comes in on the same side?" Lowell asked with a sneer.

"He can't," I enlightened him. "Closing the hedge-bush has barred entrance to that side. If you'd been paying attention, you'd know that."

"Christina is absolutely right," Ralph said. "The second person will come in on the other side of the trellis.

Believing that he or she is the first person, the second person will reach through the trellis with both hands. The Jailer will grasp that person with his hands and the second arrival will thus become the Prisoner. At this point, Horace the footman will come out from behind the semicircular bar and open the hedge doors on either side of the clearing so that subsequent arrivals will have entry to the clearing.''

"Isn't that clearing going to be pretty crowded when everybody starts finding their way there?" Bryan Kennedy wondered.

"Not really. You see, there is a formula by which people may leave the clearing after they have had a drink there. It has to do with the point of the game."

"You're sure there is a point?" Lowell snickered.

"Each new arrival"—Ralph ignored him—"must go up to the person on his side of the trellis and whisper in that person's ear his guess as to whether they are Jailer or Prisoner. If he or she guesses right, they are free to leave and to try to find their way out of the maze. This, by the way, may be a lot trickier than finding your way to the center."

"Suppose the new arrival guesses wrong?" Lady Violet asked.

"Then he must replace the person—either Jailer or Prisoner—holding hands through the trellis. The wrong guesser becomes, in effect, the new Jailer, or the new Prisoner."

"What happens to the old Jailer? The old Prisoner?" Malcolm wanted to know.

"They are free to find their way out of the maze."

"Who is winning in this compete?" Prince Feydor inquired.

"The first one out of the maze is the winner," Ralph told him. "But it's not so important to be first as it is not to be last. The last one out of the maze is the loser. And not being the loser is really the purpose of the game. It's what the game is all about.''

''What about the two people at the trellis?'' I wondered. ''The last two, I mean. When are they to be allowed to leave?''

''After all the other contestants have come through the center area,'' Ralph told me.

''But how will they know?''

''Horace will tell them. He will count the people as they come through. When they've all passed, he'll inform the Jailer and the Prisoner that they are free to go.''

''Then the last Jailer and the last Prisoner are really racing against each other not to be last out of the maze,'' Bryan said.

''Not necessarily,'' Ralph answered. ''The maze is very complex. It's quite possible that the one leaving the center first could be the last to emerge. It takes up an entire half acre, after all. Reaching the center in no way ensures being able to find your way out.''

''Bread crumbs,'' Lady Violet suggested with a grin.

''Night birds,'' Ralph replied smugly. ''We've stocked the maze with them. They'll eat them as fast as you drop them.''

''By Jove!'' Lord Alfred said, his rheumy eyes sparkling in the artificial lights.

''Are we all ready, then?'' Ralph asked.

We followed him to the entrance to the hedge maze. He had told us the truth. Right from the starting point there were many paths one might follow. We milled about for a moment and then each of us chose one and started out. I veered off somewhere between Malcolm and Bryan. In less than a minute it seemed to me that I was hopelessly lost.

There were four possible exits from the hedged-in area

where I found myself. When I chose one, I immediately found myself in a new square facing three new choices. Spotlights, focused on the maze from the high oaks overlooking it on all four sides, bathed the various paths with a whiter-than-white glow that was positively eerie. Such ambience, such perplexity, bespoke the possibility of encounters with hobgoblins, demons, evil spirits, and such. With the hair creeping up the back of my neck, it was reassuring to hear the squeals and laughter and muttered imprecations of the other guests stumbling around in the surrounding hedge-paths. Particularly so when a loud, ominous rumble of thunder rolled over the black sky overhead.

The thunder was repeated, growing louder and occurring at more frequent intervals, as I made arbitrary choices and wound my way over diabolically confusing paths. I was sure I was going in circles. It didn't feel as if I was making any progress at all. Then, quite suddenly, I made what amounted to a U-turn around one of the high hedges and found myself facing the tall trellis which Ralph DeVander had described. Half of the semicircular bar was visible on my left. Horace the footman stood behind it. I closed the hedge door behind me.

A damp breeze had sprung up and I was chilled. I crossed to the bar. "Martini, please."

"Of course, miss." His insolent eyes roved lazily over my turquoise silk sheath as he stirred the ingredients. They found the wide armholes and the naked curve of my breast visible there. Then they dropped to my hands holding the miniskirt to my thighs against the wind. "Is this to your taste, miss?" He slid the cocktail across the bar.

I sipped it. "Perfect."

"Thank you, miss." His lingering gaze said I was as much to his taste as the martini was to mine.

I finished the drink quickly, crossed over to the center of the trellis and reached through the thick leaves with both hands. Immediately my fingers were clasped and held. Someone had beat me to the other side. That someone was the Jailer. I was the Prisoner.

As soon as we joined hands, Horace moved to reopen the hedge door in back of each of us. Then he returned to his place behind the bar. A moment later a woman entered on my side of the trellis.

I had seen her before, but we hadn't been introduced, and so I didn't know her name. She was shivering from the sudden chill in the air, and she headed straight for the bar to get a drink to warm her. When she'd finished it, she came up behind me. "Prisoner," she said.

"That's right," I sighed.

"Too bad for you." She gave me a farewell pat and departed from the center of the maze.

Abruptly, as if someone had overturned a bucket, rain began pouring down from the sky. Despite the fact that the breeze had been chilly, the drops were quite warm. They washed over me like a tepid shower, a balmy sensation I rather enjoyed.

The ground beneath my feet became muddy, and I began to slip and slide on my high heels. From the way the hands were pulling at me, through the hedge I gathered that the Jailer was having similar problems. As the warm rain washed over me, I kicked off my shoes, bent at the waist and widened my stance. My footing was more secure now, but my miniskirt had ridden up a bit in back and every so often a particularly hard pelting splatter of raindrops would kick up the mud and soil the backs of my naked thighs and even my bare derriere. I found myself wishing that for once I had opted for caution over sleekness of line and worn panties. But it was too late now.

I reached behind me to hold my skirt over my jutting, naked bottom as a new arrival, a man, came into the center area of the maze. "Prisoner," he whispered in my ear. And then, fleeing the rain, he was gone.

Right about then half a dozen or so people seemed to arrive at the same time. They all made for the bar and Horace was kept very busy serving them. Like myself, they were soaked. I could hear others behind them, picking their way through the maze. Suddenly there was an enormous clap of thunder. An instant later all of the surrounding spotlights went out and the area was plunged into blackness. The hands tightened around mine through the hedge.

"Damn! Lightning must have taken out the generator," Ralph DeVander said.

"When will they be turned back on, ducks?" Lady Violet asked, concerned.

"Probably not until after the storm," Sissy DeVander answered.

"Typical, Ralphie. You screwed up again." Lowell Delano's sneer was unmistakable.

"How will we find our way out?" Malcolm Gold wondered.

"Don't try," Bryan Kennedy said. "The maze will be impossible without light. The safest thing to do is for all of us to stay right here."

"Then we are sticking here?" Prince Feydor asked fatalistically.

"By Jove!" Lord Alfred responded to the situation with his usual predictable comment.

There were new voices then, from both sides of the trellis, and with many of them talking at the same time, I couldn't really distinguish among them. There seemed to be from twenty to thirty people on each side of the trellis now. Everybody was milling around.

The rain had begun to ease up. The soft, warm drizzle

fell like a caressing mist. There were one or two new arrivals, but no departures. Everyone was waiting for the lights to be restored. I was constantly being bumped against the hedge and jostled by people making their way to and from the bar.

The person on the other side of the trellis held tight to my hands in the dark. Perhaps it was for security. I also felt more secure with the ongoing contact. Besides, I wasn't sure if the game would resume when the lights went on, and so I was a good sport and remained the Prisoner.

"Excuse me, sir," Horace asked. "I can't really see to mix cocktails in the dark."

"All right," Ralph DeVander told him. "Just put the bottles out on the bar and let people help themselves."

"How will we see them?" someone demanded.

"You'll have to feel for them."

There was a loud clap of thunder and then a nervous murmuring swept over the gathering. People were packed tight around me now. Bodies as warm as my own and clothing as wet as mine pressed against me. I couldn't see a thing, and I guessed nobody else could either. Still, I could sense that people were clinging together for reassurance in the blackness.

An anonymous hand reached through the hedge, above the hands already holding mine. I couldn't see it, but I most certainly felt it as the fingers closed around one of my breasts in the tight-stretched, sopping silk. First one of my breasts and then the other was squeezed gently. Rainwater splashed free of the silk. Fingertips investigated the aureole outline through the thin, wet silk. My nipples were stroked to hardness, and then twanged against the small leaves of the hedge I stood facing.

The caress by this unknown hand in the darkness aroused

me. I began to gasp and inhaled deeply. My breasts grew
to their full roundness. It tickled when they brushed against
the tendrils of my wet, blond hair hanging down over
them. A titillating ache possessed my straining nipples.

There were people all around me, but they couldn't see.
They were talking and laughing and moving about, oblivious to the hands caressing me so intimately. Their presence in the darkness excited me even more. I leaned into
the second set of invisible hands protruding through the
hedge, savoring the way the palms and fingers moved so
tantalizingly, so deliciously, over my panting, hard-tipped
breast.

Whose hands were they? They moved so knowingly, so
expertly. Malcolm Gold's, perhaps? He certainly knew the
terrain. Yes, tweaking my nipples so familiarly, they well
might have been Malcolm's hands.

But wait! There was a roughness to them, a gnarliness
even, which suggested hands used to coarser activity than
a typewriter. A polo player perhaps? Ralph DeVander?
The athletic Bryan Kennedy? Perhaps the harshness of a
servant's hands? Horace the footman? Or of age? Lord
Alfred?

Abruptly the hands were pulled back through the hedge
in the dark. My breasts panted untouched in the confines
of the wet silk. I wriggled with frustration against the
bodies around me, missing the hands.

The rain had almost stopped and there was a hot, heavy
humidity in the air. It felt vaguely tropical. I myself felt
soggy. My flesh felt sodden and uncomfortably packed in
with the sodden flesh of other humid bodies. It was strange
not being able to see that which I could feel so intensely.

There was a touch of hands clasping my ankles then.
Someone had sat down in the mud, between my feet but in
front of me, between my bent-forward body and the trellis.

The hands stroked up my legs, caressing the calves, then the knees, then the thighs. They were high under the miniskirt now, kneading the soft, tender inner flesh of my thighs, tracing the muddy rainwater which had splashed there. Then they were higher, on my hips, caressing my belly, circling my narrow waist. Stretching, the hands found the naked undersides of my breasts. The fingertips squeezed between the silk and the nipples. They stroked the naked, hot nipples.

I moaned. I writhed. My squirming ass bumped against a hand. The hand lingered a moment, and then it was gone. The damp humidity flushed my tingling cheeks. The hands on my naked breasts were driving me wild. It excited me to know that the other guests had no idea of what was happening.

*Yes,* I moaned softly inside my head, not speaking aloud. *Play with my breasts! Squeeze the nipples! Play with me in the dark where no one can see, where nobody knows what we're doing except you and me!*

I was concentrating on my breasts and the thrills sweeping over them, and so I was taken by surprise when the head of the person sitting between my wide-spaced feet rose between my legs. The face turned upward under the miniskirt and lips found the inner surfaces of my thighs. My flesh trembled and my leg muscles tensed as the kisses proceeded upward toward the swollen lips of my golden-curled pussy. A tongue tickled the silken hair, and then licked the syrup from the entrance. I squatted lower, settled over it, felt its velvet surface rub over the tip of my aroused clitty and then go higher, licking the flexed ridges of my inner pussy.

*Oh, God!* There were fireworks inside my head! It was an explosion of light in the occupied, crowded darkness, and nobody could see it but me. *Oh, God! Kiss my pussy!*

*Lick the honey! Suck my clitty! Tongue me! Oh, God! I'm coming! I'm coming!*

I wrenched hard, grinding against the face as I came. But even as my short, violent orgasm was over, the tongue kept on fucking me, the lips sucking, the teeth nibbling. I became deeply excited as I realized that mouth was determined to bring me off a second time.

It was the Jailer's hands reaching through the trellis that held me in position, but whose mouth was it? It was tickling now, driving me wild. Was that a mustache that I felt against the moist lips of my pussy? Could it be Lowell Delano with his pencil line of hair on his upper lip tormenting my pussy? Such torment would be right up his alley.

Sweet torture! Yes, it was sweet. But wait! That wasn't a mustache at all. It was only the lips fluttering against the golden curls of my pussy that made it feel like a mustache. No, it wasn't a mustache. Or was it?

The tongue! That was the giveaway. That exquisite tongue! It must be Malcolm. He knew just how to move his tongue around my clitty to bring on those surges of desire that made my head spin. But wait again! Malcolm didn't suck like that—so exotically.

Prince Feydor? I pictured that sensual, Balkan mouth lapping at my cunt. Yes, it could be. But I couldn't be sure.

As the hungry mouth continued to lap my honey, the hands slid down from my breasts and over my ass. They pinched my plump and flaming buttocks hard. Lord Alfred! He was crazy for behinds. Such a pinch would be quite typical of him.

A stiff finger went between my cheeks and tickled me there. The tongue licked deep inside my cunt. A vision of

Bryan Kennedy—silver hair, athlete's body—flashed through my mind. I held onto the vision as my wet pussy slapped against the mouth assaulting it. Yes, Bryan—for the moment, at least—was my cunt-lapper of choice.

The finger deep in my anus turned suddenly brutal. On the screen of my mind Bryan's face and body were replaced by Horace the footman. Yes, Horace would be cruel to a guest, given the opportunity; I had seen it in his eyes when he looked at the rich women at the party, myself included. He would ream their asses royally and lick their juices dry. Just the way it felt for me right now . . .

Savagely, violently, in pain, I came again. I clenched my thighs around that impertinent head and jerked hard against the gobbling mouth. *OH, GOD! . . . I . . . will . . . strangle . . . him!* And I squeezed with an intensity that left me drained.

When I regained my senses it was to find my cunt yearningly, yawningly empty. There was no longer anybody kneeling in the mud between my feet. There were no hands on my buttocks, no brutal finger twisting in my anus. It was still pitch black. The people were still milling around me at close quarters, oblivious to what had transpired, muttering about how long it was taking to get the lights back on.

I shifted position. Still holding mine, the hands on the other side of the trellis clutched more tightly. I bent lower. My back was beginning to ache. My pussy was a little sore but still vibrating, still hungry. A tongue, after all, is not a prick.

*A big, stiff, hard prick!* That's what I wanted inside me. I wanted to fuck with everybody around me without knowing what was happening. *Hairy balls bouncing against my ass and a hard cock plowing in and out of my inflamed cunt! Fucking in the dark in the middle of the unknowing crowd! Fucking! Yes, that's what I ached for now!*

As if in response to some telepathic communication, still another pair of hands slid under my miniskirt and grasped my hips from behind. Nails dug into my hips and drew blood. Lowell Delano? It was the kind of thing he'd do. I detested Lowell, and yet I was intrigued, excited. It would not be the first time I had fucked a man I detested and been turned on by doing it.

Lips grazed the pulse at the base of my neck. The caress was sensual, knowing. Malcolm! Who else had a mouth as carnal as that?

Prince Feydor! That's who! Surely that was his curly black beard I felt brushing my shoulders through the wet silk of my dress. Or was it the breeze? Or perhaps Lord Alfred's droopy mustache.

Hard thigh muscles pressed against my outthrust ass, pushing the silk of the miniskirt against the plump cheeks. Such strength! Was that the outline of giant genitals that I discerned? Could it be Horace, the well-hung footman? My host, the sportsman Ralph DeVander? The athletic Bryan Kennedy?

An anonymous cock slid up and down the cleft of my behind through trouser material and miniskirt silk. Hands circled me and once again my stiff, aroused nipples were played with through the wet silk. A tongue licked my ear. The cock hardened and flattened out between its owner's belly and my ass. I wiggled and moaned. How could I be hot again so soon? I don't know. I just know I was. *Fuck me!* I begged inside my head. *Really fuck me!*

One of the hands moved down between my legs. It stroked the honey-dampened insides of my thighs. Fingertips touched the swollen, burning lips of my pussy. One finger went between the lips, moved up, twisting, stirring, teasing the clitty, frigging higher . . . higher . . .

*Fuck me! . . . Oh, please! Please! . . . Please fuck me!*

Abruptly both hands released me. I could feel the knuckles bumping against my ass and knew from the movements that trousers were being unzipped and lowered. A naked hard-on grazed the silk over my ass.

*His cock is out! There are people all around us in the darkness and his naked cock is out where any one of them might bump into it. He is going to fuck me in the middle of all these people!*

But whose cock? Who was going to fuck me? Who was it? Malcolm? Ralph? Lowell? Horace the footman? Lord Alfred? Prince Feydor? Virile, silver-haired Bryan Kennedy?

And then the cock was sliding between the lips of my pussy and I stopped wondering. I gave myself up to the pure, delirious sensation of being fucked. Hands squeezed my breasts. Hairy balls bounced against my flaming behind. The big, thick cock pushed up higher. Its underside rubbed my sensitive clitty. I pushed backwards and the tip of that wondrous prick flattened against the entrance to my womb. Then, slowly it pulled out, then went back in again, and then out . . . and in . . . and out . . . and in . . .

*Ahh!* The faster it moved, the faster I moved. "Fuck, Christina! Fuck!" I was beyond recognizing the voice in my ear. I rolled my hot ass over his groin and jerked back and forth against his swaying, bouncing balls. "Fuck, Christina! Spin your hungry pussy around my hard cock! Screw! That's right! That's right! Fuck!"

It was slower now, harder, deeper. We were both grunting. Did the others hear? I was beyond caring. Besides, I wanted them to know! No, I didn't! Yes, I did! No, I really didn't! "Fuck, Christina! Fuck!" That baseball bat of a prick battered my sore, hungry, aching, insatiable pussy. "Fuck, Christina!" I fucked! Oh, how I fucked!

"I'm coming!" I tried to whisper. I don't know whether I succeeded or not. "I'm coming!"

"Then come sucking this up your cunt!" A hot, creamy spurt geysered high up inside me. It was followed by a second and then a third. I lost count as my pussy contracted in a series of long drawn-out orgasms. I squealed as the scalding cream filled my frantically climaxing pussy.

And then it was over. The burning prick was withdrawn, the sopping balls backed away. I felt his jism running out of me and down between my still-trembling thighs. My lover was gone. My anonymous lover was once again just another member of the unseen crowd.

"This is silly," I managed to say. "When the lights go back on, we're all going to go out of here in a group. The game is over. Let's let go of each other."

"All right." Surprisingly, the voice from the other side of the trellis was female. My hands were released.

Somehow I managed to clean myself up and to straighten up my clothing. The turquoise silk was drying on my body in such a way as to render it semitransparent. I realized this the moment the lights were turned back on. Many of the male heads turned to look at my charms appreciatively.

Although this group included Bryan Kennedy and Prince Feydor and Ralph DeVander as well as Horace the footman, Lord Alfred and even Lowell Delano and Malcolm, I was much too weary to respond. Had one of them been my anonymous lover? I wondered, but somehow I didn't really care.

The experience, darlings, had been truly transcendental. To identify the man might well have spoiled it. Yes, it was enough to know that my instincts had been right, despite all the overwhelming evidence from the other women in my group. Reality, the realization of one's dreams, can be every bit as thrilling and satisfying as one's fantasy. It may not have worked out for the others, but it had for me. Yes, the ecstasy was there, even as I had dreamed it would be. Ah yes, darlings. Even more so!

I couldn't wait to get to the next meeting of our women's consciousness-raising group so that I could tell them!